One Fatal Secret

Jane Isaac is married to a retired detective and they live in rural Northamptonshire, UK with their dogs. She is the author of three critically acclaimed detective series. Several of her books have reached the top 3 on Amazon's Kindle chart. *One Fatal Secret* is her latest psychological thriller.

D1079734

Also by Jane Isaac

One Good Lie
One Fatal Secret

ONE FATAL SECRET

JANE ISAAC

10 CANELO

First published in the United Kingdom in 2022 by

Canelo
Unit 9, 5th Floor
Cargo Works, 1–2 Hatfields
London, SE1 9PG
United Kingdom

Copyright © Jane Isaac 2022

The moral right of Jane Isaac to be identified as the creator of this work has been asserted in accordance with the Copyright, Designs and Patents Act, 1988.

All rights reserved. No part of this publication may be reproduced or transmitted in any form or by any means, electronic or mechanical, including photocopy, recording, or any information storage and retrieval system, without permission in writing from the publisher.

A CIP catalogue record for this book is available from the British Library.

Print ISBN 978 1 80032 404 6
Ebook ISBN 978 1 80032 403 9

This book is a work of fiction. Names, characters, businesses, organizations, places and events are either the product of the author's imagination or are used fictitiously. Any resemblance to actual persons, living or dead, events or locales is entirely coincidental.

Look for more great books at www.canelo.co

Printed and bound in Great Britain by Clays Ltd, Elcograf S.p.A.

MIX
Paper from
responsible sources
FSC® C018072

For Emma.

One of the strongest and most inspiring women I know.

Prologue

Nicole peers at the nose of the gun nudging the side of her ribcage and suppresses a shudder.

Beyond the car's blackened windows, a couple wanders aimlessly, hand in hand, along the pavement. A woman pushes a stroller, hair flying back in the wind. A group of teenage boys in baggy jeans and hoodies jostle shoulders. London's Oxford Street clogged with Saturday afternoon shoppers, but... A fresh wave of fear skitters down her spine. They cannot help her.

She steals a glance at the gunman sitting beside her. Suited and booted. Thick hands. Dark hair gelled back from his face. The broad neck of the driver in front. Both men wearing sunglasses, despite the dull day outside.

The clock on the dash reads 2.23 p.m. Was it really only twenty minutes ago that she was racing along the pavement in Highgate, sandals clacking on the stone, desperately trying to beat the clock so that her kids weren't late for a birthday party? Katie tripping over the hem of a Cinderella dress that was far too long. Finlay in a bear suit, roaring at every passer-by. She could still smell the fresh scent of their apple shampoo as she kissed their crowns and hugged them goodbye. Still picture their little faces, blooming with hope and excitement, as they disappeared into the house. So young. So innocent. So much growing still to do.

The car rumbles over a pothole, shattering the images. Replacing them with what happened afterwards. A month ago, she'd have screamed and hollered if a man had accosted her in the street and bundled her into a nearby vehicle. But that was before the crash. Before life changed irrevocably.

The car slows in the congested traffic. The man with impossibly thick hands shifts in his seat beside her. The urge to do something, to catch someone's eye, to appeal for help, is primal. But, even without a gun digging into her side, the last thing Nicole can afford to do is attract attention. Not from the public, and certainly not from the police.

Her nails dig deeper into the pads of her hands. Her abductors have taken her phone. No one knows who she is with. No one knows where she is going.

No one is coming to save her.

Chapter 1

Nicole didn't hear the doorbell. She was outside, sitting with her parents on the patio, gazing up at the cornflower-blue sky. A rich breeze carried the heat from garden to garden. Perfect evening for a barbeque.

Well... it would be perfect. She tried to ignore her mother's disapproving stare as she checked her phone, cursing her husband for the umpteenth time. It was her father's seventieth birthday celebration. Ethan had promised to be home an hour ago, and still hadn't arrived. He wasn't answering her calls or messages either. She heaved a heavy sigh. It wasn't unusual for him to be late; he was often caught up at work. But today, of all days, she'd hoped for more. Especially after the year they'd all had.

Her father's hand trembled slightly as he picked up his glass and finished the last drop of wine. He'd shrunk to a shadow of his former self this past year. The cancer eating away at his body, the chemotherapy raging through his system. He was in remission now, but for how long? None of them knew what the future held, and she'd so wanted this evening to be special. A perfect celebration for her father with his family around him.

'No news?' her mother snapped.

Nicole slid her hand from the phone. 'He's been held up.' The lie slipped out of her mouth too easily. She cursed Ethan again, wishing he didn't switch his phone to silent. 'I can't be interrupted when I'm in meetings,' he kept saying. She

3

understood that. But tonight was different. She couldn't have impressed the importance on him enough this past week.

'Oh, really?' Alice tucked a curtain of grey hair behind her ear, leaned her slender frame back in the chair and gave a sarcastic sniff. Only too happy to display her constant disapproval of Ethan's tardiness, his absence at dinner parties, his late arrivals. She'd never much approved of her son-in-law, but now she scarcely had time for him when he was present, and Ethan did little to ease the situation.

Inwardly seething, Nicole sat tall, resolute. She wasn't about to be drawn into an argument. Today was all about her dad. She moved around the table, enveloped her father in a hug, a lump forming in her throat as his bony elbows pressed into her back. 'Another glass of wine?' she asked, pulling back, kissing his papery cheek.

He smiled, held up his glass. 'That would be lovely, thank you.'

It wasn't until Nicole walked back into the kitchen, wine glass in hand, that she heard the voice coming from the front of the house. The distinctive, familiar booming tone that reached up from the pit of his stomach. She swept along the hallway, sandals squeaking on the tiles as she approached her daughter, Katie, holding the front door open a crack.

'Hey,' Nicole said, sliding her arm around her six-year-old's shoulder and pulling the door open wider to reveal David Harrison, Ethan's boss. His sleek wife of thirty years, Olivia, standing beside him in a beige trouser suit, impeccably dressed as always. 'I wasn't expecting you two. Dad will be thrilled!'

David tugged at his collar. He was wearing the same navy shirt he wore when they last saw each other, at his house in the Cotswolds, two weeks ago. She could still picture him that evening, seducing his guests with his wide grin, charm oozing out of every pore. Though there was none of that charm this evening. None of that diamond sparkle in his eye. Today, his face looked tight, his fifty-year-old skin pale.

She looked past him, almost expecting Ethan to appear with a sheepish grin. Presenting the Harrisons as his last-minute surprise, a reprieve for his late arrival. David was godfather to Finlay. The Harrisons were practically family, after all.

Instead of returning her smile, David cleared his throat. A muscle twitched in Olivia's cheek. 'You haven't heard,' he said.

'What?' Nicole's chest tightened. 'Has something happened? What is it, David?'

'Perhaps we could come in,' Olivia said. 'And have a private word.' She shifted her gaze to Katie, lowering her voice to a whisper. 'It's important, love.'

Nicole's mouth dried. *It's about Ethan. It has to be. Oh, God. I hope he's okay.* 'Of course.'

She moved aside for the Harrisons to enter, just in time for an excited Finlay to arrive at the bottom of the stairs and hurl himself at his godfather. David wrapped his arms around the young boy and ruffled his hair, while Nicole went in search of her parents' assistance, leaving the children to fill the hall with their enthusiastic chatter. *Are you staying for dinner? Can you join the party?*

It took all Nicole's mother's powers of persuasion to coax the children away and usher them into the front room – the promise of special television time until dinner was ready, a rare treat, the only lure.

Nicole's father took one look at the Harrisons' sombre faces and stayed with his daughter. He followed her as she guided her guests down the hallway, past the sweeping staircase, the enlarged black and white prints of the children as toddlers adorning the walls.

In the kitchen, David waited beside the door, pushing it to a close when they were all inside.

Nicole passed her gaze from one to another. 'Are you going to tell me what's going on?'

'Please, sit down,' Olivia said, gesturing to the table at the end of the room.

A swirl of bile in her throat. It was odd being invited to sit in her own house. Nicole walked past the shiny white cupboards, the dark granite work surface glinting in the afternoon sunshine. She took a seat at the farmhouse table beside the back door — the one she'd bid for at auction the week they moved into this house. Her father sat beside her; the Harrisons took the chairs opposite. So formal, so tense.

David swallowed, the Adam's apple in his throat wobbling. He seemed to be struggling to find the right words. 'I received a phone call half an hour ago,' he said, his voice low. 'Air traffic control lost contact with the company jet at 1.28 p.m. this afternoon. The plane disappeared off their radar, seconds afterwards.'

Nicole's heart thumped her chest. 'W-what?'

'They believe something might have gone wrong.'

'Like what?' She shook her head, trying to dispel the scenarios worming their way in. 'An accident?'

'Possibly.'

'No!' She gripped the arm of the chair. An accident. A crash. Injuries... Surely not. They travelled that route all the time from the office in Nantes. Ethan loved the independence of flying privately, just a few of them aboard, the small plane taking them closer to the elements, not to mention avoiding the queues and delays scheduled flights attracted. 'I don't understand.' He was due back in the UK mid-afternoon. 'I'll just pop into the office and drop everything off,' he'd said when she had spoken with him last night, 'then I'll head straight home.' She thought he'd been distracted. It wouldn't be the first time...

'Guernsey Air Traffic Control have dispatched search and rescue.'

'Oh my God!' She pressed a hand to her chest.

'Look, let's not panic.' David held up his hands. 'I know this is hard, but please... please try not to worry. It's possible they switched flight paths or made an emergency landing somewhere. We still don't know the full details yet.'

'Was there something wrong with the plane?'

'No! Not that I'm aware of. It was up to date with its checks.'

The ensuing beat of silence was heavy, loaded.

'What then?' Nicole's throat started to contract. 'What did the police say exactly? Did they put out a call for help?'

'As far as I'm aware, no alarms were raised. But I was only given limited information.' He glanced at the door. 'I did wonder if the police would be here by now. They contacted me as the private jet owner to request your details so they could alert you that Ethan was missing. I came over as soon as I heard.'

'The rescue team. They haven't found any…?' She couldn't bring herself to say the word.

'Wreckage.' David's face pained as he uttered the word. 'No, not that I'm aware. The police will be here soon. They'll be able to tell us more.'

She checked the clock. It was now 5.33 p.m. The plane had disappeared over four hours ago.

Her hands slid to the seat beneath her, snaking their way under the cushions, clinging to the sides of the wooden chair. 'Who was on board?'

'Ethan was the only passenger on the flight schedule. Conrad piloting.'

Just the two of them.

An unbidden image of a hospital corridor came to mind. Nicole picking the skin around her fingernails. Ethan's protective arm around her shoulders, holding her tight. Conrad plying them with coffee and cold drinks. Finlay, just a toddler then, fighting for his life after a midnight dash to A&E. Meningitis, the doctor said. The next few hours crucial. As soon as they had heard, Conrad had furiously driven Ethan across London from where he was entertaining a client to be with Nicole, then insisted on staying by their side. Refusing to leave until their precious son was out of danger. Conrad wasn't just the company pilot or Ethan's colleague, he was a dear family friend. Always there when they needed him. And a father too. A father and a husband. Oh, God… Ania.

7

'I've just telephoned Ania,' David said, guessing her thoughts. 'I was hoping to get to you both first, before the police arrived.'

Nicole pressed a fist to her mouth, imagining Ania, Conrad's wife, sitting at her kitchen table listening to the same news. The tall Pole with raven-black hair tied into its usual knot on top of her head. They weren't the best of friends. But still… She wouldn't wish this on anybody.

The tablecloth flapped outside in the soft breeze. Katie squealed with laughter in the front room. This was surreal. Like something that happened in a TV drama. Not on a warm Friday evening in Highgate.

A pan lid rattled on the stove: the potatoes for her salad. Her father jumped up, pulled the pan off the ring. In its shiny surface, Nicole watched his reflection as he moved back to the table. Gripped the hand she let fall. Quizzed the Harrisons, asking all the salient questions. But she couldn't hear his words. It was as if someone had turned down the volume.

Her husband was missing. She looked down, released her hand from her father's grip and rested it on her stomach. She desperately hoped Ethan was okay. He had to be. Because she needed to see him. There was something particularly important she had to tell him.

Chapter 2

In Leytonstone, Ania Gilbert dropped the phone into the cradle and pressed her back against the cold wood of the front door, hot tears filling her eyes as she faced her narrow hallway.

How could Conrad be missing? She'd only spoken with him this morning. It was raining in Nantes, he was looking forward to coming home to sunshine. Talked about maybe driving out to the country, taking a picnic. The basket was on the kitchen table, all ready.

A scraping, then a bump above. Ania froze. Her boys were tussling on the bedroom floor. She could almost see their bright blue eyes, their scruffy hair that never sat flat no matter how she had it cut, the freckles that spotted their noses. So young. Adventurous. Carefree. What was she to say to them?

Fireworks of anxiety sparked in her chest. Anxiety and... anger. How dare David Harrison telephone her and deliver this information? Where were the police?

A tear escaped. She swiped it from her cheek, then slid down the door, the sharp bristles of the doormat penetrating the denim of her jeans. It was poky and dark with the downstairs doors closed – the only light a thin slice, reaching down the stairs from the landing window. Another tear welled beneath her eye.

Missing meant any number of things, didn't it? He could be clinging to a life raft in the middle of the English Channel. Treading water, injured, desperately hoping to be saved.

An opaque memory flitted into her mind. Conrad on Wednesday morning, standing in the bathroom in his pants,

9

having a wet shave as he often did before a trip. Encouraging her to take her shower in the cubicle behind him to save time – family mornings, sharing a bathroom, always a rush – then moaning when the mirror steamed up. She'd surveyed the contours of his back while she towelled herself dry, the slight tuck in at his waist. He looked sporty, athletic – a man in his prime.

The last time she saw him.

A sob caught in her throat. Who would have thought their week would end like this? Her sitting in a murky hallway, clinging to the edge of a precipice. Holding on by her fingernails as she waited to hear whether he was still alive. The sob burst. She pressed her hand to her mouth.

Her gaze fell on a photo on the wall of she and Conrad in their early twenties – one of their earliest snapshots as a couple – sitting in The Angel on Islington High Street. Him with hair that flopped across his forehead and that old denim jacket he used to wear. She just back from a summer holiday in Ibiza. Bronzed skin, hair swept back into a ponytail. Skinny jeans clinging to thighs that were two sizes smaller in those days. A white crop top that showed off a perfectly flat stomach; a diamond stud in her navel, now long gone.

Ania dropped her head into her hands. Was that only eight years ago? How different things were in those days. Easy. Uncomplicated. She with ambitions to become a teacher. He was working as a delivery driver, but it was only temporary. His dream was to train as a pilot. He wanted to fly people all over the world.

Her gaze glued itself longingly to their younger selves. That was before they had children and bought this home together. Before Conrad started chauffeuring at Harrison Dunbar Associates and David, the owner, bought a company plane and sponsored her husband to do his pilot exams. Ania sniffed as more tears traced her cheeks. She'd fought against Conrad training that way. Flying for an airline was one thing. Being beholden to the CEO of an international finance company and flying a small single-engine craft quite another. She'd tried to encourage him to save up, take flying lessons privately, but Conrad couldn't wait.

Another tear leaked out as she recalled the liberties that were taken: the holidays they'd cancelled or postponed at the last minute because Conrad was 'needed for an urgent flight'. The children's assemblies and birthday parties he'd missed. She'd lost count of the number of times she'd had to pick up the pieces, placate disappointed little faces because Daddy had been called away.

And now this. The company plane disappears over the English Channel. And with Ethan Jameson as a passenger. It couldn't get any worse.

Chapter 3

Nicole stroked Finlay's crown and watched his eyes droop to a close. They'd postponed the birthday celebrations, but she refused to tell her children about the missing plane. She wouldn't have them upset, not until she knew what they were dealing with, and the ease with which they had swallowed her excuse – Daddy was delayed in France – cut her to the bone. Because he was so often delayed, so often late. Their disappointment only tempered by the steely presence of the Harrisons, who'd fired up the barbeque and distracted the kids by trying to catch butterflies with bandy nets when the police had arrived. The children hovering around the buddleia, oblivious to their mother sitting in the front room with police officers discussing their missing father.

For Nicole, the evening had been tortuous. Trying to appear upbeat for Katie and Finlay while all the time feeling like a knife had been inserted in her chest, its tip turning a notch with every passing minute. Before they left, the police had told her that air traffic control had lost contact with the plane over the English Channel. Which meant they either crash-landed in the water or managed to limp to the nearest land mass and make an emergency landing.

And now she was left waiting. Constantly listening for the door, the phone. Jumping at every sound, desperately waiting for the next update.

Finlay's breathing eased into a steady rhythm. She leaned forward, pecked his forehead and retreated out of the room.

It was quiet and still on the landing. Katie's soft snoring filtered through her open bedroom door. The babble of the Harrisons' voices reached up from the front room, where they were sitting with her parents, anxiously awaiting news.

Nicole took a moment to relish the calm, slumping down onto the top step of the stairs. Resting her back against the cold plaster of the wall. She never did this. Never took the time to sit on the floor. Never paused to think. There was always so much to do – prepare for work, cook dinner, stack the dishwasher, get the children's clothes ready for school in the morning. But this was the first time she'd been alone all evening, the first time she'd had a chance to consider the possibilities swimming around her mind.

The staircase curved onto an open landing. Tucked away here, on the top step, she couldn't see the hallway below, and anyone down there couldn't see her either. She pulled her phone out of her pocket. The screen lit as she checked it again, a tremor running through her hands. No new messages. It was nearly 8.30 p.m.

Light streamed onto the landing from the arched window. Her mother moaned about Ethan's persistent tardiness, said he walked all over her. Nicole had lost count of the times she'd hinted her daughter would be better off on her own. But her mother didn't know Ethan like Nicole did. She was never around when he was kind and sweet and gentle. She didn't see him play hide-and-seek with the kids or chase them down the garden. And houses in Highgate didn't come cheap. Ethan worked in finance. He put in long hours to enable her to work part-time, to be there for the kids while they were young. For Ethan, it was all about family. His family.

Hot tears pricked her eyes as she rested a hand on her stomach. She hadn't told Ethan about the baby slowly growing inside her yet. It was only confirmed yesterday and was supposed to be a surprise, some happy news for the weekend, a secret for them both to share.

The tears swelled, burning Nicole's eyes as she leaned her head against the wall. They'd always meant to have another child, they'd planned to, but…

A familiar ball of fear tightened in her chest. She'd sailed through pregnancy with Katie and Finlay, working up to the days before they were both born. Then everything had gone wrong.

She recalled the early-morning knot in her chest as she walked to the bathroom, just under a year ago. She was eight weeks gone. They'd just had a party the weekend before and told her parents. The raindrops collecting on the window, snail trailing down the glass as she felt her third child slipping away.

A blip, the doctor had said. It happens sometimes.

Fast-forward eight months. Another early morning. Another bucketload of heartache. She had been ten weeks when she lost her next child. Almost outside the twelve-week danger zone.

She gripped the edge of the step. She couldn't go through that again, especially not on her own.

On her own. She shuddered, biley acid shooting into her mouth. Surely it wouldn't come to that.

The chime of the doorbell rang through the house, jolting her forward. She knew she should go down and answer the door, but a raw fear inside rooted her to the spot. What if it was bad news?

A movement downstairs. She recognised her mother's shuffles along the hallway. Nicole held her breath.

The front door opened, sending a rush of cool air inside.

'Is Mrs Jameson at home?' A low voice, a gravelly tone winged its way up the stairs.

The police were back.

—

'I'm so sorry, Mrs Gilbert.'

Ania stared at the fresh-faced officer, the crisp shirt beneath his fleece newly ironed. His trousers starched, as if he was barely out of training. A sombre colleague stood beside him at the fireplace, dark skin glistening under the low lighting.

Time froze. Ania sat perfectly still, her mouth agape. They'd just told her they'd found a body. Her husband was dead.

Blanka reached across and took her hand, squeezing her fingers until they whitened. Her dear best friend, the closest thing she had to family in the UK, who'd come as soon as Ania had called her, regardless of the late hour and the fact that she'd just completed a twelve-hour shift at the hospital. Sitting with her, consoling her, mopping her tears.

'How can you be sure it's Conrad?' Blanka asked. The Polish inflection in her voice was stronger than Ania's, more guttural. 'You said yourself, there were other people on the flight schedule.'

A thread of hope. The body they'd found could just have easily been Ethan, or someone else, fallen from a passing boat. Or perhaps there was a mistake with the schedule and another person was on board...

The officer looked directly at Ania. 'You mentioned your husband had a tattoo.'

'Yes...' Her voice was sore from crying, husky. 'A Celtic symbol on his forearm.' She pointed to the downy hairs on her own arm. 'It has the children's names in it.'

The officer gave a sober nod, apologised again, and Ania's heart shrank. She could only stare as he asked for Conrad's toothbrush – for a formal DNA match.

'It's the green one,' she said, as Blanka heaved herself up and led the officer upstairs to the bathroom. Leaving Ania with his colleague, still beside the fireplace.

The other officer continued to talk about 'the incident', as he called it. But his words washed over her, only snippets of information feeding through. He couldn't comment on the specifics or what state the plane was in. 'We still need to establish the facts,' he said. He went on to talk about Air Accident Investigation opening an inquiry and Ania's mind whirled, her body numb. It all sounded so formal, so final.

'Wait,' she said, interrupting him mid flow. A sudden moment of clarity, presenting itself through the haze in her head. Snapping her back to the present. 'What about Ethan Jameson, the other passenger?'

'He hasn't been found,' the officer said. 'They're still looking for him.'

Chapter 4

Pain. A strangled scream inside her chest. Trapped, unable to find a way out as the days tumbled into one another.

Nicole rolled onto her back and stared at the bedroom ceiling. It was Tuesday. Ethan was still missing. Four nights had passed, three full days. The police came and went. Drank cups of tea made by her mother and sat on Nicole's sofas. Checking they were okay, that they had support. Updating them on the 'inquiry', as it was now called. The wreckage was caught in an underwater valley. It was difficult for divers to get close enough to examine it properly due to rapid and unpredictable water currents. She imagined the broken wing of a plane, a cockpit on its side. Fish swimming in and out like the wrecks she had seen on nature programmes on television.

The aroma of freshly brewed coffee and buttered toast wafted up the stairs – her father's mid-morning snack. The clatter of breakfast bowls being loaded into the dishwasher followed as her mother cleaned and tidied. The endless babble of Radio 4 in the kitchen – the sound of her childhood. Her parents hadn't left since the news of the crash on Friday. Popping home only to pick up a few 'essentials'. They were wonderful with the children, constantly coming up with different games, colouring competitions, films to watch. Nicole had to force herself to get out of bed each morning, place one foot in front of the other, to be there for her kids. At least her parents' presence enabled her to sneak off for quiet moments, to think, to cry, to despair, and for that she was grateful. Because she didn't want her children witnessing her pain. But she was wracked with guilt too. Her father was still weak. He needed to rest, to have her mother's undivided care. They couldn't continue like this for long.

She rolled onto her side, a lump crystallising in her chest as she stared at Finlay's red dragon, the soft toy he slept with. Her children's little eyes had grown to saucers on Saturday, when she'd knelt before them and explained that Daddy's plane had to make an emergency landing in the sea. They looked so small, their feet dangling off the end of the sofa as she had tried to explain. She couldn't tell them much more because she knew so little herself. And she couldn't mention the word 'crash'. Crash denoted injuries, debris. Crash sounded frightening. And, as scary as it was, she didn't want her kids petrified. So, she told them the plane had made an emergency landing. Katie had cried when she said Conrad had sadly died. Finlay had gripped her wrist when he heard his father had broken out, and the child had taken to sleeping in her bed ever since.

She felt awful, fudging up a lie to her children, some story that sounded as though it came straight out of a novel. That at any moment Ethan would walk through the front door, the hero of the hour. But was it really a story? Nobody knew exactly what had happened, or even whether he was still alive. Although, as each day passed, even she had to admit that the chances of him surviving grew slimmer and slimmer.

She folded her arms across her stomach. Almost eight weeks. By Nicole's reckoning, she was almost eight weeks pregnant, her unborn child the size of a raspberry, and she still hadn't told anyone apart from her GP and midwife. She couldn't. Her mother would fuss, make her rest and she wasn't about to let that happen. Finlay and Katie required her full attention right now. It wouldn't be fair to ask them to compete with the prospect of a new sibling. Not when their father was missing.

She thought of Ania and her boys. Their dark hole of grief. Were they sleeping in her bed too? She felt compelled to call her. They'd be drawn together through this cruel twist of fate. She meant to. Kept telling herself she would. Just as soon as they found Ethan.

18

Her phone erupted, dancing on her bedside table. 'Carla' flashed up on the screen.

It was 10.30 a.m. Nicole should be at work now. Interviewing potential clients for new opportunities. Searching for just the right fit for a particular position. Recruitment hadn't exactly been her dream job when she left university, but she'd grown to love it and working for Jackson's, a small company – focusing mainly on corporate headhunting – she relished the challenges it presented.

She clicked to answer. Carla Jackson wasn't only her MD, she was also her friend.

'Hey. How are you?' Carla's familiar American drawl sent a warm feeling through Nicole. In the eight years they'd worked together, they'd become close. Exchanging snapshots of daily life over coffee, chatting about what they'd been up to at the weekend. Offloading and confiding, opening their hearts to one another. Carla was the one person Nicole could be brutally honest with. The one person she trusted.

'I'm okay.'

'What's the update?' That was one of the things Nicole liked about Carla. She cut to the chase.

'Still the same.'

'God, you must be beside yourself. Are you sure there isn't anything I can do?'

'No. My folks are still here, helping out with the kids.'

'How are you holding up?'

'Taking it one hour at a time.' A phone rang in the background. 'What's going on there?' Nicole asked.

'The usual… I managed to renegotiate the package on the Wilson's position. Sounds like Burlington's going to take it.'

This was a position they'd been working on for months. 'That's good.'

'I think so. Look, I won't keep you, hun. Try to get some rest. You know where I am if you need me. Even if it's just to scream or holler.'

Nicole's eyes welled. The offer was like a mug of hot chocolate on a winter's evening. 'You've a business to run.'

'You're my best friend. Anything, okay? I mean it. And don't even think about work. We'll be here when you need us.'

The doorbell sounded. 'I've got to go,' Nicole said.

Voices filled the hallway as Nicole thanked her boss and rang off. A rich Birmingham accent: the detective supporting them as Family Liaison Officer. What was her name? Sherry, Sheila. Sharon, that was it. By the time Nicole had gathered herself and descended the stairs, the detective was standing beside her mother in the kitchen.

'Morning, Nicole,' Sharon said. The detective looked at home in her long purple skirt, floral blouse tucked in at the waist, dark curls pinned back from her forehead. Glass of water in her hand. Not at all formal. 'How are you doing?'

Nicole swept a weary hand down her face. How was she supposed to be doing? She was all over the place, veering from wanting to scream and shout – to articulate the desperation clawing at her insides – to hiding under the bedclothes. 'Is there any news?'

The woman placed the glass down on the kitchen surface. 'Why don't you sit down?'

'Why?' With Sharon there were always questions, always scrutiny, and, as much as Nicole tried to ignore it, there was something about the police officer's persistent presence in her home that niggled her.

Nicole's father entered the kitchen from the garden. He nodded an acknowledgement at the detective and stood beside his daughter, glancing quizzically from one to the other.

'I'm tired,' Nicole said to the detective. 'Have you got any news?' The last thing she could bear was another 'tea and sympathy' visit.

Sharon sidestepped the question. 'I understand,' she said.

Nicole huffed. She doubted Sharon understood at all. Not really. She wondered how many other family kitchens she'd stood in with the same empathetic expression, offering the same advice. But she'd probably never been in the situation herself, never had to deal with someone vanishing. Someone close. Never had to wake each morning, insides hollow, clinging on to a tiny thread of hope that today would be the day that would herald good news. Only to have your hopes dashed.

Sharon talked about how the police were supporting the crash investigation team, how they were working together to establish what had happened.

Nicole rubbed another hand down her face. She'd heard all this before. She was considering going back up to the solace of her bedroom, when the detective said, 'So, we're calling off the search.'

'W-what?' The words hit her like a juggernaut.

'The air rescue team have done everything they can. The chances of anyone surviving that long in the water—'

'Are what?' Nicole interrupted.

'Practically impossible, I'm told. I'm so sorry.'

Nicole's legs weakened. She grabbed the kitchen worktop. Waving off her father's hand of assistance. The room fell silent as three brains attempted to process the information. No. They couldn't call off the search. They hadn't found Ethan. He could still be out there somewhere, waiting...

'I'll make drinks,' her mother said eventually, moving towards the kettle.

Nicole watched her mother open the cupboard and busy herself with the teapot. There was no hope... There had to be hope, didn't there? Surely there was still a chance?

'There's something else,' the detective said. She pulled out a chair. 'You really do need to sit down.'

Chapter 5

Ania was reading with Robert when the doorbell chimed. At five, his tastes were for superheroes and pirates, and it was a struggle to say the words with her usual enthusiasm. It was 11.03 a.m. and their dinner, hearty but simple lamb stew, simmered on the stove. Simple was all she was capable of. She'd kept the boys off school and was forcing herself to stick to her routine, day to day, devoting every waking hour to her children. The news of their father's death had hit them hard. Robert clung to her, barely leaving her side, but it was Patryk that really bothered her. Whenever Conrad's name came up, he changed the subject or left the room and she'd discovered his sheets in the washing basket earlier – he'd started wetting the bed again. Blanka had taken him to the park this morning, to distract him with some goal practice, but she was worried about him.

Two years younger than his brother, Robert was a different kettle of fish. The notion of dying, of going to heaven, like another place to him. Somewhere you drove to or travelled to on holiday. He couldn't understand why they couldn't visit his dad and when she tried to explain, he became upset and then angry, pounding her with his fists until he collapsed into sobs. It was harrowing, but at least the grief was coming out. Which is why she relished these occasional moments of calm, when she and Robert cuddled up together.

The doorbell rang again. In the four days since the crash, she'd come to dread that sound, fearing more bad news. She used to measure everything by the kids' ages. Robert was two when she got sunstroke at the zoo. Patryk was five when he

22

broke his arm, falling from a climbing frame. In future, it would be the crash. Before the crash. After the crash.

Ania recognised the silhouette of the officer behind the glass door panel before she opened the door, Robert at her heel.

'Hello, little man,' the officer said. Robert hid behind Ania's legs as he bent down. 'You're not shy, are you?'

Ania ruffled Robert's hair and manoeuvred them both aside for the detective to enter. 'Why don't we put the telly on?' she said to her son. 'You can watch SpongeBob, while I speak with the officer.'

The boy's face brightened. He followed his mother into the front room, where she settled him in front of the television.

Back in the kitchen, Ania checked the detective's drinks preference, invited him to sit and flicked the switch on the kettle.

'We're releasing Conrad's body,' he said gently.

Ania steadied herself against the side. They'd been in limbo these past few days. Waiting for Conrad to be flown back to London, for the post-mortem to take place. At least now she could make the arrangements with the funeral director.

'Thank you,' she said. The kettle switched itself off. She busied herself making drinks, the relief in the room palpable.

'How are you doing?' he asked.

'Pardon?'

'I'm just checking to see if there's anything you need. We could send someone from Victim Support.'

'I don't need anyone, thanks. Me and the boys, we're fine.' They were far from fine, she knew that, but she wasn't about to invite a stranger into her home. She'd already dismissed the family liaison officer. No. They were better off together.

'Okay,' he said. He waited until she placed the mugs of coffee on the table before he continued. 'There are a few other questions I need to ask.'

Ania sat opposite him and wrapped her hands around the mug, the warmth of the coffee seeping through the china, soothing her tense fingers.

'The post-mortem showed traces of Zopiclone in Conrad's body.'

'What?' Coffee slopped onto the table as she jolted forward. Ania placed the mug down, ignoring the spillage.

'It's a prescribed sleeping pill.'

'I know what it is.'

'Did Conrad take Zopiclone?'

'No.' She was shaking her head, but even as she spoke the word, a tiny voice clawed up from within – *he used to.*

'Has he ever taken it?'

Ania swallowed. 'A couple of years ago, after his parents died, he suffered a depressive episode. Had to take some time off work, was struggling to sleep. The doctor prescribed them to help. He took them on and off for a couple of months.'

'Are you sure he hasn't taken any recently?'

'Of course I am. I'd have known.' She dredged up memories of the last few months. He'd certainly been away a lot. But there weren't any signs he was experiencing sleeping problems when he was home.

'Do you have any in the house?'

A shiver travelled down Ania's back. *What is he insinuating?* She couldn't be sure there were none there. Clearing out old medicines wasn't a priority. And with sleeping pills… Well, you never knew when you might need them. 'I don't know.'

Surely, they didn't think Conrad would take sleeping pills before a flight. He'd never do that. He was always so careful. Her throat tightened. Surely, they didn't think the crash was his fault.

The chair scraped against the tiles as she pushed it away from the table. She was out of the door before she dared take another breath. The honeyed tones of the characters on Robert's television programme filled the hallway as she dashed through, taking the stairs, two at a time. In the bathroom, she headed for the cabinet above the sink. Ignoring the dental floss, spare soaps and toothpaste that littered the bottom shelf. The perfumes and

24

aftershaves lining the shelf above. Instead moving to the top shelf, where they stored the medicines, safely out of reach from little hands. She pulled out a blister pack of paracetamol, an unopened box of ibuprofen. Moved aside a packet of stronger painkillers her doctor had prescribed when she'd jarred her neck after a car accident last year, a box of plasters. And then she found them. A half-used blister pack of Zopiclone, the box missing. She wanted that box. A part of her wanted to show they were old, perhaps even out of date... She scrabbled about amongst the multivitamins, the indigestion tablets, fingers urgently searching, but it wasn't to be found.

The blister pack was curled at the end, the little pockets squashed where tablets had been pressed out. She grabbed it and turned to find the detective at the door.

'Conrad could never have taken these before a flight,' she said. The plastic crackled as her grip tightened. 'He wouldn't.'

Chapter 6

Blanka opened the front door and took her time checking up and down the road. The street light outside lit the front garden in a dull hue. 'I think they've gone,' she said.

It was almost 9 p.m. on Wednesday. News of the sleeping drug had reached the papers that morning. A leak, the police had said when they'd called. A leak they were looking into. But it didn't stop articles headed, *Traces of Zopiclone Found in Pilot's System* or *Pilot Under the Influence of Drugs*, spreading across the internet like wildfire. Scathing, vile headlines. Wounding headlines that sent Ania reeling. If they weren't bad enough, from first light a group of journalists had gathered at the end of her pathway. Watching, waiting. Shoving a microphone in her face when she'd gone out to the funeral director's earlier. Trying to get her reaction to the devastating news. Had they no shame?

Blanka stepped back into the hallway and wrestled on her jacket. 'Are you sure you are going to be okay?'

Blanka had been amazing since last Friday. Cleaning, cooking, staying over, helping with the children. Ever since they'd been toddlers, growing up in the same street, attending the same schools, they'd looked out for one another. And when they'd left Poland and travelled to England together in their late teens in search of work, the bond only deepened.

'I'll be fine,' Ania said. 'As you say, they've gone.'

Blanka's eyebrows fused in concern. With her bleached blonde hair scraped back, accentuating her dark eyes and angular face, Blanka looked fierce. And she could be fierce.

But she was also loyal, soft and caring to the core – the sister Ania had never had. 'I can phone in, take some more leave.'

'You've taken five days already. You have to work sometime.'

Blanka cast an uncertain glance to the ceiling, to where the boys were sleeping upstairs.

'They're fast asleep,' Ania said. 'I'll probably head up myself soon.'

'You sure?'

'I'm positive.' She gave her friend a gentle nudge. 'Go.'

'All right. You call me, okay? If you need anything. Anything at all.'

'I will. I promise.'

Ania watched her friend wander up the pathway, give one final wave and disappear into the night. She peered up the road herself, before she closed the door, pulled the chain across. Then took a deep breath and stared down the empty hallway.

She was accustomed to being here alone with the boys. They'd lived their lives organising family outings and events around Conrad's work schedule. *We'll save that for when Daddy comes home. Let's do that before Daddy goes away.* When he was home, he filled the house with his chatter, his cheeky teasing, his games. Running up and down the stairs, playing hide-and-seek with the kids. Many a time, she'd joked about having three children, not two – she'd married a big kid. She used to look forward to these rare moments of quiet, cherishing the evenings she had to herself when he was absent, and the boys were in bed.

But tonight, the silence was deafening.

She padded into the front room, collected a few toy cars strewn across the hearth rug, a jigsaw spilling out of its box, and piled them in the corner. Then drew the curtains, switched on the lamp and sat on the sofa. She needed to rest; she'd been running on adrenaline since the news on Friday. A permanent dull ache pulsed at her temple. It was bad enough dealing with losing Conrad, the million and one memories echoing around her head, without being thrust into the public eye over question marks regarding his fitness to fly. That afternoon, she'd been subjected to another police visit, and more questions. Humiliating, crushing questions. *What was Conrad's mood like recently? Could he have been anxious or depressed?* Surely, they didn't think he'd crashed the plane on purpose. No! Conrad would never do that. She knew her husband. He wasn't depressed. Overstretched maybe, with the demands at work. But, depressed? No way.

The issue over the sleeping pills was like an infected wound, weeping within her.

Admittedly, Conrad hadn't been immediately open with her last time he was having problems but she'd spotted the signs herself. Witnessed the restless nights. The warm milk at 2 a.m. Him taking a pillow and a throw down to the sofa so that he didn't disturb her. The pallid skin, the dark circles under his eyes, the crushing fatigue, the mood swings. Eventually, she'd persuaded him to go to the doctor, to get help. The relief when eventually things improved.

Yet she'd seen none of that recently. He looked well. He was a little sombre last Wednesday, but he was always sombre before he went on a trip, a reflection of the friction it caused in the household. Especially when it was announced at the last minute, as this trip was.

She thought back to a week ago last Saturday, a family walk through Epping Forest. They'd taken the boys to McDonald's afterwards. She drove. On the way home, Conrad had taken a phone call and seemed distracted. She remembered quizzing him, worried he'd be dashing off to work, and he'd said it was only Ethan. An issue with a client. They'd been interrupted by Robert, messing with the door. He was constantly messing with the door – trying to work out how the child safety lock worked. Now she wondered what that phone call had meant. She'd tried to question him again later, when they were home, and he'd told her that Ethan was working on a big deal. Life-changing, he called it. But the boys had interrupted them again and the moment had passed.

The window rattled in the light breeze. Had the strain of the new deal rubbed off on Conrad? Her gaze wandered haphazardly around the room. To Conrad's guitar in the corner, the pile of magazines beneath it, when something caught her eye. Sandwiched between *Pilot* and *Aviation News* was Conrad's laptop. If Conrad was stressed, there might be some indication of the source on there.

She slid off the sofa, knelt on the floor and gently eased the computer out from between the magazines. The silver casing glinted beneath the lamplight as she opened it. The keyboard was worn: only the top triangle of the A visible, the E almost unrecognisable.

She switched on the device. A photo of Patryk and Robert in swimming trunks on Cromer Beach – their holiday last year – filled the screen. A password box flashed up. She keyed in his date of birth, Conrad's go-to password. The screen changed to another photo – of Patryk this time in full football kit. A ball tucked beneath his arm, a wide grin on his face exposing two missing front teeth.

Ania wasn't really sure what she was looking for. She clicked on Internet Explorer, scrolled down to history and brought up Conrad's most recent tabs. An array of sites littered the top of the screen. Mostly about guitars and bicycles. A wistful smile. Conrad had been a guitar dabbler, self-taught. He fancied himself as a bit of an Eric Clapton. She clicked on a YouTube tab and was treated to a rendition of 'Eruption' by Eddie Van Halen. Ania slid back against the sofa and watched the song play out, her heart contracting as memories of their younger selves came back to her. Hanging out at the pub on a Friday evening, watching the open mic nights.

The song faded. She opened his email. His inbox was littered with old order confirmations and shipping details from Amazon, eBay and other online stores she didn't recognise. Conrad's 'sent' folder contained an email to David Harrison, his boss, checking the times for a recent event. Several to

Ellen, David's receptionist, confirming dates and times for an upcoming flight. Ania vaguely remembered Ellen. A short, unflappable woman with coiffed blonde hair and sky-blue eyes. Immaculate, as were most of the Harrison Dunbar lot. God, she'd hated those company events. The false hugs, the air kisses, the vacuous conversation. She used to joke to Conrad that they were immaculately wooden. It never ceased to amaze her how he managed to spend so much time with them. But Conrad loved flying. He'd do anything to pursue his passion.

She moved on, opened other emails to guitar contacts, checking tabs, comparing notes. One to Patryk's football coach arranging an old training session.

She was about to shut down the laptop when she saw something in the drafts folder addressed to David Harrison. Ania clicked on it. And froze.

> Dear David,
>
> I wish to resign from Harrison Dunbar with immediate effect.
>
> I will, of course, complete my month's notice and arrange to pay the outstanding loan to you in full, as soon as possible.
>
> Regards,
>
> Conrad

Ania flinched, as if she'd received a good hard slap on the cheek. Surely not?

She reread the few lines again. Then replayed the numerous conversations in her mind, the rows they'd had over the last few years, when she'd try to convince Conrad that David Harrison was taking advantage and the job was interfering with family life. Pleading with him to seek employment elsewhere. And every time he'd shrugged her off. David had paid half the costs of Conrad's pilot training and loaned him the other half. A loan they were slowly repaying. A loan balance that, as far as she was aware, was still hefty. And every argument had ended the same: Conrad wouldn't leave the company until the debt was clear. Before Harrison Dunbar, Conrad had been rejected by all the major airlines. David had finally given him the chance when no one else would – he felt he owed him.

The date on the email was 31 May. Only a week before the crash. Why was Conrad planning to leave now? And, more to the point, why hadn't he mentioned it to her?

Chapter 7

Nicole pressed the doorbell, stepped back and gazed up at the powder-blue frontage of Ania's house. The front door of the mid-terrace was surrounded by an arch of honeysuckle. Terracotta pots spaced neatly apart on the gravelled garden spilled over with a kaleidoscope of pastel geraniums. Net curtains veiled the windows, masking the inside.

It was Thursday. Two days after the emergency services had called off the search for Ethan. Two days since the revelation about Zopiclone, the sleeping drug, was found in Conrad's system. Two days in which she'd endured a constant maelstrom of emotions – shock, anger, disbelief – tumbling around her insides like dirty washing. Conrad was a conscientious pilot. He'd flown them back from a weekend in Paris last November, their eighth anniversary celebration, and she'd felt more turbulence on an international airline. What had he been thinking of?

Granted, they still didn't know the full details. The plane was in a tricky position, too dangerous to attempt recovery. The investigators said it might take some time to establish exactly what had happened. Some time... While Ethan's body floated idly in the water, slowly being picked away by sea life. The very notion made her chest ache.

Nicole tried the doorbell again. But whatever had happened, whatever the inquiry uncovered, she had to push aside her anger. It wasn't fair to ostracise Ania and the boys. They had all suffered enough.

She'd reached out to Ania twice in the last couple of days, left two voicemails, to no avail. The woman had ignored messages from Conrad's colleagues too. Which is why Nicole had forced herself to venture out, to check on them herself today. As much as she found Ania difficult, she hated the idea of her hiding away, guilt-ridden because of her husband's actions. Though now she was here, she was beginning to wonder...

Their first meeting, at one of Harrison Dunbar's garden parties, a few years earlier, shortly after Conrad had joined the company, climbed into her mind. Ania had looked uncomfortable that day, standing at the edge of the lawn alone. Raven-black hair piled messily onto her head, like a tall Helena Bonham Carter. Deep-red tea dress swishing around her ankles in the gentle breeze. Two young boys clinging to her side. Her husband circulating the area, doing his best to fit in with his new colleagues. Most of the Harrison employees were older, their kids grown. It was refreshing to find someone with younger children, especially when they were similar in age to her own.

Nicole had sidled up to her that day, encouraged her children to coax the Gilbert boys into a game of chase so that the two women could become acquainted.

Only Ania didn't share Nicole's enthusiasm for friendship.

'You're Ethan's wife, aren't you?' she'd said, her tone dismissive, clipped. And before Nicole could answer, she'd added, 'You need to speak with your husband. He's keeping mine out until all hours.'

And with that she had moved off to the drinks table, leaving a dazed Nicole flabbergasted. Yes, Conrad drove for Ethan. He drove for all the senior partners, and sometimes the nature of their work meant long hours. The fact that Ania felt the need to raise the issue there was astonishing.

Later, when dinner was announced, Nicole had approached the long table set out on the Harrisons' lawn, only to find Ania tampering with the place names – moving her family further away from their planned seats beside the Jamesons.

Ania had rarely ventured out to company events since, and when she did, she kept her distance. Occasionally, Conrad brought their kids himself and the children played with Katie and Finlay happily. It was all rather sad and unnecessary.

A group of teenagers bumped shoulders, laughing together, sharing a private joke as they passed on the pavement nearby, dragging Nicole back to the present.

You're doing this for Conrad, she told herself. *Looking out for his family. It's the right thing to do.*

Nicole sighed heavily and looked back at the house. The letterbox glistened in the early-afternoon sunlight. She was beginning to wonder if they were out, or that perhaps the doorbell was broken, when the net curtain was pulled back, and a face appeared at the front room window. Patryk.

Nicole smiled at the young boy and gestured at the door. Within seconds, she heard the jangling of a chain being removed. The door juddered as it opened.

'Hello, Patryk,' Nicole said. 'You remember me, Nicole. Katie and Finlay's mum.'

The child stared up at her unspeaking.

'Is Mummy at home?' she asked.

'Who is it?' a voice called from inside.

'She's having a lie-down,' the boy said.

'Patryk!' The voice again.

Footsteps descended the stairs and Ania appeared. She was dressed in black leggings and an emerald tunic. Tousled hair hung loose on her shoulders, framing a tired and drawn face. If she was surprised to see Nicole, it didn't show.

'He's not supposed to answer the door,' Ania said, angling her head past Nicole and looking up and down the street. Short, birdlike movements.

'Katie does the same. I'm always telling her not to.'

Ania ignored her. Instead making a play of sending Patryk upstairs to check on his brother.

'I'm sorry if it's a bad time,' Nicole said. Ania wasn't listening. She was looking up and down the road again. 'I just wanted to—'

'You'd better come in.' Ania reached out an arm, and guided Nicole over the threshold so quickly, she almost tripped, then closed the door.

'Is something wrong?'

'Reporters.' Ania's mouth puckered. 'We've had them knocking at the door. I don't like people looking in.'

'Ah.' Her dad had moved a bunch of journalists off her own driveway yesterday. The media was cruel when it got its teeth into a story. Plane crashes were rare, and the loss of two young professionals in their prime had pricked their curiosity. 'How are the children doing?' she asked, changing the subject.

Ania glanced at the ceiling and shrugged.

'It must be hard for them.'

'It's hard for all of us.' She led Nicole into a small front room, dominated by an oversized sofa, an armchair beneath the window. A colourful Turkish hearth rug covered the polished oak floor. 'I was so sorry to hear about Ethan,' Ania said. 'You must be...' She looked away, blinked, shook her head.

Nicole jumped in to thank her. Anything to dispel the awkwardness hanging like a foul smell in the air. 'I just wanted to come by and see how you are doing,' she said. 'If you need anything...'

'We don't.'

Nicole stared at the line of sympathy cards overlapping one another. On the windowsill, on the mantelpiece, on the sideboard. It mirrored her own front room, a family home shrouded in grief. Two men had gone. Two people ripped from their lives, leaving gaping holes behind. 'My mother thinks I should organise a memorial service,' she said softly.

Ania's face eased and when it did so, she looked surprisingly childlike. 'For Ethan?'

Nicole nodded. 'I don't know what to do. It feels... too soon. A part of me still expects him to walk through the front door.'

They both settled themselves down. Nicole on the sofa, Ania on the armchair beside the window. There was no invitation, but it just seemed automatic, natural. And for the first time Nicole felt the shutters between them open a tiny crack.

'I had to choose Conrad's coffin yesterday,' Ania said, staring into space. 'It was so clinical, like picking a piece of furniture.' She flicked her gaze to Nicole, and her eyes instantly widened. 'Oh, I'm sorry.'

'Don't be.' The thought of what had happened to Ethan's remains, of where his final resting place might be, made her nauseous. She wouldn't be choosing coffins any time soon. 'You've decided to organise the funeral then.'

'No sense in waiting. O'Hanlon's are handling it for us. The service is next Thursday in the church at the City of London Cemetery and Crem on Aldersbrook Road.'

'So soon?' Nicole was astounded. Her gran's funeral last year had taken three weeks to arrange.

'Blanka knows old man O'Hanlon's son. They fitted us in early. I'm arranging a small service, a burial. Just close-knit family and friends. Conrad's brother's coming across from Salisbury. I just want it over with now.' She stood and peered around the edge of the curtain. 'Perhaps then, they'll leave us alone.'

Nicole pressed her lips together. Harrison Dunbar was well known in the finance sector and the tragic loss of two colleagues, and then the announcement about the sleeping pills, had pushed the story to the forefront of the local news. A family piece, or even a quote, would give them a new angle. 'They'll forget about us soon,' she said quietly. 'Move on to something else.'

Ania raised her gaze, met Nicole's eyeline. 'Maybe. Did you know Conrad was planning to leave the company?'

Nicole felt a jolt in her chest. 'What?' She listened to Ania's tale about the draft resignation letter she'd found on Conrad's laptop, astounded. 'No. I had no idea.'

'Ethan didn't mention anything?'

'No. Not at all. I suppose it's possible Conrad didn't tell him.'

'Conrad didn't even tell me, but he must have had reason to write a resignation email.'

Silence fell upon them, thickening the air as Nicole struggled to make sense of the revelation. Conrad flew with Ethan regularly. They ate together when they were away, worked out in the hotel gyms together, were close. It was extraordinary he would keep something like this to himself.

Ania narrowed her eyes to a squint. 'What do you know about that deal Ethan was working on?'

The hairs on the back of Nicole's neck pricked. 'What deal?'

'Surely, Ethan mentioned it to you? Conrad said it was a special customer. There was a lot riding on it. All very confidential. Then they go away suddenly on Wednesday morning, and we don't see them again.'

Nicole opened her mouth and closed it again. Ethan hadn't mentioned anything to her about a secret deal. 'No, he didn't. And I'm not sure what you're getting at.'

'You know how much Conrad cared about his job,' Ania continued. 'Flying was his life. It doesn't make sense. The weather last Friday – it was clear. Perfect conditions. And Air Traffic Control said no distress call was put out.'

'Maybe their communications were down.'

'They still had mobile phones.'

Nicole stared at her, aghast. 'What are you suggesting?'

'I'm not sure. Something at the company—'

Nicole huffed. This was ridiculous. There was no reason, and no evidence for that matter, to cast aspersions on the company. 'Like what?'

'Like I said, I'm not sure. All I know is Conrad wouldn't resign, not just like that. He wasn't even looking for another job. *Something* must have happened.'

Nicole scratched the back of her neck. 'Who was this special client?'

'I don't know. Conrad wouldn't tell me the specifics.'

'Why don't you ask the Harrisons?'

Ania curled her lip. 'Oh, believe me. I intend to.'

Nicole recalled the Harrisons visiting her yesterday. Olivia's pale face as she handed over a bunch of flowers. David hugging her tightly. The pair of them utterly grief-stricken. Yes, David ran a tight unit, and expected a lot from his staff. But she couldn't see him involved in anything sinister. 'I'm not sure—'

'Don't you think it's strange the way David is so protective of some of his clients,' Ania gabbled on, as if she was talking to herself. 'The way he keeps everything close, in house. He made Conrad hire cars, for Christ's sake, to chauffeur the staff abroad as well as at home. Did that never strike you as odd?'

True, Nicole thought. They were careful, respectful of confidentiality. But they represented some high-profile clients. Clients whose privacy David was protecting. No. Ania was deflecting. A deflection that was making her paranoid and Nicole couldn't listen to another second of it.

'They found a sleeping drug in Conrad's system,' Nicole said quietly. She hadn't wanted to raise this, not today, especially with the press hounding them. 'I'm sorry. I know that's not what you want to believe, but if it impaired his ability to fly in some way—'

Ania's face darkened. 'It's not true. The only way Conrad would have taken drugs before a flight is if someone had given them to him without his knowledge.'

Nicole sat in the traffic on her way home, her mind racing like a Formula One car at Grand Prix. Grief was playing tricks with Ania's thoughts, her conjecture a by-product of an overactive imagination and the pressing need to plant the blame elsewhere. That was it. Of course it was. It was only natural she'd want to clear any stain on her late husband's character.

But now, as Nicole stared at the hypnotic line of brake lights rising up the hill in front, fragments of their conversation sat uncomfortably. Why hadn't Ethan told her he was working on a big deal for a special customer? Surely something that important you'd discuss with your wife. Though, Ethan was a senior partner. He worked on a lot of big deals, attracted a lot of important clients.

Ania's sharp retort on the issue of the sleeping pills jabbed at her. Was it possible Conrad was taking them secretly? Perhaps they had problems in their marriage. Ania couldn't be the easiest person to live with. Plus, they hadn't been told about the level in his system. Was it possible it was minimal, and he thought he was okay to fly?

The draft resignation was odd though.

It had been no surprise to anyone at the company when David purchased the private plane, a little under three years ago. Business was expanding, they were all travelling more. Nicole remembered how she'd puffed out her chest at the time, proud of Ethan for putting in a word for Conrad and persuading David that their chauffeur, with his enthusiasm for flying and evident loyalty, was the perfect choice to train up as company pilot. A few members of staff made noises at the time: it would have been easier to hire a freelance, cheaper too. But the nature of Harrison Dunbar's business meant working with rich clients. For some, discretion was everything. It was convenient to have someone on the inside, someone in the 'Harrison family', as David liked to call it. A situation that suited them all perfectly. Perhaps, with the experience he'd now gained, Conrad had simply been offered a better position elsewhere. But it did strike her as strange that he wouldn't mention it to his wife.

The car in front moved and braked again. Nicole edged forward. The North Circular was busier than usual for a Thursday afternoon. At this rate, it would be teatime before she got home.

At least it gave her time to think, to ponder Ania's words.

The woman didn't approve of David Harrison, that much was obvious. She disliked the way families were urged to attend events, and wine and dine occasional clients, on top of the long, unsociable hours the job demanded. Nicole reluctantly accepted the schmoozing as a part of Ethan's job. She worked hard, life was busy. A part of her quite liked to don a cocktail dress and dip her toe in the glamour, every now and again. And she'd known the Harrisons for six years now, ever since Ethan had joined the company. Suggesting something else had contributed to the plane crash, that even the company may be involved... No, that was too much of a stretch, even for Ania. She was clutching at straws. She had to be.

It was after four when Nicole finally pulled into her driveway. She parked up, leaned back into the headrest and looked up at her whitewashed semi-detached home, nestled in the heart of Swain's Lane, a stone's throw away from the busy cafes and gastropubs of Highgate. A far cry from the pebble-dashed terrace where she grew up in south London. Ten years ago, she'd never imagined herself living somewhere like this. But ever since she'd met him, Ethan had a fire in his belly. He wanted his family to live the dream. *Their* dream.

Memories of a balmy evening during freshers' week at university filled her mind. Sitting outside the student union bar under a clear sky. Drinks flowing, the atmosphere charged with excited chatter. The courses were just beginning. New friendships striking up. She'd ignored the tall blond when he'd initially approached. Guys rarely approached her and when they did, they were usually drunk, after a quick shag and best avoided. She was shocked when he ignored everyone else, bought her a drink and sat beside her. Not even the slightest bit inebriated, asking questions, showing genuine interest in her! That night, they drank shots and danced until their limbs ached, and their heads were fuzzy. He'd walked her back to her room across the sports field, their shoes stroking the dewy grass, and kissed her hand instead of snogging her face off at the door. They became inseparable afterwards.

Before uni, Nicole had few close friends. When she did venture out to occasional events, her parents had dropped her off and picked her up. Uni changed everything. For the first time in her life, she was free. Free to come and go as she pleased. Free to explore. And she explored Ethan. She'd never met anyone like him, so gregarious and fun, but focused and fiercely ambitious. 'We can do anything we want if we work hard enough,' he said. She'd always wanted to move out of London, buy a family home in the country. Together they could do it. Together they were indestructible.

A lump climbed into her throat as a slideshow of their life after university passed in front of her. The dreary flat they rented as postgrads with the damp bedroom wall, the bathroom window that never quite closed properly and rattled in the wind. 'We'll be out of here in no time,' Ethan had said. 'It's only temporary.' Everything was only temporary with Ethan, his eye permanently on the next big thing. They moved several times in the early years of their marriage. Until Katie was born, and they found this home. 'The next one will be the big one, I promise,' Ethan had said with a twinkle in his eye as they stood surrounded by boxes in the hallway on that first evening. 'The next time we move, I'll have my own company and we'll have our house in the country. Our forever home.'

Nicole closed her eyes, swallowed the lump back deep into her windpipe and climbed out of the car. If the last week had taught her anything, it was that nothing was forever.

The road was unusually busy outside. Cars whooshed past, pedestrians filled the pavement. A tall passer-by in dark clothing, a low-peaked baseball cap masking his face, hovered at the end of her drive, typing into his phone. Nicole ignored him and busied herself with reaching into the car to retrieve her bag and jacket. At least yesterday's reporters hadn't returned.

When she looked up again, the man was still there, less than fifteen metres away. His presence throwing a long shadow up the driveway. And he was staring straight at her.

A cold shiver danced around Nicole's neckline. 'Can I help you?' she asked.

He said nothing, but his gaze hooked hers. Cold, steely.

'I said, can I help you?' Nicole repeated, enunciating every syllable.

He didn't answer. Instead, he tore his gaze away, tapped something else into his phone. Then cast her one last cursory glance from beneath the peak of his cap and moved off.

Nicole stood on the driveway watching him a moment, with far more bravado than she felt, before she slammed the car door and scurried into the house. Perhaps she'd been wrong about the reporters.

Chapter 9

Ania climbed out of the taxi and looked up at the red-brick converted factory in front of her. David and Olivia Harrison divided their time between their country home in the Cotswolds and their Docklands apartment and this Saturday morning they were in London. She knew that because she'd taken precautions, called ahead. The taxi to West London was expensive enough; she couldn't afford a wasted journey.

She stepped across the cobbled street, pressed the keypad beside the entrance. Seconds later, Olivia's high-pitched voice answered, 'Ania, sweetheart. Come straight up.'

Inside, the foyer was vast. The light of a chandelier bounced off the marble flooring, the reflection of its abundant crystals sparkling in the shiny gold lift. A winding staircase swept away to the side.

Olivia was waiting at the door, lips pressed together anxiously, when Ania stepped out of the lift on the top floor. She was wearing a lemon linen shift dress that showed off her willowy figure. David behind, a stripy shirt hanging loose over a pair of cream trousers. Immaculate, as usual, even on a Saturday.

'Darling, you should have let us come to you!' Olivia cried.

She'd said much the same when Ania had phoned earlier. But Ania had insisted. She didn't want them to come to her. She didn't want her children witnessing this conversation. Plus, she'd gone out of her way to avoid the Harrisons when Conrad was alive. She certainly didn't want them in her house now that he'd died. Which is why she'd ignored their messages this past week, let Blanka field their calls. No. The only reason she was here this morning was to find out what had been going on at the company, to confront David about the resignation. To get answers to the questions whirling around her mind.

Ania stiffened as Olivia encased her in a tight hug.

'How are you doing?' David asked when Olivia released her. He leaned forward awkwardly, pecked her on the cheek. 'And the boys? We can't begin to imagine what you must be going through.'

'We're coping.' She didn't have time for their sympathy, their pity.

They motioned for her to follow them, down a bright hallway, lit by an atrium window above. Another door led directly into a spacious open-plan area, light and airy due to the cream walls, the milk-white carpet, the folding glass doors leading out onto a decked balcony overlooking the River Thames beyond. Inside, a kitchen filled one end, edged with a long breakfast bar and high stools. Two leather sofas were arranged at an angle in the middle, a copy of the *The Times* folded on the coffee table between them. Ania's gaze fell upon the wrought-iron spiral staircase in the corner, which she guessed must lead to the famous roof terrace Conrad had talked about, where the Harrisons hosted evening drinks with guests and clients.

'Please, take a seat,' Olivia said, motioning to one of the sofas. 'Can I get you a drink?'

Ania declined. She didn't have long. She'd left the kids with Blanka, who needed to leave for work at lunchtime.

They settled themselves down, the Harrisons on the sofa opposite.

'We got something for the boys,' Olivia said. She lifted a Harrods bag from the side of the sofa and passed it across. The contents were wrapped in shiny silver. 'A couple of remote-controlled cars. Might take their minds off things for a while, poor little mites.'

'That's very generous of you,' Ania said blankly. She looked out onto the sunlight sparkling off the river below. She couldn't help wondering how many times Conrad had been in this room. How many times he'd sat on this sofa, and stared at that view.

She opened her mouth to speak, but before she could do so, David cut in. 'Have you thought about the funeral?'

'It's all arranged.'

'Ah.'

A beat passed before Ania passed on the details. She didn't want them there, but she couldn't see any way of avoiding it. They were bound to find out from someone else.

'What about the wake?' Olivia asked, clasping her hands together. 'We'd like to help.'

'We're having a quiet one at home. Family only.'

David cleared his throat awkwardly. If they were put out, they weren't about to show it. 'Right. Well, I've got Henry sorting out the life insurance policy. I'm sure you'll find it generous.'

Is that what they thought she'd come to talk about? Money? Ania couldn't give a bloody damn about money. They'd get by somehow. She could go back to work, get another job as a teaching assistant, maybe even study for her degree this time. No, this had nothing to do with money.

'I just wanted to reassure you,' he continued. 'You'll have no worries on the financial front. You've enough to think about.'

Ania felt her hackles lift a notch. They had no idea what she had to think about. 'We still have to pay back the loan for Conrad's flight training yet,' she said, crisply.

'I don't think we need to worry about that now,' he replied. 'Few gave their time to the company like Conrad. You know how much we thought of him.'

The words touched a nerve. 'If you thought so highly of him, why was he planning to leave?'

Olivia's jaw dropped. She looked to her husband. But Ania's gaze was fixed directly on David. His body language changed. Tensed. A flicker of confusion played across his face. Confusion and something else. Something Ania couldn't read.

'I don't know what you're talking about,' he said, tramlines furrowing his brow.

She told them about the draft resignation note she'd found. 'What do you think prompted that?'

David's face scrunched further, as if he wasn't sure where this was going. 'I have no idea.' He looked to his wife, then back to Ania. 'We've been talking about changing the Cirrus next year. Upgrading. He was involved in the decision about what to buy next. He certainly gave me no indication he was planning on leaving.'

If Nicole had told them about her trip to Ania's, warned them of their discussion, they were doing a good job of feigning surprise. She imagined them at Nicole's house, drinking coffee, passing on presents for the Jameson children. Though they'd have received a very different reception there. It was clear Ethan was the golden boy at the firm. From what Ania had heard from Conrad, his family were treated like royalty.

Ania ploughed forward. 'What was the trip to Nantes about?'

'Just a routine business trip, a client Ethan was working with.'

'Which client?'

David jerked his head back. 'You know I can't tell you that, dear. It's confidential.'

The word *dear* went through her. 'I don't see why not. It's not like it would make much difference now.' She didn't give him time to answer. 'Only, I know Ethan was working on something particular before he died. Conrad told me. A big account. There was a lot riding on it. It must have caused quite a stir in the company.'

'Ethan worked on a lot of big accounts.' David shifted in his seat. 'I'm sorry, Ania, what exactly are you getting at?'

'They were called away very suddenly on Wednesday.'

'As is often the case. Our clients expect a personal service.' He straightened and, even with Ania's above-average height, appeared to tower over her.

But Ania sat tall. 'I'm trying to understand why my husband drafted a letter of resignation, then a week later he's dead. Why there was a sleeping drug found in his system when he hasn't taken sleeping pills in over a year.'

Olivia's hand flew to her chest. 'Oh, sweetheart, it was an accident! A terrible tragic accident.'

The tension in the room tightened.

If Ania had looked away, she'd have missed it. For a split second, David shot her a look of venom, fire ablaze in his eyes. He glanced at his wife, quickly recovered his composure and sat forward. 'We're all hurting,' he said. 'Conrad and Ethan were like sons to me. I'm devastated to hear that he was thinking of leaving the company. Believe me, I had no idea. But it has no bearing on what happened.' His face pained. 'You're letting your mind run away with you, Ania. You can't possibly think—'

'Frankly, I don't know what to think,' Ania cut in. The Harrisons stopped short, both pairs of eyes on her as she passed her gaze between the two. 'I don't know what to think or who to believe.'

Chapter 10

Ania sat at her kitchen table surrounded by nests of paperwork – the contents of Conrad's bedside cabinet, the cupboard in the front room dresser, their kitchen drawers. It was Monday morning and, after her visit to the Harrisons on Saturday, she'd started the process of going through their paperwork, desperately searching for some clue as to Conrad's mood and movements up to the crash. She didn't believe David Harrison when he'd implied the trip to Nantes was nothing out of the ordinary, that it was business as usual. Maybe the trip wasn't unusual, but something else had been going on, she was convinced of it. Though all she'd found so far were piles of paid bills, delivery notes from eBay and other online stores, and little mementoes and old birthday cards from the children.

A shriek sounded from the front room. The kids were getting restless. She'd planned to keep them off school for another week, until after the funeral, although she was now beginning to wonder whether it was such a good idea.

She looked back at the table in front of her, moved aside an old key ring and opened a *Congratulations on Your Wedding Anniversary* card from Blanka, smiling at the greeting inside, written in Polish. Blanka was fiercely proud of their heritage and keen to pass it on to Ania's boys, cooking them pierogi (stuffed dumplings) or szarlotka (Polish apple cake), and teaching them Polish words and phrases. Ania had lost count of the times she'd said, 'You should talk to them in Polish, raise them bilingual.' When they were born, Ania had intended to. But Patryk didn't speak until he was two, and she worried she was confusing him. Then Robert came along, and life was so busy. Plus, she and Blanka had made a concerted effort to speak to one another in English the moment they arrived in the UK, even they barely conversed in their native language these days – a fact which, deep down, suited Ania just fine. Because Poland didn't hold happy memories for her like it did for Blanka.

She read through the greeting again, cast the card aside and worked her way through the last pile of unchecked papers, putting to one side another delivery note – this time for guitar plectrums – and that's when she spotted it. A photograph. *How did this get in here?* A distant longing filled her chest as she looked down at the smiling face of her mother, leaning up against the oversized oak front door of the apartment she was raised in, back home in Warsaw. Oh, how she wished she could talk to her, to share the troubles, the strain of the last week. A note had attached itself to the back. She peeled it away, unfolded it. And her heart turned to stone.

It was from her brother, Piotr. Addressed to Conrad. Just a few scrawled lines in broken English, asking him to get in touch. A contact number below. No date. A fire burned in her chest. She didn't want this in her house. She'd worked hard to put Piotr and his sinister mis-dealings behind her. She didn't want this anywhere near her family. She rushed to the bin, ripped the note in half, then half again, and dropped it inside. The bin clanged, metal against metal, as it snapped shut.

Another shriek from the boys. Ania exhaled a long sigh, pushed all thoughts of her brother out of her mind, and wandered into the front room. Robert scooted past her up the stairs. Patryk was standing on the armchair, staring out of the window.

'You have to stop fighting with Robert,' she said.

The child ignored her. 'That man,' he said, pointing at the road outside. 'He's there again.'

'Patryk, get down from the window.'

The net swung back into place as Patryk slid to the floor. 'That man you were talking about yesterday. He's out there again,' he repeated.

At that moment, Robert shouted down the stairs, calling for his mother.

Another exasperated sigh. Ania glanced at the window, then down at her son. 'Thank you for letting me know. Now go and see what your brother wants, will you?'

Patryk let out a long groan and sauntered out of the room. She waited for him to go, then crossed to the window and peered around the side of the curtain, squinting through the sunlight at the busy street. It was nearly lunchtime, the sky a brilliant azure blue. A pair of women wandered along the pavement on the other side of the road; a man walked a Labrador behind them. A lorry trundled past, followed by a motorbike. And then she saw him: the short man in the dark trousers and blue shirt, leaning against the plane tree diagonally opposite, staring directly at her house. Sunglasses masked his eyes. Wheels of sweat showed beneath his armpits. He'd been there a while.

He'd been there yesterday too. And on Saturday evening.

A ball of anger rose in Ania's chest. She was sick of people hanging about. Nicole Jameson had said there were reporters outside her place too, trying to get a soundbite, something to accompany their next news piece. How long must they endure this? Had these people never heard of family privacy? They'd clearly never lost anyone dear.

A soft thud upstairs. A peal of laughter. Her boys were wrestling again. She needed to go up and sort them out, but... another glance outside. She couldn't let this go. She dropped the curtain back into place, marched out into the hallway and pushed her feet into her shoes. She'd had enough. It was about time her family were left alone to grieve.

The man looked up as Ania flew out of the front door, leaving it open.

'Hey!' she shouted across the road. Within seconds, she was at her gate, fiddling with the catch. A woman had stopped to watch. A group of teenagers on the other side of the road turned.

The man didn't answer.

'I want to speak to you,' Ania yelled. A stream of cars passed, one after the other. She stamped her feet, searched for a gap in the traffic.

The man casually slunk off, as if he hadn't heard her. More people stopped to watch, clogging the pavement.

'Hey!' Ania called. 'Leave my family alone!' The blast of a passing lorry snatched her words. She gritted her teeth, waited for it to pass, then rushed across the road, only to find it empty.

Ania placed her hands on her hips and looked up and down the road. Where had he gone? He couldn't have disappeared into thin air.

People started to move off now the show was over.

Ania touched the forearm of a boy wheeling a bicycle along the path. He only looked about fourteen. 'Did you see where that man went?' she asked.

He paled, wide-eyed. Said nothing.

She suddenly realised how firm her grip was and released it. He jumped on the bike and sped off. She turned and stopped a woman pushing a buggy. 'The man in the blue shirt,' she said, pointing at the tree. 'He was just there. Did you see him?'

The woman shook her head, looked at her as if she was crazy, and made off.

Ania turned on her heels 360 degrees. Reporters didn't run away. They didn't make themselves scarce when you approached them. If anything, quite the contrary.

She stepped back a few paces. Her front door was open; her boys were alone. She raced back across the road, zigzagging through the traffic. Ania was out of breath by the time she reached her gate. Only to find the boys, sitting on the stairs, staring out at her. Frightened little faces. Had they witnessed the whole thing?

She wasn't standing for this a moment longer. She reached into her pocket and pulled out her phone. She didn't care where they were from or who they were, she wouldn't have her children upset.

Chapter 11

'Are you sure it was the same man you saw yesterday?' the officer asked. She was a large woman, her uniform polo shirt stretched across her stomach as she perched on the edge of Ania's sofa. A petite colleague beside her typed the details into a tablet.

The police had responded within ten minutes. Two female officers. One searched the street, the other looked around the house, the yard out back. When they were confident all was clear, they had moved into the house and settled themselves on Ania's sofa.

'Of course she's sure,' Blanka said. She'd arrived amid the commotion.

The officer asked again for the man's description and took down the details. 'And you didn't see in which direction he made off?'

'No, I told you.' Ania was getting exasperated now. She'd taken her time to talk them through the plane crash and losing Conrad. If they were aware of the incident, they didn't let on. She'd told them about the journalists hanging about afterwards. Gone through the earlier event in minute detail. She'd even told them about Conrad's draft resignation note, her visit to the Harrisons and her disbelief over him taking Zopiclone, yet they still felt the need to ask more questions.

'And he hasn't spoken to you at all, even when he's been here before?'

'No. He didn't answer me today. As soon as I shouted across the road and tried to approach him, he vanished.' She cursed herself for not thinking to take a photograph.

The officers exchanged a glance.

'What?'

They ignored her question. 'He hasn't knocked the door, approached the boys, or possibly even your friend?'

'She's already said, no,' Blanka replied.

'And you don't know him?'

'What does that mean?' Blanka again.

'We have to ask the question,' the officer said.

Blanka placed a protective arm around Ania's shoulder. 'We don't know him. Do you think he is from the press?'

Ania shrank back. All weekend, Nicole's visit coupled with that to the Harrisons on Saturday had buzzed around her head. Something was amiss. She felt it in the pit of her stomach. And David Harrison's reluctance to discuss the trip to the company offices in Nantes or to talk about what Ethan was working on before he died only reinforced her concern. What secrets was he hiding?

But, just like the blank faces of the officers opposite, Blanka didn't buy her suspicion about the Harrisons either. She thought she should take whatever life insurance they offered and put it all behind her.

The slim officer looked at Blanka. 'It's possible he was from the press,' she said. 'Though I imagine he would show an ID card.'

'So, what are you going to do about it?'

Another traded glance. The large officer turned to Ania. 'Has anything else given you cause for alarm? Phone calls? Have you had any threats?'

Ania shook her head.

The officer looked at the floor, long and hard, before she continued. 'Look, Mrs Gilbert, I know you've been through a difficult time—'

'That's got nothing to do with it.'

'We can't control who stands on the pavement. It is possible this man was waiting for someone or carrying out a survey. It's a busy road, there could be a perfectly innocent explanation.'

Is that what they thought? That she was a grieving widow, gone off her head at some innocent man, waiting for someone in the street. 'He didn't take his eyes off the house.'

'You said he was wearing sunglasses.'

'Yes, but he was facing here.'

Sensing her agitation, the petite officer held up a calming hand. 'Be assured, we take allegations like these very seriously.'

'So, what will you do?' Blanka pressed.

The officer turned to Ania in response. 'We'll record the occurrence.'

Ania swiped her hand down the front of her face. 'The occurrence?'

'As I say, there could be an innocent explanation. I don't want you to worry unduly. We will be checking our records and CCTV around the area with a view to identifying the man and establishing what he was doing here. We'll be back in touch when we know more, and we'll feed it back to the inquiry into your husband's death. In the meantime, I'd ask you to be extra vigilant. Always keep your phone with you and don't go out alone. If you see the man again, get a photo if it's safe to do so, and if he approaches you or your family, call us immediately.'

Chapter 12

A tsunami of pain. Lower abdominal. Excruciating.

Nicole dropped to her knees and clutched her stomach. She was at home, on the landing. She'd been making her way to the bathroom when her legs gave way, leaving her hunched in the shard of light seeping through the window. Face red hot.

No. No. No. Please, no! Not again.

She started to crawl, the thick pile of the carpet catching at her knees. Another cramp stalled her. She hugged herself again.

The pain was unbearable now. Rivulets of sweat coursed down her back. She gulped a breath. Her vision began to blur.

A chiming in the distance. Nicole ignored it. Holding on to her stomach, wrapping her arms around herself as if the movement might somehow lessen the pain and keep the baby inside.

Several beats passed.

Another chime, louder this time. She jolted forward. Eyelids fluttering open, Nicole drew a sharp intake of breath. She was at home, in her bed. Her hand shot to her tummy. A dream. It was only a dream. A cruel twisted dream.

Her neck was damp, her back clammy, but she didn't care. She was still almost nine weeks pregnant. Another three weeks to go until her ultrasound.

A long breath whooshed out. Thank God.

Nicole nestled back into the pillows, waiting for her breaths to regulate. Imagining the chug, chug, chug of her baby's quickened heartbeat. What was her child destined to look like? Would they be stocky and blond like Ethan and Finlay, or would they be petite and wrestle daily with chestnut curls like she and Katie? Would they go through the night from three or four months, or still interrupt her sleep in their toddler years? Not that it mattered. Because, more than anything, she wanted this baby, this little piece of her and Ethan. She wanted to raise it, nurture it, watch it grow. She wanted it so bad, her head hurt and her chest ached.

Perhaps she should finally tell her family. But, as comforting as it would be to share the load, something stopped her. It wouldn't be prudent. Not until the twelve-week scan confirmed everything was okay. Her loved ones had enough grief, enough heartache to deal with. She couldn't put them through any more.

The clock on the bedside table read 11.36 a.m. The doorbell sounded again. She vaguely recalled her parents talking about taking the kids to the park. She hauled herself up. She'd been so tired recently, so fatigued. This early trimester taking everything out of her. At least she hadn't suffered the sickness – that had been a devil with Finlay.

As she made her way down the stairs, she recognised the silhouette of Sharon, the family liaison officer, through the glass panel in the front door.

'Morning!' Sharon said brightly as she opened the door. 'Can I come in?' She stepped forward as she spoke. She was coming in anyway.

'Is there some news?' Nicole asked, raking a hand through her bed hair, desperately trying to smooth it out as they walked through to the sitting room.

'I'm just here to give you an update and see how you are all doing.'

Nicole inhaled, long and deep. A welfare call was the last thing she needed, especially as there was nothing anyone could do for them.

Sharon declined her offer of drinks and settled herself into the sofa, chatting about the investigation. AAIB were progressing with the inquiry. The plane was still stuck in the Channel. Nothing new. 'Is there anything you would like to talk to me about?' Sharon asked eventually.

The question, out of the blue as it came, knocked Nicole sideways. They hadn't spoken since Sharon had delivered the news that they were calling off the search for Ethan's body. 'Like what?'

'I don't know. Sometimes things happen. People think of questions or information when I'm not here.'

'What sort of information?' The woman talked in riddles.

Sharon ignored the question, asked how the children were coping.

'Okay. My parents are helping.'

'I take it your callers have dropped off,' she said, looking towards the window.

She was referring to the reporters. Nicole nodded.

'Good.' She licked her lips and pressed them together. 'No one else hanging around?'

Nicole narrowed her eyes. A brief flashback. The man in the baseball cap the other day. She considered mentioning it, but... she had no reason to believe he was doing anything wrong, and he hadn't been back. 'No,' she said. 'Why do you ask?'

'Colleagues received a report of harassment at Ania Gilbert's. She claimed a man had been hanging around, watching the house.'

Nicole stiffened. She hadn't heard a whisper from Ania since her visit. When Olivia and David saw her at the weekend, Olivia said afterwards that Ania had looked frail, ill, the grief taking its toll mentally and physically. 'Oh my God! Are she and the boys all right?'

'I've been assured they are all fine. We couldn't trace the individual, but the family weren't approached or threatened in any way. We're not unduly concerned. It is possible it was a misunderstanding. It may even be a rogue reporter, watching from afar. I just wanted to check you were all right.' Sharon stood. 'There's nothing else you want to tell me?'

Nicole frowned. 'No.'

'Well, you have my number. Don't hesitate to call if you need anything.'

She was at the door when she turned, opened her mouth, then closed it again. As if she was about to say something and stopped herself at the last minute. 'I'll get off then.'

Nicole thought of Ania as she watched the liaison officer walk down the drive. She should reach out to her again, the woman was clearly struggling. But it was Sharon's visit that clung to her like superglue as she closed the door. It felt odd, out of kilter. She had the distinct feeling that the detective was trying to tell her something, but she had no idea what.

Chapter 13

Ania checked the front door lock and chain for the third time that evening. It was cool out in the hallway, a thin draught seeping in where the door seal was broken at the bottom.

'It's locked.'

Ania jumped and spun round. To face Blanka, standing at the bottom of the stairs. 'I was just checking.'

'Again.' Blanka gave her hard stare. 'You okay?'

'Fine.'

'You sure? I can stay up a bit later with you if you like?'

'No. You've got work tomorrow.' She looked beat. It was good of Blanka to move in with them for a while, to help with the children, but she was working. She needed her sleep. 'Go to bed. I'll be fine.'

Blanka looked uncertain. 'The doctor told you to rest,' she said.

'And I'm just about to.'

She watched Blanka climb the stairs. At the top, the woman turned and glanced back at Ania before she disappeared into the back bedroom.

She was worried, Ania understood that. But she could do without the head tilts, the soppy eyes. It was the same with the doctor this morning. She'd only made the appointment because her neck pain had flared up, the stress igniting an old whiplash injury. He'd given her something for the pain, then fired questions at her. How was she coping? Did she need any help with the children? No, she didn't need help. What Ania needed was answers. Answers to the questions ringing in her head.

She hadn't found anything amongst Conrad's possessions to explain the abrupt draft resignation and the inquiry into the crash had gone quiet. When she'd phoned for an update yesterday, she'd been assured that they were looking into everything, every aspect of the day, both before, during and after the flight. Which presumably meant they'd speak to David Harrison and investigate what the men had flown over to Nantes for. At least they were being thorough. But their final remark had been like a fist to her gut. It would likely be months before they reached a conclusion. How could it possibly take months?

Ania waited until she heard Blanka's bedroom door close, then moved into the kitchen and checked the rear door lock and the window locks. When she was certain all was secure, she exhaled long and hard.

Back in the front room, she peered around the edge of the curtain into the street outside. It was almost 10.30 p.m. The lines of vehicles parked outside threw low shadows on the houses opposite. Street lights illuminated the pavement in pools of amber. A taxi rumbled past. Another shiver, deeper this time, reached into her bones. Was someone still lurking out there in the darkness, watching them?

Ania pulled away from the window and lowered herself into the armchair. She hadn't seen the man she'd tried to accost outside the other day since the police visit. But something didn't feel right. Every time she looked out of the window, every time she went out to her car, or arrived back home, she felt the heat of eyes upon her. Surely, she wasn't imagining it.

She pictured the police officer's face when she'd called by earlier. Reassuring Ania in her soothing voice that colleagues were circulating the description of the man she'd spotted outside, and they wouldn't give up. Reiterating the spiel about safeguarding herself and her family, remaining vigilant.

Confirming that, however relevant, all details would be fed back to the main inquiry.

However relevant. The police didn't believe her. Nicole hadn't believed her either, when she came last week, putting any presence outside down to journalists. Even Blanka, who'd been so supportive in front of the officers, who'd helped with the boys and stayed close, was now giving her odd looks. Looks that betrayed her growing concern for her friend's mental stability.

No one believed her. And why would they? There was nothing to suggest the man was doing anything illegal.

So, why did she feel so edgy?

Ania had never been the sort to be easily spooked. When she first moved to England, in her late teens, she and Blanka had rented rooms in some very suspect houses, with neighbours that banged on the door, and came and went at all hours. In one flat, they were trading drugs next door, visitors injecting heroin in the corridors. She lived on a busy road now, was accustomed to the low murmur of traffic outside her window. Yet every car engine, every voice, every creak and bump was making her jump. And no matter how hard she tried, she couldn't shake off the notion that she was being watched. If this was paranoia, the ghouls of grief playing tricks with her mind, she couldn't imagine anything worse.

Her gaze travelled to the crayons strewn across the coffee table beside her. That morning, she'd helped Robert draw a brightly coloured picture of his dad in football kit with his boys either side. Patryk wrote a letter in his disjointed hand-writing, telling his dad not to worry because he would look after everyone. They'd given them to Blanka to take to the funeral director's, along with the family portrait of them all from Conrad's bedside table. All to accompany Conrad on his final journey at the funeral tomorrow. It was heart-wrenching.

Ania collected up the crayons and placed them in the box in the cupboard beneath the television, then switched off the light and made her way upstairs. Pausing beside the crack in Patryk's doorway to listen to the ebb and flow of his breaths. Popping into Robert's room to pull the duvet he'd kicked off back up to his chin. Her usual night-time routine.

In her bedroom, she glanced up and down the street outside again, drew the curtains and then opened Conrad's wardrobe and inhaled, long and slow. Even his smell was fading. She ran her hand down the piles of hoodies and jeans on the shelves. At odds with the suits and dinner jackets and crisply ironed shirts hanging on the rail beside. The old and the new. The old Conrad, always more comfortable in jeans and sweatpants, only one to wear a suit at weddings and funerals. Until he joined Harrison Dunbar. Everything changed then. His clothes. His demeanour. The circles he mixed in. David invested in him, made his dream of flying possible, and changed him in the process.

Ania wrapped her arms around herself. Why, oh why, didn't Conrad tell her he was planning to leave? There was a time when they were open, told each other everything. Admittedly, he was more reluctant to talk about work of late, especially after the rows about it intruding into family life. But he'd mentioned the importance of Ethan's new deal. Surely, he'd discuss something as fundamental as changing his job.

Excited voices outside pulled her back to the window. Two young women were squaring up to each other in jest as they passed on the other side of street.

Was it possible Blanka was right? Was she overreacting?

She stepped away from the window and was lowering herself onto the edge of the bed when David's comment about repayment of the loan he'd given Conrad for half of the pilot training fees nudged her. '*I don't think we need to worry about that now.*' It was close to forty thousand pounds when they took it out three years ago. They'd agreed a monthly deduction of four hundred pounds to be taken direct from Conrad's wages. Even so, over half of it must still be outstanding. Was he writing it off, or implying the life insurance would? Whatever the situation, it wedged itself uncomfortably in her chest. It was almost as if he was trying to buy her silence.

Chapter 14

The stone church at the City of London Cemetery always felt chilly, no matter the time of year, and the sunlight, streaming through the lattice windows, did nothing to ease the situation. Nicole pulled her jacket across her chest and suppressed a shiver. As she did so, she felt Olivia's bony elbow at her side. There was barely any room to move between Olivia Harrison and the end of the pew.

She glanced down at the service booklet in her hands. Conrad Robert Gilbert stared back at her. Ash brown curls quiffed away from his face. His usual toothy grin, green eyes sparkling. He looked strong. Happy. Alive. Like a young Harry Connick Jr. Nicole shifted position, the wood cool and hard beneath her. The service was short. Two hymns, a couple of readings and a eulogy. It would be over in half an hour. She could manage half an hour, couldn't she?

More people were spilling into the church and forming a thin row at the back. She could see several Harrison Dunbar employees. Susan, David's secretary, sat in the row in front. Ellen, the receptionist, behind. Henry, the company accountant, across the other side beside the font. Various office staff and customers too, dotted around the church. '…a small service, a burial,' Ania had said. 'Just close-knit family and friends.' What would she make of all this?

The organ sounded. The church hushed. Nicole recognised the opening notes of 'You'll Never Walk Alone'. Heads turned. She followed them. Just in time to catch a light oak coffin enter, shouldered by six sombre-looking pallbearers. Olivia took her hand. The grip was warm, tender. But Nicole couldn't look away, her gaze glued to the wooden box travelling down the aisle. The box that contained Conrad's broken remains.

Her heart ached. Ethan would never have this. She couldn't arrange a burial or a cremation. Ethan would never have a final resting place, somewhere physical where she could take the children to mourn. Because they didn't have his body.

Ania entered the church behind, head bowed, in a long black dress that swept the floor. Dark hair pinned up on top of her head. She looked brittle, fragile. Like a piece of glass that might shatter at any moment. She was holding the hand of her youngest. Blanka, her friend, walked behind with Patryk. The two boys staring ahead, a pair of deer caught in headlamps.

Ania looked as if she'd lost half a stone in the past week. Nicole could only imagine what a horrendous burden it must be, wondering if your husband died and killed a passenger due to his own negligence. She worried about them. Blanka worked long hours and Ania needed people around her at times like this, to help with the children, with sorting the house, with building a life without Conrad. Nicole had her parents; she didn't know what she'd do without their support. There was so much to organise, Ania shouldn't be alone.

Nicole looked back at the coffin. It felt like someone had reached into her chest and grabbed her heart, their grip tightening by the second. Her vision blurred. Jagged lines appeared at the edge of her vision.

The procession was at the front of the church now, the coffin lowered gently onto the stand. The family streaming into the front pew.

'Excuse me,' Nicole said to Olivia. 'I just need to pop out.'

Olivia looked anxious. 'Are you okay?'

'I'm fine. I just need some air.'

'I'll come with you.'

'No, please.' She squeezed the woman's hand, then released herself. 'I'll come and find you afterwards.' And with that she scurried out of the pew and out of the church.

Chapter 15

The fresh air outside was like a drug. Nicole pressed her back into the old church wall. Chipped and pitted edges of stone digging into her as she gulped breath after breath. Waiting for her pulse to slow, and her body to calm. The organ was winding up, the congregation quietening. The mist began to clear. The heat in her cheeks cooled.

After the recent coverage, she had wondered if there might be reporters or photographers watching, but the cemetery was clear – the journalists' interest obviously taken elsewhere.

It was a bright day, the sun high in the sky. She retrieved her sunglasses from her bag and put them on. Then watched a couple of magpies flap about above a nearby yew tree, their movements perfectly synchronised. Should she go back inside? She could hear the vicar's voice amplified by the microphone, though couldn't quite make out the words. And the thought of being back in there, of looking at that coffin again, of listening to him talk about Conrad's life, induced a fresh wave of nausea.

No. It would be better for everybody if she stayed outside.

Time passed as she wandered around the cemetery, examining the different graves. The weathered headstones, barely decipherable, the wonky ones, the large tombs with statues. Tended graves with fresh flowers. Those forgotten, overgrown, the grass reaching up the headstones. Cemeteries had always intrigued Nicole. Every one of these little patches marking the passing of a loved one. Somebody's brother, father, son, sister, mother.

Her parents popped into her mind. When she'd left earlier, her mother had been picking flowers from the garden with the children and fixing them in an old-fashioned press. The press Nicole herself had used as a child. Alice was in her element, with a needy family around her. Nicole her only child, she'd struggled with her leaving home and, later, after her grandchildren were born, she'd persuaded Nicole's father to move across London, so that they could be nearby. She relished the opportunity to look after everyone, help the family heal and, in turn, they looked forward to her comforting stews and pies, her soothing words at the dinner table.

'Nicole?'

Nicole jumped. She hadn't heard anyone behind her. She turned abruptly to face a tall, stocky man with dark features. He wore a black suit, but then so did every other man in the vicinity. The jacket button strained at his overhanging paunch. Sunglasses covered his eyes, jet-black hair swept back from his forehead. 'Can I help you?' she asked.

'Nicole Jameson?'

Nicole lifted her sunglasses onto her head, expecting him to do the same. He didn't. Instead, he stroked his square jaw and the five o'clock shadow coating his chin even though it was only late morning.

'I'm sorry, do I know you?' she asked. It was disconcerting with his eyes covered.

'I doubt it. John Sampson,' he said, extending a hand. 'I... was associated with your husband.'

'Oh.' She shook his hand. His grip was firm, warm. The skin rough. The knuckles thick and strong.

She waited for him to pass on his condolences, tell her what a good guy Ethan was, how he'd gone the extra mile for his clients. Another sympathy call – they'd filled her Facebook timeline for the past two weeks. She was surprised when his face hardened. And even more surprised by his next question.

'What do you know about Ethan's associations, Mrs Jameson?'

'I'm sorry?' The words, seeming to appear from nowhere, shook her.

'How much do you know about your husband's business connections?'

Singing filled the air. 'Abide with Me'. The final hymn. The congregation would be exiting the church shortly. Nicole looked over her shoulder for David or one of the other Harrison Dunbar crew to bail her out. He was talking about the company. This was their area. But they were still inside.

'Not much,' she said warily. 'He pretty much kept his clients to himself, with a few exceptions.'

'So, you didn't know what he was mixed up in?'

Mixed up in? This was starting to feel threatening. And dodgy. 'I'm sorry. Who did you say you were?'

'John Sampson. I'm an intelligence agent. I work for the government.'

Nicole froze. Was this for real? 'W-what do you mean? Why are you interested in Ethan?'

'Your husband kept some interesting company,' he said, sidestepping her question.

Nicole blinked, long and hard. This was bizarre. Like she was in some strange dream and at any moment she might wake. 'I don't know quite what you are saying.'

'Now's not the right time.' He held out a hand, clasped hers again. 'I just wanted to introduce myself,' he said. 'We should talk. Give me a call when you are ready.'

Nicole withdrew her hand to find he'd pressed something into her palm. A business card.

'Let's keep this between ourselves for now,' he added, leaning in so close she could smell nicotine on his breath. 'Don't mention it to anyone.' A short glance at the church. 'Especially not that lot.'

What was he talking about? The church was emptying now. She peered around the people, spotted several Harrison Dunbar employees. When she turned back, Sampson was gone.

Nicole desperately craned her neck, this way and that. Then shuffled through the bodies gathering around her. Nothing. Where was he? She rushed to the front of the building, squinted down the long Church Avenue to the main gate. And there he was, striding towards the exit.

'Hey!' she called, holding up the card, apologising as she gently shoved people out of the way to race after him. By the time she'd reached the gate, he had vanished.

She checked the road, either way. A car raced past, and another. She looked down at the card, still in her hand. White, with the words J. P. Sampson, a mobile number beneath, written in black. An email address on the other side. What did he mean by Ethan 'kept some interesting company'? What did they think Ethan had been involved in? And what did he mean when he asked her to tell no one, *especially not that lot*? Who was he referring to? Employees of Harrison Dunbar, or someone else connected to Conrad?

She pulled her phone out of her pocket, typed out a quick text to Olivia.

Decided to make my way home. I'm fine, please don't worry x

She didn't want to alarm them, and she didn't want to be followed. She shoved the mobile into her pocket.

Nicole didn't feel herself dislodge the business card, didn't hear it slip out of her pocket. She didn't notice it float to the ground as she made off up the road.

Chapter 16

Nicole sat in the far corner of Joe's Cafe, on Romford Road, and stared at the tree outline shaped into the foam on the top of her latte. She couldn't go home, couldn't face her parents, her children. Instead, she'd called a cab and directed the driver towards the North Circular, away from the cemetery. It wasn't until they were on Romford Road, and she spotted the cafe, that she had asked the driver to pull over. She needed time to order her thoughts. Alone.

Should she call Sharon, her liaison officer, or – blood pounded her head – did Sharon already know about the intelligence agent? Surely the agencies would pass information between one another. Was that why the detective had been so on edge, so cagey with her questions yesterday?

Who was John Sampson? Did he work for MI5 or MI6? If the intelligence services were looking into Ethan's business transactions, why was she only hearing about this now?

Her mobile erupted on the table. Nicole jumped, pressing a hand to her stomach to calm her frayed nerves. The man at the next table looked across, his gaze lingering as the phone continued to ring, lit with a familiar name: Olivia Harrison.

Nicole tore her gaze away from the man beside her, stole a breath and tried to sound upbeat as she answered, 'Hello.'

'Nicole, darling. I got your text. Are you all right?' Nicole imagined Olivia standing outside the main cemetery gate in her Hobbs suit, perfectly manicured hands holding the phone pressed to her ear. David beside her. Had they caught the end of Nicole's exchange in the cemetery? Seen the agent leave?

The sound of a car passing filtered down the line. 'I'm fine. I just needed a bit of space.'

'Where are you now? We'll come and pick you up, give you a lift home.'

'I'm almost back, thank you.'

'Shall we come by? I'm worried about you.'

Nicole fought to keep her voice even. 'There's no need, really.'

'Okay, if you are sure.' Her tone was raspy, uncertain. 'I'll call you tomorrow.'

She shouldn't have left so suddenly. It was bad enough nipping out of the church to get some air, but running off like that, especially given their comments about Ania's mental health... It looked bad. As if *she* wasn't coping either.

Nicole ended the call, sat back in her chair and stared at the ceiling, Ania's suspicions about the crash flashing in and out of her mind. The blame she laid at Harrison Dunbar's door. Blame Nicole had dismissed, suspicions she'd ignored.

And now, this...

Ethan had been David's star partner. He brought in most of the new clients. If Ethan had mixed with *interesting* associates, if it was linked to work, David would know about it. But why had nobody said anything to her? And why would the intelligence services be concerned? It sounded illicit, as if Ethan had been involved in something serious, possibly criminal. Ethan usually shied away from anything illegal. He was the type of person who scrutinised the small print on contracts, even online software agreements that Nicole would ordinarily auto-click 'agree' on without reading, to make sure he complied.

She dug her hand in her pocket, searched for the business card. Tried the other pocket. Pulled out a tissue, a used car parking ticket. She jumped up, checked both pockets again. Ignoring the man at the next table gaping at her. She opened her bag, pulled out a hairbrush, her purse, one of Katie's hair ties. Nothing. She searched the floor, eyes darting from the door to the table. No! She'd only gone and bloody lost it.

Nicole cursed her clumsiness. How could she lose the card? Now she had no means of contacting John Sampson and finding out more. She toyed with going back to the cemetery to search for it. But so many people had trampled across the area. Someone else might have picked it up. Or she may have dropped it in the taxi.

She grabbed her phone again, googled John Sampson. It was a popular name with numerous listings. A professor of psychology in the US, a singer with music on YouTube. Facebook, Instagram users. Over one hundred LinkedIn profiles. She scrolled along a row of images. None of them fitted the dark-haired man in the suit she'd spoken to earlier. Though she supposed if he was working for the government, behind the scenes, his profile wouldn't be easily accessible online. Was that even his real name?

This was bizarre. Surreal. Like something out of a Tom Clancy novel. Admittedly, she didn't know much about Ethan's work. Apart from the occasional clients she met at Harrison Dunbar events, he rarely discussed his clients at home. He might moan about the odd difficult customer, but he rarely gave names or went into detail and, anyway, she usually switched off. Life was too busy. They had the children. She had her work. And he was often travelling, away. When he was home, it was family time.

John Sampson had asked about Ethan but was this specifically about him or were the intelligence services looking at the company? Harrison Dunbar was international, the rules in the financial industry were tight. Perhaps they bent them occasionally or had made some dubious investments.

Nicole googled 'Harrison Dunbar'. Immediately, a link to their website graced the screen, followed by a Wikipedia entry about David Harrison, listing him as the founder of the company in 1996. In 2003, he won Young Entrepreneur of the Year. It went on to talk about him growing up in Coventry. Son of a market trader, his mother worked part-time at the local supermarket.

Her shoulders dipped. She knew all this. She flicked back to the main search, changed her criteria to 'Harrison Dunbar news articles'. There was a stream about the crash, the tragic loss of two employees. An older piece about an after-dinner speech David had given to candidates from the Prince's Trust. Another of David handing a cheque to a children's charity. Her gaze rested on a piece on a financial site, from a few years ago, reporting the authorities investigating David Harrison for alleged insider dealing. Allegations later dismissed. Allegations Ethan had claimed were brought about by a disgruntled competitor. *Insufficient evidence of impropriety*, the article relayed. Ethan had been dismissive of the inquiry at the time. 'It happens all the while,' he had said. 'Harrison Dunbar are good at what they do, successful. There's always someone looking to dent the company's reputation.'

Nicole wrapped her hands around the mug, the heat from the drink calming her trembling nerves. The exchange in the cemetery filled her with disquiet. Could this be another allegation of impropriety, or worse, dodgy dealing? Again, she was reminded of Ania pointing the finger at the business, the resignation letter Conrad had written before he died. Was Ania right? Was there something else going on? If there was, she owed it to Ethan to find out, to expose it, and she knew exactly where to start looking. She just needed to get rid of her parents first. There was no way she wanted them caught up in whatever was going on.

Chapter 17

The door to Ethan's study opened with a low squeal. Nicole checked over her shoulder, listened for the soft breaths of her children, sleeping in the rooms nearby, and stepped inside.

Her parents had been reluctant to pack up and leave earlier. Despite her holding her chin high and thanking them, telling them it was time for her and the children to move forward and return to some kind of routine. For them to go home and look after one another. They'd hesitated. They were worried. She was worried too. But it was the right thing to do, for everyone. Her dad had an oncology appointment coming up, he needed her mother's care. And, after the exchange in the cemetery, Nicole needed time alone. To search for answers.

The room housed an antique Georgian desk with a wine leather inset, and a matching leather captain's chair with wheels that sank into the thick pile of the cream carpet below. A portrait of the family, taken when the children were young, Finlay a babe in her arms, hung on the far wall above the bookcase. This was Ethan's private space, the place he disappeared to when he worked from home. If she was to find out anything about Ethan's associations or his clients outside the Harrison Dunbar offices, it would be here.

The air smelt musty and stale. Nicole was instantly drawn to the window. It was closed. Ethan never closed the window. It was awkward to get to, with his oak desk pressed against the wall beneath. Many a time she'd suggested he move the desk, put it against the far wall, opposite the door, and he'd always refused. He liked the view of the back garden and the apple tree below.

Her mother must have closed the window. Just as she'd moved or 'tidied' Nicole's kitchen cupboards. It was a job to find anything; she'd had to hunt around to find the Marmite for Finlay's sandwiches earlier.

She brushed a finger over a silver framed photo of Katie and Finlay as toddlers beside a row of paperbacks at the back of the desk. *7 Habits of Highly Effective People. How to Win Friends and Influence People. Think and Grow Rich.* Ethan's motivational books.

The leather of his chair felt cold beneath her thighs, and soft and squishy as she lowered herself into it. A pang of sadness. Perhaps if Ethan had relaxed more, been less driven, he wouldn't have felt the need to dash off to address every client's whim. He wouldn't have taken the plane that day. And he'd still be with her now...

Nicole swallowed and pushed the thoughts to the back of her mind. She flipped open a blue A4 exercise book on the side of the desk. It was empty, the lined pages clear. Several pages had been torn out. She ran her finger along the ragged edge.

She turned to Ethan's tablet, hidden beneath the book. Ethan had been protective of his devices. *There's confidential information on there. Client details.* She slid the tablet towards her. His phone and his laptop would have been with him on the plane. This was his personal tablet, for gaming and YouTube, though she had occasionally found him working on it too.

She switched on the iPad, her stomach dipping to her toes. No light, nothing. The battery must be dead. She rolled the chair back and looked down at the rows of drawers, tugging at the top one. It was locked.

Nicole eased back in the chair and faced the garden. The branches of the apple tree swayed in the gentle breeze. Ethan kept all his personal keys with him. But... The desk used to belong to her father. They had inherited it when he retired.

She remembered they'd had to employ a locksmith to put the lock on the drawers. And she'd asked them to make a spare in case it was ever mislaid. A small gold key, a bit like a window lock. Where had she put it?

She made her way out of the room and down the stairs to the key rack in the hall. The metal tinkled together as she worked her way through the garage keys, spare car keys, shed keys. They seemed to have a key for everything. But there was nothing that resembled the desk key. She was about to give up when she knocked a messy ring of window keys off the bottom shelf and spotted something glisten amongst them as they hit the floor. That had to be it.

In the kitchen, she went through her cables. Working through a tangled mess of old phone, computer, toothbrush, camera chargers. Wondering why she kept them when she was sure she didn't have half the appliances anymore. Eventually, she pulled out a cable that might fit the tablet, raced upstairs and plugged it in. A red light appeared on the side. She gave it a few moments to warm up and turned back to the drawers. She slid the key into the lock and, yes, it opened!

The top drawer was loaded with paperwork. Old bank statements, held together with a bulldog clip. Share certificates. Exam certificates. The next was full of pens, highlighters, Post-it pads, paper clips. A box of drawing pins had broken and the pins tapped together as they rolled across the wooden base.

The bottom drawer caught as she pulled it, opening to a narrow gap. Nicole fed her hand through and had to jiggle it about to free up a folder that had wedged itself at an angle at the back. The buff folder ripped as she retrieved it. She smoothed out the corners. It was their mortgage agreement. Why Ethan felt the need to keep hard copies of this material when most things were stored online these days was beyond her. Beneath it was a notebook. Lines of figures written inside that made little sense. She flicked through the pages of scrawl. Something stood out on one of the pages – ZegloV-sw7. The black biro was heavy, as if Ethan had been talking on the phone, distracted, and written over the letters several times. It looked like a code of some sort.

She turned back to the iPad and fired it up. The screen lit, a deep blue. A password box in the middle. Nicole bit her lip, trying to guess what combination Ethan would use. She typed in the children's names to no avail. Tried Blink-182, his favourite band at uni. She looked back at the notebook, then typed in ZegloV-sw7 – it had to be worth a try. Nothing.

Frustrated, Nicole turned back and leafed through the paperwork. It was all boring, financial stuff – investment projections, more statements. Personal. Nothing relating to a client. She picked up the notebook, about to place it back when something slipped out from between the pages and floated to the floor.

An A5 piece of white card: a lunchtime restaurant menu. *On Board* written in silver at the top. *Fine cuisine* beneath it, with a sketch of a yacht. A selection of starters, mains and sweets. An address in central London and a telephone number along the bottom. She flipped it over. On the back was a handwritten note in blue: *Thanks for today, it meant the world. Looking forward to next time! Mags x*

Nicole's heart lurched. She sat back in her chair and stared at the menu. Who the hell was Mags?

Chapter 18

Ania dropped her sunglasses down over her eyes and stepped over the threshold of the supermarket. The funeral yesterday had passed in a blur. She had no idea who'd attended. The Harrisons were bound to have been there. Nicole Jameson too. Other colleagues of Conrad's from work. But she hadn't been able to face any of them after the service. It was as much as she could do to serve sandwiches to Conrad's brother's family at home before they travelled back to Salisbury.

She rubbed the tight muscles at the back of her neck, grabbed a trolley. Food shopping was the last thing she felt like doing this Friday morning. The painkillers were making her light-headed and she still felt jittery, as if she was being watched. But when she had put this to Blanka earlier, when she had tried to excuse herself from the trip, the woman had pulled a face, as if her friend was imagining things. She needed to step up, be strong for her kids. Show her friend she was at least trying to hold it all together.

The store was busy inside. Ania worked through her list methodically, taking care to keep her head down and avoid the eyes of other shoppers — she wasn't in the mood for conversation.

Patryk jumped onto the end of the trolley and Blanka indulged him by pushing it fast, letting it spin. The boys chuckled. Ania felt her shoulders slacken as Robert begged for a turn.

Time passed. She was almost at the end of her list when she reached the cereal aisle. Robert wanted Coco Pops. Patryk, Weetabix.

'Why don't you choose one each?' she said. 'As a treat.' She watched as Blanka helped the boys look through the different varieties. She couldn't remember when she'd last seen them so diverted and she couldn't help but lift her glasses onto her head and smile to herself.

The boys were just working through the boxes, making their selection when she heard a husky voice call out, 'Ania. Ania, is that you?'

Sweat prickled Ania's scalp. She turned towards the voice, and froze. It was Sarah. A former analyst at Harrison Dunbar, Sarah had resigned last summer after only six months at the company. Ania looked from her family to Sarah. She didn't want to make small talk with one of Conrad's old colleagues, but the aisle was brimming, Sarah's trolley was wedged in front of hers and there was nowhere to go.

'I was sorry to hear about Conrad,' Sarah said. She was a short woman with sleek, shoulder-length ginger hair tucked behind her ears, long mascara-black lashes and a clear translucent complexion.

Ania gave a nod – all she could manage.

'How are you coping?'

A fleeting glance at her boys. They were kneeling on the floor with Blanka, examining something beneath the shelving. She ought to tell them to get up, the floor would make their clothes dirty. 'We're doing our best.'

'Conrad was great,' Sarah said. 'I really am so sorry for you all. It's such a tragedy.'

'Thanks.' The aisle thinned. The boys were still on the floor – Patryk reaching underneath the shelf, Blanka goading him on.

Sarah's face eased. 'Look, if you need anything, let me know, won't you?' she said. 'I lost my dad suddenly last year. I know what it's like. People either avoid you or are awkward because they don't know what to say. I'd be happy to exchange numbers. The Harrison crowd can be a bit stiff.'

The woman's generosity of spirit touched Ania. Most Harrison Dunbar employees would spot her and surreptitiously walk the other way, just as they did at the few company events she'd attended. A fact that suited Ania just fine. But Sarah was different.

She recalled a company event at the Harrisons' Cirencester house last summer. The last event Ania had attended. She hadn't wanted to go. She hated the shallow conversation, the pretensions. The coldness of the other families because her bohemian clothes were different to theirs and she spoke her mind. She'd refused initially, until Conrad had pleaded with her. 'Just this one. It's important. David wants everyone there, to show a united front. And, please, be on your best behaviour.' She'd only spoken a couple of words to a client, an Irish woman with a harsh tongue and hooded eyes. She had no idea what she'd said, but whatever it was, the woman was ushered away. And Ania was left alone on the sidelines again, while her boys played with the Jameson children. Until Sarah came over and chatted to her about vintage clothes. Sarah had never really fitted the Harrison mould either.

'Thank you,' Ania said. 'That's really kind.' She keyed Sarah's number into her phone.

Sarah pressed her lips together, then looked down at her hands, as if she was about to make a move when a thought wriggled into Ania's head. Sarah might have an insight into how Harrison Dunbar worked, who their clients were.

'Maybe we could have coffee.' The words dripped from Ania's mouth in tandem with her thoughts.

Sarah smiled. 'That would be lovely.'

At that moment, the boys came running over. 'Look,' Patryk said to his mother. He held out his hand and in the middle of his palm nestled a shiny pound coin.

Ania tore herself away from Sarah. 'You found that! I wondered what you were reaching for under those shelves. How clever. We should find something for you to spend it on.'

Both boys cheered.

'Listen, I'd better go.' Sarah reached across and squeezed Ania's arm. 'You take care.'

'Thank you.' Ania held up her phone. 'I'll call you soon.'

'Who was that?' Blanka asked, joining them.

'Just a mum from the school,' Ania lied, shrugging it off. No sense in bothering Blanka, she was worried enough about them all.

She turned away, lips edging into a satisfying smile. A chat with Sarah was just what she needed.

Chapter 19

Harrison Dunbar's waiting area was two large sofas, separated by an oak coffee table with a glass top, beside the reception desk. A floor-to-ceiling window looked down into Portsoken Street in London's financial district. Nicole poured herself a latte from the coffee machine and stood beside the glass, watching the traffic pass below. Cars and vans punctuated by black cabs, a red double-decker bus. Pedestrians hurried in all directions, going about their business like an army of ants.

Don't mention it to anyone. She'd turned over the intelligence agent's words in her mind, again and again, since their encounter yesterday, a growing sense of anger clouding her vision. Why the need for such secrecy? What did they think Ethan was involved in? But she wasn't about to be intimidated by someone from the intelligence service casting aspersions about her dead husband. She'd known David for six years. They'd barbequed at each other's houses, celebrated last New Year's Eve together. He was godfather to her son, for Christ's sake. She wanted to confront him. Which is why she found herself standing in reception, waiting for him this morning. She hadn't called ahead or given notice of her visit because she wanted to watch David and gauge his reaction as she shared the exchange in the cemetery. If there was something awry, she'd see it in his face. And if the intelligence service contacted her again, she'd be ready, prepared.

Nicole took a sip of coffee. Mags. Another name that had floated around her head like an errant feather all night. A distinctive name. The note she'd found was handwritten, personal, and the combination of it being so well hidden, inside a notebook in Ethan's desk, and the kiss at the end of the message made her uneasy. He'd never mentioned the name Mags to her. Was it possible her husband had been having an affair? The very suggestion knocked her sideways.

She thought back to Ethan's tardiness, the school assemblies he'd missed, his late arrival at dinners and get-togethers. But then... Ethan was always late. He was always working. Wasn't he?

Ellen, the receptionist, finished a call and looked up. Blue eyes sparkling as she spoke. 'I just need to pop a file downstairs,' she said. 'Are you sure I can't get you anything before I go? David shouldn't be too much longer.'

Nicole shook her head and watched the woman go. She'd asked for contact details for Mags when she came in, hoping she might possibly be a client or a business associate, but Ellen had looked at her blankly and said she didn't recognise the name. It didn't help not having a surname. Ellen assured her she'd ask about, but her response was disconcerting. Ethan's social life revolved around his work. Ellen had been employed here over twenty years, was front of house. Surely, if Mags was a contact or a client, she would know of her.

Nicole finished the drink, placed the cup in the bin and checked her watch again. David's office was on the next floor up, on the same floor as Ethan's. Perhaps she should take the stairs, quietly make her own way up there. Steal a peek into Ethan's office while she was at it. Maybe she'd find some answers there.

A flight of stairs later and Nicole stepped out into a corridor, a soft Axminster carpet underfoot. David Harrison's room was at the other end, beside the lift. In the middle was a conference room where they held their staff meetings. At this end were the senior partners' rooms.

Nicole's breath caught in her throat as she looked up at the black nameplate on the door of the first office. Ethan Jameson,

Senior Partner – etched in gold letters. She slipped inside, taking care to close the door quietly behind her.

It was only when she turned to face the room that she gasped.

Apart from Ethan's desk in front of the window, the room was completely bare. The noticeboard, the painting of Old Town Bay she'd commissioned for him after a holiday to the Isles of Scilly, all removed. No cabinets. No computer. No personal effects. It hadn't occurred to her that someone would clear it out this quickly.

Nicole's insides hollowed as she wandered over to the desk and swept the tips of her fingers along the oak top. And, as she sank into the chair, it all came back. The morning of Ethan's first day in the job. Him standing in their bedroom, turning this way and that while checking the cut of his new Hugo Boss suit in the mirror. 'It's the perfect chance to make contacts, learn everything I need to know in readiness for setting up my own company one day,' he'd said. Ethan didn't want to work for David Harrison for the rest of his life. He wanted to be the next David Harrison. The tears came from nowhere, streaming down her cheeks as she imagined the hours her husband had spent sitting in this very chair, poring over this desk. Last time he was here he was alive and well. Now he was gone.

She reached down, tried the drawers. They were locked. Nobody was going to find anything in here, somebody had made sure of that. She pulled a tissue from her bag and wiped beneath her eyes, desperately hoping she hadn't smudged too much of her mascara. Then, without thinking, she bent down, pulled the bin from beneath the desk and dropped her tissue into it.

'Nicole!'

Nicole jerked back at the booming voice.

She hadn't heard David Harrison walk down the corridor and open the door. She looked up to find him filling the doorway, an imposing figure in a black suit, a crisp grey shirt, a navy tie.

His face softened. 'Nicole, dear. I'm so sorry. I didn't mean to make you jump. I just wasn't expecting to find you in here.'

'I wanted to see it,' she said. 'One last time.' At least a part of that was true. Her face flamed. She pulled out another tissue, pressed it to her eyes.

'Come on.' He beckoned her towards him, enveloped her in a tight hug. 'Come into my office,' he said, placing a hand in the small of her back as they parted. 'We'll talk there.'

David's office resembled a plush hotel suite. A leather sofa sat at one end beside a bookcase lined with hardback books arranged in height order. A low table surrounded by easy chairs at the other. An open laptop and a telephone graced the desk in the middle, the glass-walled backdrop of London behind.

'I wasn't expecting Ethan's room to be empty,' Nicole said quietly as she stepped inside.

'I'm sorry.' David paused. He closed his eyes a second. 'I had Ellen clear it on Monday. It was difficult, you know, for everyone.'

'Of course.'

'We've kept his personal items. Let me know when you're ready, and we'll drop them over.' He approached his desk and immediately rang down to reception. 'Ellen, organise some coffee for us, will you? And send out for some of those pastries from the bakery across the road.'

'No,' Nicole mouthed. 'Don't go to any trouble.' In truth, she could murder a pastry, but she didn't want to stay any longer than necessary.

'It's no trouble at all.' His voice was as smooth as silk. 'The team will eat them if you don't.' He broke out into a warm smile as he rang off. 'You should have called! I wouldn't have kept you waiting if I'd known you were coming.'

'It's fine. I was just in the area running some errands,' she lied. 'Thought I'd drop by.'

'I'm glad you did.' He motioned for her to take a chair.

'I wanted to thank you, and Olivia, for accompanying me to Conrad's funeral. I didn't get a chance to say goodbye properly at the church.'

'We were worried about you, dashing off like that.' He lowered himself into a seat beside her. 'It can't have been easy yesterday.'

'I'm fine. I was more concerned for Ania.'

'Yes.' His eyes dropped to the floor. 'It was a good service though. Conrad would have approved.'

He asked about her parents, the children, and she indulged his small talk. When she told him about how the kids had trotted into school happily that morning, unfazed by their first day back, their teachers assuring her they would keep a watchful eye and phone her if they were concerned, he nodded.

'Excellent,' he said. 'It'll do them good to be amongst friends. Be a good distraction.'

'I think so.' She crossed her legs, clasped her hands together tightly. 'Can I ask what Ethan was working on before he died?' she asked eventually.

David looked momentarily taken aback. 'Funny. Ania asked me the same thing.' His eyelashes fluttered. 'He flew to Nantes to meet a regular client.'

'He told me he was working on something special. It sounded exciting.' The lie slithered around her mouth like an annoying hair.

'All of our clients are special. As you know, Ethan attracted some of our top earners. To be honest, I'm not really sure how we're going to manage without him.'

They were interrupted by a knock at the door. Ellen appeared with coffees and a plate of pastries balanced on a cream tray. 'I've made you another latte,' she said, smiling at Nicole. 'No sugar, right?'

Nicole nodded and waited for Ellen to serve the drinks and leave the office before she continued. 'Actually, something rather strange happened in the cemetery after I left the service yesterday,' she said. She made a play of stirring her latte.

David took his coffee and eased back into his chair. 'Go on.'

She took her time telling him about the man who'd approached her, relaying their conversation verbatim. When she described the 'intelligence agent' making off at the cemetery, his eyes narrowed to tiny holes. 'They've got a damn cheek,' he interrupted.

'Who?'

He placed down his coffee. 'Do you still have the business card he gave you?'

'No, it slipped out of my pocket.'

He looked away, thought for a moment. 'Do you remember the full name?'

'John. John Sampson. I googled his name afterwards, to check he was who he said—'

'He wasn't.'

'I beg your pardon.'

David grimaced. 'I'm sorry, my dear. I'm afraid you've been a victim of unscrupulous business practices.'

Nicole bristled. 'I'm not with you.'

'John Sampson, or the man calling himself such, was a competitor digging for information.'

Nicole baulked. Not for a second had this thought occurred to her. 'You're not serious?'

'Oh, yes, I am. I'm sure you know that Harrison Dunbar has some very wealthy clients. Our competitors will try anything to poach. But to speak to a grieving widow at a friend's funeral...' He shook his head. 'That's a low ball.'

Nicole felt heat creep up her neck. She was usually so astute, a reasonable judge of character. The man hadn't come across heavy-handed. In fact, quite the contrary. 'Are you positive?' she said. 'I mean, is it possible that Ethan was mixed up in something? Or maybe one of his customers—'

'I'm convinced. It's not the first time. Will was approached the other month. They're after names, client details.'

The report in the financial press about alleged insider dealing nudged her. Ethan's later explanation of the allegation being posed by a competitor looking to discredit them. 'I just thought with Conrad planning to leave, there might be something to it.'

'I don't know why Conrad was planning to leave,' David cut in, 'even if he was. But I'm sure that's what this is about.' He sighed, picked up the plate of pastries and offered them to Nicole. 'When you are successful, like Ethan, there is always someone trying to pull you down.'

Nicole took a Danish but didn't put it to her mouth. She held it out in mid-air, replaying the incident in her mind, desperately searching for clues, indicators to substantiate David's claim. The dark suit, the sunglasses, the firm hand-shake. Whoever it was didn't want to be identified. The way he vanished when the church emptied. The minimal details on the business card he'd pressed into her hand.

David asked her for a description of John Sampson and took down the details. 'I'll get my people to look into this. You won't be bothered again.'

'What do you mean? What people?'

'I just mean we'll put word out in the industry. This is unacceptable behaviour.' A muscle twitched in his jaw. He was angry. Angry at competitors trying to steal his business? Or angry at something else? He looked away, took a sip of his coffee. 'While we're on the subject, I'd like to come out and clear Ethan's home office for you this weekend.'

'What? Why?'

'I'm sure it isn't an exercise you want to do yourself. Ethan was a great one for working out of hours. He'll have paperwork dotted about—'

'There isn't any paperwork in his home office, not work-related anyway,' she said. 'I've already been through it.'

For a split second, David looked taken aback. 'Ah. Well, I'm sure there must be some devices. Let me take a look, just to be sure.'

Nicole's internal antennae twitched. 'There's no need. I told you, there's nothing there. What's this about, David?'

'It's nothing, really.' His face eased and there was a humbleness to his expression, an almost paternal sense of protection. 'We're just trying to locate everything. Ethan often worked remotely and kept files with him. Let me know if there's anything else you need. You know we're only too happy to help.'

'There is something actually.' She pushed her concerns about the intelligence agent aside, placed the Danish pastry on the serviette on her lap and asked him about Mags. 'She was a friend of Ethan's,' Nicole said, keeping the note she'd found on the restaurant menu to herself. 'Do you know where I might find her?'

David straightened. 'No, I've never heard that name.'

Frustration crowded Nicole. She took a bite of the pastry. It clung to the top of her mouth as he waffled on about a life insurance policy. 'Henry will be in touch soon with figures,' he said.

Nicole waited until she had swallowed her mouthful before she thanked him.

David placed his mug down, leaned forward and pressed a hand on her shoulder. 'We look after our own.'

Chapter 20

Less than fifteen minutes later, Nicole climbed out of the taxi, paid the driver and glanced up at the restaurant in front of her. Shielding her eyes from the sunshine to view the fascia. *On Board* was crafted in black italics on a cream background. She pulled the menu out of her pocket and unfolded it. The same pencil drawing of a yacht.

Her head was still whirling after her meeting with David. She wasn't sure what to believe, but she wasn't about to make the trip into town this morning without visiting here too.

She slipped the card back into her bag, taking care to zip it into the side pocket – she didn't want to lose this one – and pushed open the door. The nautical theme continued inside, watercolours of yachts and seaside scenes adorning the wood-panelled walls. Miniature main and jib sails swept across the ceiling. A ship's wheel formed the front of the maître d's greeting station.

The tables – fifteen or so, Nicole guessed – arranged at angles, filling the small area, were empty. The opening times on the door read 12–2 p.m., 5–11 p.m. It was only 1.35. She was about to call out when a slim woman dressed in a black fitted shirt and trousers appeared. Short dark hair cropped to her head. The maître d'. She was followed by a waitress with blonde pigtails.

'I'm sorry,' the maître d' said as she approached. 'We've stopped serving lunch. We're setting up for evening service.'

'I apologise for coming in late,' Nicole said. 'I was just after a coffee.'

The waitress grabbed a pile of tablecloths and moved away.

The maître d' checked her watch, uncertain.

'Only my late husband used to come here,' Nicole said. She glanced at a table for two in the window. It was bare. 'I don't suppose you could manage a latte?'

The woman's shoulders slackened. She extended an arm to the table Nicole was viewing. 'We only have half an hour or so.'

'I won't keep you. I have to get to the school anyway, to pick up my children.'

The woman nodded and called for the waitress to prepare a latte. 'Who was your husband?' she asked, guiding Nicole to the table. 'Maybe I knew him.'

'Ethan. Ethan Jameson,' Nicole replied. 'He was killed in a plane crash the week before last.' The words caught in her throat. *Killed*. It was the first time she'd spoken that word aloud to a stranger and the realisation made it sound so real, so final.

The maître d's face fell. 'Oh, I read about that. I'm so sorry.'

'Did you know him?'

'I don't think so.'

Nicole brought up a photo on her phone and passed it across.

The woman examined it for several seconds. 'No, I'm sorry. I've only been here a short time.'

At that moment, the waitress emerged with the latte and placed it down in front of Nicole. The maître d' showed her the photo and asked her if she knew the man. 'I don't recognise him.' Her pigtails danced as she shook her head. 'We get a lot of diners pass through here though.'

'Of course,' Nicole said. 'I'm just retracing his steps. Visiting his favourite haunts. Actually, it was a friend of his that recommended *On Board*. Mags.' She searched their faces, yearning for any hint of recognition, but they both looked at her blankly. 'You might know her as Maggie or Margaret. Um…' She waved her hand in the air, as if she couldn't recall the surname.

They shook their heads.

Nicole thanked them, doing her best to curb the trepidation rising within. Ethan's work colleagues didn't know Mags. The restaurant where they ate didn't know of her. Why was she proving so difficult to track down? 'How long have you been open?' she asked the waitress.

'Almost two years. I'm afraid we get very busy. We can't remember everyone. Sorry.'

The women moved off. So, the message was written within the last two years.

On Board was a small restaurant in a quiet side street. Easily accessible from Piccadilly Circus Tube station. Nicole tried to imagine them sitting at a table together with glasses of wine, perusing the menu. Was Mags blonde, or dark like Nicole? Again, the question of an affair raised its ugly head, sharpening the air. Surely, she'd have known if Ethan was having an affair? There would have been signs: a change in his behaviour, his timekeeping. He'd have been more secretive. Though... Her heart thumped her chest. She was reminded of the numerous calls and messages that he'd either ignored or failed to respond to of late. There was always an excuse – *I was with a client. I was in a meeting.* But was he, really? Whichever way she looked at it, his job would have provided the perfect mask for someone having a secret relationship.

And where was Mags now? Was she grieving Ethan's loss, like Nicole?

The sun was stronger now, bouncing off the paving outside. *Did you sit here?* She glanced around. *Or did you pick one of the tables at the back, away from the street?* Her gaze rested on a circular table in the far corner near the kitchen. Tucked away, intimate. Hot tears burned her eyes.

Her phone bleeped twice, breaking her abstraction. Two messages.

The first was Carla.

Glass of wine, Monday evening? Shall we say 8?

The second was Tamsin, Ethan's sister.

> How are you all doing? Sending lots of love xxx

Nicole pictured Tamsin, Ethan's only family after his mum had passed away a couple of years ago. Her long blonde hair, her wide smile, her slender frame. Tamsin, who had met her boyfriend in a gap year after university and followed him back to South Africa. The relationship broke up soon afterwards, although not before Tamsin fell in love with Cape Town and set up home there. The cracks in Tamsin's voice when she'd phoned to tell her of Ethan's passing rang out in Nicole's head. It was so difficult with her being so far away.

She clicked off her phone, she'd reply to Tamsin and Carla later, and looked out of the window, her mind switching back to Mags. She wanted to believe Mags was a client, but something about the message suggested more. Maybe she should try Ania. Perhaps Conrad had mentioned something.

The waitress bustled around, dressing the tables in clean blue and white tablecloths. Nicole grabbed a dinner menu from a nearby table. Lobster squid ink ravioli with a parmesan crisp. Tempura king prawns. *Fine dining*. The sort of food Nicole loved. The sort of food they ate when they went out without the children, yet Ethan had never brought her here.

She placed the menu back on the next table and sipped her drink, flinching as the hot milk burnt her tongue. She was beginning to wonder whether she really knew her husband at all.

Chapter 21

'I'm sorry, Mrs Gilbert, I can't help you.'

Ania gritted her teeth, ended the call and chucked her phone across the bed, twisting a biro in and out of the fingers of her other hand. Even Conrad's GP was refusing to help. What was the point of adhering to patient confidentiality after death?

She stared at the scrawl of names on the notepad beside her, struck through the doctor's name, and cursed. She'd called everyone she knew. Everyone she and Conrad had been associated with. Diligently working through the list of contacts on her phone. And she'd got nowhere. No one had any idea what Ethan had been working on before he died, why the two men had dashed off to France, and why Conrad had suddenly decided to leave the company. Thank goodness she'd managed to text Sarah and arrange a coffee next week. Because she was running out of ideas.

Her eyes started to droop. She laid her head back on the pillow. As soon as they'd arrived home from the supermarket she'd taken to her bed; these painkillers really weren't agreeing with her. She was just drifting off to sleep when her mobile trilled, waking her with a start. It was Nicole.

'Hello.' She didn't make any attempt to curb her slurred tone.

'Hi,' Nicole said. 'I'm sorry, I didn't get a chance to talk to you yesterday. How are you all doing?'

'As well as can be expected.' Irritation nipped at Ania. What could the woman want now? She'd made it quite clear she didn't share Ania's suspicions about the crash and it wasn't as if they were friends.

'Listen, the kids have been talking about Patryk and Robert. I just wondered if you wanted to meet at the park tomorrow morning. Might help take their minds off things.'

'Okay.' She stretched out the word, warily. 'What time?'

'Say, 10.30. At Langthorne Park? I can meet you on the bench, beside the play area.'

'We'll see you there.'

Ania clicked to end the call. Odd. The kids had only met a few times, they weren't particularly close. Was it possible Nicole was beginning to share her doubts over the crash? Ania didn't trust Nicole, she was far too thick with the Harrisons. But… what if the other woman had uncovered something? She couldn't afford to ignore her either.

'Who was that?' Blanka said, appearing at her bedroom doorway.

'Nicole Jameson. She wants to meet with the kids tomorrow for a play date.'

Blanka frowned. 'I thought you were going to stay away from the Harrison Dunbar set. They've caused enough trouble over the years.'

Ania shrugged. 'It's just a play date. The fresh air will do the kids good.'

'Hm. You didn't take your tablet,' Blanka said, changing the subject. She held out a hand, a white pill in her palm.

Ania pressed a hand to her forehead. 'I'm not sure I want it. They're wiping me out.'

'That's the idea, to help you sleep, give your brain and your body a rest. Come on.' She moved her hand closer.

Ania didn't want to take the tablet. Ever since she'd started them, they'd made her sluggish, zombie like. But she didn't have the strength to argue, and she didn't want to upset her friend. Blanka was worried about her. Worried she was spiralling into grief-stricken depression, losing all rational thought.

Was she depressed? Probably. If the permanent stone in her chest was anything to go by, she was certainly swamped in grief.

But she needed to show her friend she was trying. Aside from the boys, Blanka was all she had now. She couldn't afford to lose her confidence.

She took the pill, placed it in her mouth, then picked up the glass of water on her bedside table.

'I'll sort the boys out tonight,' Blanka said. 'You get some rest.'

Ania gave a thankful nod and watched her friend leave the bedroom. She was just taking the tablet out of her mouth and placing it in her bedside drawer when an idea swooped in. She moved off the bed, glanced over her shoulder at the tightly shut door, and opened Conrad's wardrobe. An array of shirts and trousers stared back at her. Sooner or later, she'd need to clear them out, but not yet. Not now.

She looked across at the work suits. Conrad often hung them up after wearing them, they only went to the cleaner's every week or so.

Ania started with the trousers, working her way through the pockets. She pulled a packet of tissues out of one, a paper clip bent out of shape from another. Most were empty.

She moved along the line. Nothing. Her shoulders drooped.

She switched to the jackets. Trying the inside pockets. Another paper clip, a safety pin. An old ticket for the NCP at Leytonstone station. Another receipt, curled at the corner. She smoothed out the receipt. And her chest bolted. It was a fuel receipt from a petrol station on the fourth of June. Conrad and Ethan left for Nantes on Wednesday the fifth. She peered closer at the address. South Wood Services. Just outside St Albans. She knew it well because Conrad used to take her out there regularly. He'd lived in Redbourn for a while as a child, called it his happy place. They often drove to junction 9, spent time navigating the backstreets of Redbourn, then took the road into St Albans city and picnicked in the cathedral grounds. Sometimes they'd fuel up at this station on their way back. It was small, privately owned.

St Albans was where Conrad had proposed. Surprising Ania by going down on one knee on the bridge in Verulamium Park, the backdrop of the old city wall in the distance.

What was Conrad doing in St Albans on the Tuesday before he died? And why hadn't he told her he was there?

Chapter 22

The children were racing around the car. Finlay running after Katie, who shrieked like a gull and sped up if he got too close.

'Careful!' Nicole said. She loaded their jackets into the boot. The morning clouds were darkening overhead, thick with the promise of rain. Certainly not conducive to outdoors play.

Nicole dashed back into the house and brought out their wellington boots, just in case.

'Right, kids, in you get,' she said. 'You don't want to be late for Patryk and Robert, do you?' Finlay hadn't batted an eyelid last night when she'd told them about the arrangement to meet Ania and the boys. Any excuse to go to the park. Katie had asked if they would have to talk about their dads and Nicole said no, not if they didn't want to, and that the idea was to play and enjoy themselves. That's what their dads would have wanted. Though – she checked her watch again – with the Saturday-morning traffic they needed to leave now if they were going to be there for 10.30.

She couldn't erase the note from Mags from her mind – she desperately hoped Ania had some answers.

She was strapping the children in, wrestling with Finlay's catch, when she heard a tapping. She glanced out of the rear window, her stomach dropping as she spotted a hunched figure with a stick entering the driveway. It was Irene, her elderly neighbour from across the road.

Irene was ninety-three, a fact she liked to remind people of on a regular basis, widowed and lived alone in the house opposite. She walked with a limp after a fall, two years ago, the stick she used to steady herself a permanent accompaniment.

'Usual June weather,' Irene said cordially, lifting her stick to the sky by way of an introduction. In her other hand, she was cradling a round tin with a tea towel draped over the top.

Nicole tensed. She really did need to make a move but getting away from Irene wasn't easy and she didn't want to hurt her neighbour's feelings. They hadn't spoken since the crash, not apart from Irene briefly offering her condolences when Nicole was leaving for Conrad's funeral on Thursday. She'd have been late that day too, if it hadn't been for Olivia Harrison chivvying her into the car.

Poor Irene. She'd been so active when they had moved into the road, five years ago. Always stopping Nicole in the street to regale tales of meeting friends for lunch, or plays she'd seen at the theatre. An eccentric woman who wore bright clothes and dyed her fringe pink, she'd taken in parcels when they were out, shared coffees with Nicole and offered to mind the children when they were little. But after she fell and broke her ankle a couple of years ago, she became unsteady on her legs and aged rapidly. Her hair had thinned, liver spots dotted her face, and even leaving the house was an effort these days. Nicole helped with her weekly shop and odd jobs; if she made a Sunday roast, she took a plate of food round. Which is why, now, as Nicole eyed the tin in Irene's arms, guilt pinched her. She'd neglected the poor woman since Ethan's crash. Irene had no family, apart from a niece in Dubai. She hadn't even considered who else was looking after her.

'Looks like rain to me,' Nicole said, forcing a smile. 'Sorry, I'm just on my way out.'

'Oh, no problem, dear, I've a pot of tea brewing myself,' Irene rasped. 'I just brought you this.'

Another pinch of guilt. Nicole took the tin and thanked her.

'It's a chocolate cake for the children.' The thin skin around her eyes crinkled into folds as she pressed a cold hand to Nicole's forearm. 'Thought they could do with a bit of chocolate. You all could.'

The gesture brought tears to Nicole's eyes. She'd spent the last few years looking out for the old woman, and now she was looking out for them. 'Thank you.' There was so much more she could say, but she was afraid that if she opened her mouth again, she'd dissolve into a blubbering wreck. Irene was a reserved, proud woman. Not at all the tea and sympathy sort.

'You get off now,' Irene said. 'I've got a whole list of jobs to be getting on with.' She started to make off down the drive, her stick tapping the tarmac, when she stopped, as if she had suddenly remembered something, and turned back. 'Did that man catch you yesterday?'

Nicole frowned. 'What man?'

'The one in the black BMW. He wasn't sure which house you lived at. Had a parcel to deliver. Very badly addressed, by all accounts.'

Nicole frowned, tossing her head from side to side. She hadn't received a parcel. 'When was this?'

'Yesterday morning, about eleven-thirty.'

When she was in town. 'No, I was out.'

'Oh, he said he needed your signature. Was quite particular. Perhaps he'll come back today.' And with that she lifted her stick in a farewell gesture and made off, down the drive.

Nicole watched until the old woman was safely back in her house opposite, before she carried the cake inside and set it down on the kitchen surface. They hadn't been expecting a delivery yesterday. Strange that the driver hadn't left a card. As she made her way out of the house, another thought needled her. *A black BMW.* It seemed an odd choice for a delivery driver.

Chapter 23

Ania was sitting on the bench in the children's play area when Nicole arrived, watching her boys on the basket swing. She was wearing a paisley blue maxi dress and, with her hair tied back in a ponytail, she looked sallow. And so thin.

'Hey,' Nicole said as she approached. Katie and Finlay greeted Ania, then immediately ran off to play with the boys. Nicole lowered herself onto the bench and placed the children's coats beside her, grateful that the wind had picked up, brushing the rainclouds aside. Hopefully, they'd have a dry morning. 'How are you doing?' she said to Ania.

Ania shrugged. The usual frosty reception.

She looked weary, gaunt. As if she hadn't slept in a week and it was making her ill. 'Are you sure you're all right?' Nicole said. 'Only... I hope you don't mind me saying this, but you look—'

'Tired,' Ania said, finishing the sentence. 'I'm shattered.'

'I'm sorry.'

She lifted another shoulder, let it drop. 'My neck problem has flared up. Blanka made me go and see the doctor for stronger painkillers. I don't know, the stuff he's given me... It's making me woozy.'

They watched the children run from the swing to the climbing frame.

'We've arranged Ethan's memorial,' Nicole said in an attempt to soften the atmosphere. 'Well, Mum's done most of it.' After listening to almost a fortnight of her mother's nagging – 'People want to be able to pay their respects' – Nicole had finally acquiesced and given her the green light to organise a memorial service. She knew her mother meant well, but selecting hymns and arranging a service so soon, especially with the ongoing inquiry, was tortuous. 'It's next Thursday at St Michael's on South Grove at eleven o'clock. Then back to the house afterwards. We'd love you to come. And the boys, of course.'

'Thank you.' Ania nodded, then checked over her shoulder as if she was looking for someone.

Nicole followed her gaze. There was nothing there. 'The police came to see me,' she added. 'They said you'd reported a man hanging around, outside the house. Are you all okay?'

'We're fine. There was a guy watching us. I take it you've had nothing?'

Nicole shook her head reassuringly. Nothing she could put her finger on anyway. 'Has he been back?'

'I haven't seen him since I called the police.'

'What did he look like?'

Ania shifted in her seat again, she seemed on edge. 'Short. Stocky. Dark hair.'

Not the guy from the cemetery then. Or the baseball cap wearer Nicole had seen at the end of her drive. Should she say anything to Ania about the intelligence agent? She was tempted to, but... She didn't have any proof he was from the intelligence service. She cursed herself again for losing the business card. And David's explanation about him being a competitor masquerading as an agent, looking to poach business, sounded plausible. No. It wasn't worth worrying Ania with it, especially when she looked so poorly.

'I told the officers my suspicions about the crash: the sleeping pills, the resignation letter, the sudden trip,' Ania said. 'Everything. They've passed it all through to the inquiry.'

'That's good. If there is anything wrong, the investigators will pick it up.'

'I doubt it.'

'What do you mean?'

'Well, how do we know David, or anyone else at Harrison Dunbar for that matter, is going to tell them the truth?'

A shot of adrenaline pumped through Nicole. 'Why wouldn't they?'

'I bumped into Sarah at the supermarket,' Ania added, avoiding the question. 'Arranged to meet up with her next week.'

'Are you talking about Sarah Newton?' Nicole was reminded of the young analyst who'd worked at Harrison Dunbar for six months or so last year. The short woman, with the sleek red hair. She could never understand why she'd left so suddenly.

Ania nodded. 'She should be able to give me a better insight into the company.'

The wind rustled through the leaves above. It sounded like the trees were whispering secrets to each other, just out of earshot. Ania was still on edge. Shifting in her seat. Looking over her shoulder. And it was making Nicole uncomfortable.

'I went to see David yesterday,' Nicole said. 'Confronted him about what Ethan was working on before he died.'

Ania twisted in her seat, lifting a brow at her emphasis on the word 'confronted'. For the first time, she looked genuinely interested. 'And?'

'There was nothing special, nothing out of the ordinary.'

'That's what he told me.'

'He was quite indignant. I really don't think there is anything.'

'Well, he'd be unlikely to tell you if there was, wouldn't he?'

Nicole huffed inwardly. Ania's obsession with the company was starting to wear thin. The Harrisons were friends, for goodness' sake. She'd know if anything was going on. 'Can I ask you something?' She didn't wait for a reply. 'Hear me out here. Is it possible that Conrad was stressed, that something else outside the company pushed him to take sleeping pills or leave his job?'

'He wasn't taking sleeping pills.'

Nicole flinched as Ania enunciated every syllable. 'I just meant that maybe there was something bothering him that he felt he couldn't tell you.'

'There wasn't.'

The air tightened between them.

The kids doubled up as they shot down the slide. Katie waved to Nicole before she descended with Robert. 'I'm wondering if Ethan was having an affair,' she said quietly. Speaking the words aloud made them sharp, raw. And pained her like a fresh kick in the gut.

Ania frowned. 'What makes you say that?'

She passed on her discovery of the menu, the note on the back. Her trip to the restaurant.

'Could be a client,' Ania said. 'Or even a friend. Mags could be a nickname.'

'Did Conrad ever mention her to you?'

'No.'

'What? Not at all?'

Disappointment rained down as Ania blinked and shook her head. She squirmed in her seat.

'Honestly, I can't see Ethan having time for an affair,' Ania said, staring ahead at the children. 'He was always bloody working. Mind you…'

'What?'

'Well.' Ania sniffed. 'I wouldn't put anything past any of them in that company.'

Here we go again. Nicole resisted the temptation to roll her eyes.

'Everything is so cloak-and-dagger. So in-house, so secretive. I mean, when was the last time somebody left?'

Nicole thought hard. In the six years since Ethan had joined them, she couldn't recall anyone, apart from Sarah. And *she* barely counted, she'd only been there a short time. 'They're a good employer. They look after their staff.'

'Or they have a hold over them.'

'Oh, come on, Ania—'

Ania rounded on her, and the fire in her eyes stopped Nicole in her tracks. 'You're not listening to what I'm saying. There's something going on there.'

'And you know that for sure, do you?'

'Yes, I do. Why else would somebody be standing outside my house, watching?'

'He could have been a reporter. And you said yourself, he hasn't returned.'

'No. I said, I haven't seen him. Doesn't mean he isn't still there. You know how busy my road is. There's something wrong with all of this, something awry. Mark my words, somebody, somewhere, has secrets to hide. And what's more, they're not going to stop until they're sure that no one else can reveal them. Which includes you and me.'

Chapter 24

Nicole drove home in a state of flux. *Somebody, somewhere, has secrets to hide.* What did Ania mean? Was this another one of her sweeping, unfounded statements? She'd refused to expand, intent on meeting with Sarah and delving as deep as she could into Harrison Dunbar's business. Obsessed with finding something. Problem was, it was all still speculation. But Ania's demeanour *did* bother her. The woman couldn't sit still, couldn't relax, and it filled Nicole with disquiet.

And she still hadn't found out anything about the elusive Mags.

The kids were bickering in the back of the car. Fighting over a comic they'd found in the seat well. Tugging it back and forth. A rip filled the car as the paper tore.

She turned, called back at them, 'That's enough, guys!'

Nicole didn't see the child step out onto the zebra crossing. She'd only turned her head for a second to speak to the kids.

'Mum!' Katie's voice shrieked.

Nicole was just twisting back to the road when she saw the little face. Blonde ponytail, flapping in the wind. She slammed the brake. The car skidded to a halt, inches from the bewildered little girl. She could have only been about Finlay's age.

The child's mother rushed into the road. Katie screamed. Nicole couldn't breathe. Tears filled her eyes as she watched the mother drop to her knees, hug her daughter. Check her over. She didn't appear hurt.

The car fell silent as Nicole opened the door and slid out of the driver's seat. 'I'm so sorry,' she said, stumbling towards them. The words splintered as they fell out of her mouth.

The child's mother scooped up her little one. The child looked at Nicole, wide-eyed.

'You stupid cow!' the mother said, hiking her bag up onto her other shoulder. 'It's a zebra crossing.'

'I'm so sorry,' Nicole repeated. Tears spilling out, rolling down her cheeks. 'I didn't see her.'

'Because you weren't looking!'

Nicole choked. 'I'm really sorry. Is she okay?'

The woman crossed to the pavement and placed the child down. She was fine. 'You shouldn't be allowed on the road,' the mother said. She took her daughter's hand, cast back one more disapproving glance, and made off.

People started to gather on the pavement opposite. A line of vehicles sat behind Nicole's, horns filling the air. Nicole ignored all of them. She dashed back to her car and climbed inside. 'It's all fine,' she said to the kids. 'No one's hurt.' The engine roared as she turned it over.

She navigated the next few streets in silence. Slowly, carefully. Nerves somersaulting in her chest. She was letting everything get to her. Focusing on the million and one scenarios colliding in her mind. And in doing that, her concentration had lapsed. How could she let that happen? With her children in the car. Her unborn baby... She needed to get a grip. Forget what Ania had said, forget she'd ever read the name Mags. She needed to concentrate on her family.

–

By the time they arrived in Swain's Lane, the atmosphere in the car had calmed. Nicole let them all into the house, pausing in the hallway to remove her jacket and help Finlay take off his shoes. She tidied away their things, moved through the house and opened the back door. Marvelling at how the kids ran into the garden, still full of energy after a morning of climbing and playing, the incident in the car a distant memory. Yet her nerves were still jangling.

Back in the hallway, Katie's jacket had slipped off the peg. Nicole was just hanging it up when she felt a presence. As if someone else had been there. She sniffed the air, searching for signs of her mother's floral perfume. Had her parents popped over? They hadn't mentioned they were coming. And, if so, why hadn't they sent a text or left a note?

As Nicole entered the front room, a chill stroked the back of her neck. She shook it away. She must be imagining things. She was about to go into the kitchen and make a cup of tea when she noticed something on the mantel. The silver-framed photograph of them all was placed face down. Odd. She was pretty sure it had been standing upright when she'd left earlier. She picked it up, turned it over in her hand. Looked around. The rest of the room appeared fine, everything in its place.

She glanced over her shoulder, went back into the kitchen to check on the children. Finlay was on the swing, Katie pushing him. She called down the garden, asked them whether they'd moved the photograph. Finlay looked at her blankly. Katie shrugged. Nicole's eyes swept the lawn, searching the high fencing encasing the garden.

She moved down the side of the house. It was clear. The gate locked; the padlock held fast. But something was bothering her. Something still drew her back into the house, to check each room. The dining room, the front room, the playroom. The bedrooms and bathrooms upstairs. Nothing. She was imagining things. She had to be.

She stood beside her bedroom window. The road outside was empty apart from a car parked at the kerb, opposite her driveway. A black saloon: she couldn't gauge the make. The driver inside wore a baseball cap and sunglasses, and… The hairs on the back of her arms upended. They were staring straight back at her, their gaze long and unwavering.

Irene's tale about the delivery driver in a black BMW tripped into her mind. Whoever this was, they were making no attempt to deliver a parcel. They weren't even set on leaving the car.

She thought about Ania's alleged stalker. Someone had been watching her too. Were they connected to the man in the cemetery? An annoying competitor, a persistent journalist, or someone else?

Nicole raced downstairs and pushed her feet into her sandals at the bottom. Well, she wasn't going to be intimidated by people outside her own home. She'd sort this out, once and for all. As she moved down the drive, her step quickened to a jog. She grew closer, puffing ragged breaths. It was difficult to say whether the person in the car was male or female. They didn't look like the guy at the end of her drive the other day, or the man in the cemetery – the baseball cap was brown, not navy and they were more slimline – but whoever it was had short, cropped hair. They wore an open-necked white shirt. Shades across their eyes. She was almost at the pavement when the engine roared and wheels screeched against the tarmac. The car rocked as it zoomed down the road, leaving a roll of dust in its wake.

'Hey!' Nicole called as the car disappeared out of sight. She placed her hands on her hips. Should she call the police? But what could she tell them? There were no restrictions here, people could park where they liked. And... Nicole cursed. She hadn't even caught the number plate.

She thought again of Ania's alleged stalker, her account of the police reaction. They'd asked if she'd been approached or contacted or threatened, and Nicole had faced none of these things. No. She was making too much of it. Ania's paranoia was rubbing off. There was nothing to suggest she or the children were in danger. Was there?

Chapter 25

Ania sat on the bench in her back yard, the glass of wine she was holding chilling her hand. The sun was setting, splashes of amber and yellow brightening the pale blue sky. She'd cooked dinner and put the kids to bed, but she couldn't shrug off her earlier conversation with Nicole. The woman was deluded. How could she not think there was something else going on here? And how dare she suggest there might have been something awry in Conrad's personal life? Ania would have known. He would have told her.

Though – a sneaky thought crept in – he hadn't told her he was planning to resign. And he hadn't told her about the trip to St Albans.

She hadn't told Nicole about the trip to St Albans either. No. That was one piece of information she was keeping close. She placed her free hand in her cardigan pocket and pulled out the petrol receipt, unravelling it in her hand. There had been no one on the investigation available to speak with her when she'd called the police that afternoon. She recalled the female constable's voice as Ania explained finding the receipt, that it was out of character for Conrad to visit St Albans, his special place, and not mention it to her. And only the day before he flew to Nantes. 'I'll make a note, pass it through. An officer will contact you if they feel it's relevant.'

Relevant. There was that word again. The police didn't care. They weren't interested what her husband had been up to three days before he lost his life. It was like they'd already made up their mind – Conrad had taken a sleeping pill, he must have caused the crash. They were just going through the motions now, waiting for the air accident inquiry to play out. But Ania wasn't about to accept that. She stared again at the note. Well, if they weren't prepared to help her, she'd make her own enquiries.

She googled South Wood Services' telephone number, surprised at how easily the details popped up, and pressed dial.

The phone rang out six, seven, eight times. She was about to ring off when a voice filled the line. 'South Wood Services, Pauline speaking. How can I help you?'

'Yeah, hi.' Ania hesitated a second, unsure of what to say next. 'Um... My name's Ania Gilbert. My husband bought petrol at your station at...' She paused and glanced down at the receipt. '15.05 on Tuesday the fourth of June.' Ania cringed. Today was the twenty-second of June. It seemed such a long time ago.

'Okay. Is there a problem?'

'Not a problem as such.' Another hesitation. God, this was proving more difficult than she'd thought. 'It's just that he died on the Friday afterwards. You might have read about it in the news. A plane crash. Conrad Gilbert.'

'No, I'm sorry.'

'All right, well, I'm just trying to track down his movements in the week beforehand, find out who he spent time with, that sort of thing. And I found a receipt in his pocket showing he visited your station, bought petrol from you. Is there anyone there that I could speak with about this?'

The line went quiet. Ania could just imagine the woman at the other end of the line pulling a 'I've got a right one here' face to her colleague.

'The police are looking into things, naturally,' Ania said. 'To find out what happened, what caused the crash.' Oh, she was making such a mess of this! 'I'm just helping out where I can. I'd like to know if there was anyone with him that day.'

'We get a lot of people pass through here,' the woman said. 'It's impossible to remember, especially that long ago. I'm sorry.'

'Would you at least be able to tell me who was working that day? Perhaps I could speak with them?'

'I'm afraid not. Look, I am sorry for your loss, I really am, but I can't give out staff details.'

'But you do have CCTV, don't you? It would show when he attended, whether there was anyone with him?'

'Yes, we do. You need to contact the police. We can only share these details with them. I'm so sorry.'

The line went dead.

Ania closed her eyes, pressing her eyelids hard together. Why was no one prepared to help?

What had Conrad been doing in St Albans? She was reminded again of Nicole probing about problems at home.

No, there were no problems at home. Maybe Conrad had been secretive about his work, but home life was different. At home, they talked things through. They'd always talked things through. They were a family.

Though he hadn't told her about the note from Piotr she'd found amongst his paperwork.

Dirty fear crystallised in her chest. Fear and something else. Pain. When she allowed herself to think of it, the heartache of cutting ties with her brother, of leaving her old life behind, still sliced through her like a knife. And the wound felt especially raw now, after losing Conrad so suddenly.

Piotr, her only sibling. The older brother she'd looked up to, revered. They'd fought and bickered as kids, but Piotr always came good when it counted, and he could be so thoughtful, so loving. Tears filled her eyes as she remembered the abandoned cat he brought home when she was six because she'd always wanted a pet. A little ball of black and white fluff they'd named Kulka. Then there was the time when the older girls from the corner shop threatened her and Blanka and took their dinner money. It took Piotr less than ten minutes to recover the cash, and he'd followed them on their walk to school for weeks afterwards. And the convertible car he'd borrowed from a friend to celebrate her sixteenth birthday. Oh, how they'd raced through the city streets that day, the wind in their hair, like royalty! The ache in her heart spread across her chest. Piotr was almost the perfect brother. Until it all went horribly wrong.

The idea of him secretly communicating with Conrad, bypassing her, was like a spear to the soul. How dare he? After everything that had happened between them.

She took a sip of wine. There was no date on the note. It must have been old. Years even. It had to be. Conrad had obviously forgotten all about it. Because Conrad was nothing like her brother. She finished the last drops of wine in her glass, stood and walked back into the house. No, nothing like her brother at all.

Chapter 26

At precisely 10.20 a.m. on Monday morning, Ania slid through the entrance of Scott's Coffee House on High Street, Leytonstone. She didn't pay any attention to the man in the trench coat who walked in behind her. It was another rainy day and all she wanted to do was to shrug off her wet jacket, get a coffee and warm up in readiness for her meeting Sarah.

It wasn't until she'd ordered a flat white and had found a table, dropping her bag at her feet, that she felt a hand on her shoulder.

'Mrs Ania Gilbert?' The man was tall, slim, blond. A handsome face. Soft blue eyes.

Ania frowned. 'Who are you?'

'I thought I recognised you. Ben Anstill, *Waltham News*.' He proffered a card. 'I just—'

'No,' Ania interjected, stepping back, shaking her head. *Is he for real?*

'Listen, I'm writing a piece about Harrison Dunbar. I wondered if you would like to add a few words. I'm sure our readers would be interested to hear what you have to say, especially after...'

Ania wasn't listening. She was looking to the door then back to him. 'Have you been following me?'

'No, not at all. I was in the area. Just passing. I saw you in here, recognised you from the photo in the news.'

The photo. The one time they'd snapped her and Conrad at an old Harrison Dunbar event. Heaven only knew where the press had dredged that up from. 'I don't want to talk to you.'

At that moment, the barista walked across and delivered her coffee. 'Everything all right?' he said, looking from one to the other.

Ania shook her head. 'No. No, it's not.'

Concern crumpled the journalist's features. 'I can see this isn't a good time. I'll leave you my card,' he said, holding it up. 'Call me.'

'Just go!' She waved him away, then turned her back on him, her blood boiling. How dare he? Just when she was starting to relax. Could she go nowhere?

The reporter backed out of the cafe. The barista checked she was okay and when she nodded, he retreated to the counter. Leaving Ania to sink into her chair. An old Bee Gees track filled the room.

How could she let this happen?

She looked at the raindrops clustering in groups on the window. Yesterday had been fine. More than fine. She and Blanka had taken the children back to Langthorne Park and the sun had been so strong they'd had to smother the boys in sunscreen and shelter under the shade of an ancient oak to have their picnic.

Ania's shoulders loosened as she recalled them lounging on the grass, eating their crisps and sandwiches. She hadn't wanted to go, she still felt uncomfortable outside the house, but Blanka had persuaded her, and, in the end, she was pleased she did because it was one of those balmy days when time stands still, and life's daily troubles seem to trickle away. The park was almost empty; bees buzzed in and out of the flowers, birds sang in the trees. No one stared. No one bothered them. And, for the first time since he'd lost his father, Patryk ran around with his brother, dribbling his football. Happy, carefree. She'd rolled her shoulders, listening to the cartilage pop and crack. Even her neck was starting to loosen.

But today she'd let her guard down. Been less careful. Who else was out there watching?

Coming here was a mistake. She pulled her jacket off the back of her chair, was leaning down to gather up her bag when she felt a whoosh of cold air. The door had opened again.

'Hey,' Sarah said, rushing towards her. 'Sorry I'm late.' Her hair was wet and clumped on her shoulders. 'I missed the bus.' She looked at the bag and jacket bunched into Ania's arms. 'Are you okay?'

Ania shared her experience with the reporter.

'Scum,' Sarah said, following Ania's eyeline back to the door. The street was empty outside, the journalist long gone. 'Honestly, I don't know how they could stoop so low.' She took off her jacket, placed it on the back of a chair. 'You are going to stay for a coffee, aren't you? Come on. It'll be fine. Just you and me.'

Ania wasn't sure. Her nerves rattled in her chest. But she'd come here, arranged to meet Sarah because she wanted to question her. There was no sense in leaving now. She hung up her jacket, eased back into her chair.

Sarah ordered them coffees and wittered on about her mother phoning as she was leaving the house, making her miss the bus. 'She always rings on my landline. I don't know why. She knows I have a mobile!' She pulled a face and they both laughed, the tension in the air diffusing.

Ania had wondered if their meeting might be awkward. It wasn't as if they were friends. This was the first time they'd chatted together properly outside a Harrison Dunbar event, and they'd only met at one of those. But Sarah was one of those warm, naturally funny people and, within no time, she felt calmer.

'How are you managing?' Sarah asked, sipping her coffee.

'We're doing okay,' Ania replied. 'Taking it one day at a time.' She placed down her mug. 'So, what are you doing now?' She was dying to ask Sarah about company connections, but she didn't want to put her off. *Softly, softly*, her inner voice cautioned. *Take it easy, build her trust.*

'I've applied for a job as a business analyst with the Co-op food chain. Similar sort of thing as I was doing with Harrison Dunbar. Got an interview next week.'

'That's brilliant,' Ania said with as much enthusiasm as she could muster. 'Good luck!'

'Thanks.' She crossed her fingers. 'Hopefully, it'll work out. I can just imagine my dad's face if I have another disaster.'

Disaster. That was an interesting word.

'I'm sure he just wants you to be happy.'

'Hm, I guess.' Sarah reached underneath her hair and scratched the back of her neck. 'Problem is, I'm the first from the family to go to uni. He was thrilled when I got the place at Durham to study geography. And getting a graduate job in the city, he thought I was made. I can't tell you how disappointed he was when I told him it wasn't for me.'

Ania sipped her coffee. 'What was it about the position you didn't like?' she asked casually.

'Sorry?'

'What made you resign? You must like being an analyst if you're looking to do the same job elsewhere.'

Sarah pulled the sleeves of her cardigan over her hands. For the first time since she'd entered the cafe, she looked uncomfortable.

'I'm sorry,' Ania said. 'It's just, in all the time Conrad was with Harrison Dunbar, you're the only person I know who has left.'

Sarah wrinkled her nose. 'It was a number of things. I'd rather not talk about it...'

They sipped their coffees quietly.

'Conrad was planning to leave,' Ania said eventually.

'What?' Sarah's jaw dropped. The coffee mug she'd lifted to her lips was now held out in mid-air.

Ania told her about the draft note of resignation she'd found.

'Oh, I'm surprised. I thought it suited him there.'

'So did I. I mean, he always planned to leave when he'd paid back the loan for the pilot's course. But not now.' She lowered her voice a notch. 'There were a few things he wasn't comfortable with.' She left the statement hanging in the air, lifting her mug to her lips. 'Perhaps you had the same reasons.'

Ania held on to the silence, thickening between them.

'It was more an ethical decision for me,' Sarah said. 'Before I joined them, I wasn't familiar with the interests of some of their clients.' Sarah's eyes flicked from side to side. She was clearly choosing her words carefully. She looked up, met Ania's eye. 'Clients whose morals don't match my own, shall we say.'

'That's pretty much what Conrad said. From the discussions he overheard in the car, he questioned whether some of the investments were even legal.' She was fabricating, but if she was to get Sarah to speak freely, she needed to pull her into her confidence.

'Oh, I don't know about that,' Sarah replied. 'Financial services are heavily regulated.' She finished her coffee, pushed her mug away.

Ania's stomach sank. She had overdone it. Just when they were getting to the nitty-gritty too. But she wasn't about to let it go. Not when she was so close. 'That's what I used to say to Conrad. I mean, the clients I met at their parties all seemed fine enough. And he was only a glorified chauffeur, after all. What would he know?'

Sarah passed her a sideways look. Wary.

'I know,' Ania continued. 'It's the ones that don't attend the parties that Conrad was concerned about too. I mean—'

'Look, I shouldn't be talking about this,' Sarah said. She cleared her throat. 'I signed a confidentiality agreement when I left Harrison Dunbar. They are very protective over their clients and for good reason.'

'Oh, I completely get that,' Ania said. There *was* something, she could see it in Sarah's face. 'I'm just trying to understand my husband. And why he felt so strongly.' The tears that swelled in her eyes weren't all fake. She did care. She cared so much, it hurt.

Sarah softened. 'It must be difficult for you. What happened was tragic.'

'It was.' Ania pulled a tissue from her pocket and dabbed her eye.

Sarah scratched her neck again. 'You obviously know they have a front list, those the Harrisons entertain at their get-togethers, and a back list, those they don't talk about. It's only when you work there, you find out why.'

'What do you mean?' Ania had never heard of separate client lists though she wasn't about to admit it.

'Well, some of the back list clients' business interests wouldn't exactly show the company in a good light. No one wants to be connected to companies that farm palm oil or are linked to arms dealers.' Sarah's face tightened. She held up her hands. 'I've said too much. Suffice to say, if you have a conscience, it doesn't make working for them an easy ride. That's why I left. It's possible these issues bothered Conrad too.' She hesitated, bit her lip. 'You will keep this to yourself?'

Ania was quiet a moment. This wasn't what she'd been expecting. 'Of course,' she purred. 'Strictly between you and me.' She leaned in closer, as if she was sharing a secret. 'Conrad wasn't sure about David either, to be honest.' Conrad had never said anything of the sort, but Ania sniffed and glanced askance at Sarah.

Sarah's nose wrinkled again. 'David's very astute, I'll give him that.'

'Isn't he?' Ania said, conspiratorially.

'Yes. I was more intimidated by Olivia though.'

Ania blinked. 'Oh?'

'Yes. She's a piece of work, that one. Believe me, nothing goes on in that company without her knowing about it.'

Chapter 27

Nicole had just lowered herself into the bath when her mobile rang through from where she'd left it in the bedroom. She groaned, waited for it to go to voicemail, then rested back. Whoever it was, she'd call them later.

It was Monday evening and, after a fraught Saturday, spending Sunday at her parents' house with the children had done nothing to improve matters. Her father had looked pale and drawn. Her mother was testy, both of them nervous about her father's upcoming oncology appointment next week. And, as much as she tried, Nicole couldn't shake off the sense of uneasiness she had felt on Saturday.

She couldn't offload her concerns to her parents. She considered speaking with the police, the detectives on Ethan's inquiry, but she hadn't heard from Sharon again and there was something about the woman she didn't warm to. And there had been no further contact from the intelligence service, supporting David's theory that the agent wasn't genuine.

But Nicole still felt uncomfortable. Granted, the inquiry into the plane crash would look into why the men had flown to Nantes, and David couldn't keep the client details from them: if there was anything untoward, they'd find it. But the exchanges with Ania, the car outside her house... Was she making too much of the incidents? She needed to speak to somebody before she imploded. She was holding herself together for the sake of the children. She needed to offload these issues to someone she could trust. Someone who respected her confidence, who offered sound advice. Someone like Carla. Thank goodness her friend was coming round this evening.

Her mobile rang again, the tinkling ringtone travelling along the landing. Someone was persistent. *Oh, for Christ's sake, it'll wake the children!* She groaned, hauled herself out of the bath, pressed a towel to her wet chest, her feet leaving damp impressions in the carpet as she jogged to her bedroom. It was Ethan's sister, Tamsin.

'Hey,' Nicole said.

'Hey. You sound out of breath. Is this a bad time?'

Nicole patted herself down with the towel with her free hand. She considered telling her about the bath, putting her off until later, tomorrow even, but Tamsin was difficult to pin down at the best of times and rarely answered her phone. 'No, it's fine. You okay?'

'I'm afraid not. I've got some bad news.'

Nicole pressed the towel to her face. Not more bad news. 'What is it?'

'I can't come to the memorial service, I'm so sorry. I fell at work today, displaced a disc in my back.'

'Sounds painful.'

'Believe me, it's murder. Any slight movement and I'm in agony.'

'It's a shame for you to miss the service. We could help you, get a wheelchair or something.'

'I can't fly, darling. I'm flat on my back. Honestly, I'm gutted. I really wanted to be with you guys.'

Nicole desperately tried to bury her disappointment. 'Oh, that is sad. What happened?'

Tamsin rambled on about the accident and, as she listened, Nicole found her gaze wandering around the room. To Ethan's bedside table where he emptied the contents of his trouser pockets when he undressed, the floor where he left his clothes in pools at night. And, suddenly, she was overcome by a bubble of loneliness swelling inside.

'So, how are you guys?' Tamsin's voice dragged her back to the phone.

Nicole blinked away the tears gathering in her eyes and said they were coping as best they could. 'We'll miss you on Thursday.'

An awkward pause winged down the line. 'Listen, as soon as I'm better, I'll be over. And I'll be thinking of you all.'

A fresh wave of sadness washed over Nicole as she thanked Tamsin, wished her a speedy recovery and ended the call.

It wasn't as if she knew her well. Five years older than Ethan, Tamsin had lived in South Africa for the duration of Nicole's relationship with Ethan. She'd only come across for their wedding, her parents' funerals, a few short breaks. Ethan's family weren't good at keeping in touch. Apart from birthdays and Christmas, they rarely spoke. 'I know where she is if I need her,' Ethan would say. It tended to be Nicole sending Tamsin messages online, trying to maintain contact. Posting photos of the kids on Facebook and tagging her in, keeping her involved in family life. But, still, she had been looking forward to spending time with her sister-in-law.

It was pitiful to think Ethan would have no extended family at his memorial service. No one at all apart from her and the children.

Chapter 28

Carla wiped the korma sauce from her empty plate with her finger. 'Ooh, that was yummy,' she said.

Nicole placed her own plate on the floor and sank back into the deep cushions on the sofa. 'Careful, there are calories in pottery too, you know.'

'Don't joke!' Carla said and sighed. 'Do you know, I haven't touched Indian food in over a year because of this diet. It can't be good for your mental health.'

Nicole snorted as her friend reached beneath her loose shirt and undid the top button of her jeans. 'You're looking good on it though. Weight Watchers clearly agrees with you.'

'I wish I felt like it.'

Low-bellied clouds had gathered outside, signalling an early dusk. Nicole switched on the lamp in the corner, then lit a candle on the hearth, lighting the room with a soft glow.

'I'm sorry I missed the kids,' Carla said, crossing one leg over another.

'I put them to bed early. Being back at school has worn them out. Not that they'd tell you that.'

Carla laughed. 'I'll have to pop round at the weekend. Bring them sweets to keep up those sugar levels.'

Nicole rolled her eyes. Her gaze fell upon the candle. She watched it awhile, the flickering flame oddly calming.

'So, how are you?' Carla asked. 'Better than you look, I hope? And' – she eyed Nicole's glass – 'what's with the water?'

'Antibiotics,' Nicole said quickly. 'The doc thinks I've had a bug. Just got to see the course through.' She was growing adept at hiding the pregnancy now.

'What about at home? How are things here?'

'The honest truth?'

'You're talking to me now, remember.' Her American accent was rich and soothing.

'I don't know where to start.' And she didn't. Her brain was a mass of fog.

'Listen, I'm sure you'll feel better after the memorial on Thursday. It's such a shame your sister-in-law won't be able to join you.'

Nicole sighed. The misery of Tamsin's absence at Ethan's memorial lingered like a wasp sting.

'I saw your mother in Sainsbury's Local. She's worried about you, here alone with the kids.'

'She's always worried.'

'You just lost your husband, and you sent your parents home.'

'I need to do this on my own.'

Carla gave a series of quiet nods, as if she understood. Though she didn't. Not really. She'd never been married, never had children, never even suffered a bereavement of someone close, as far as Nicole was aware. She'd lived with a guy, Steve, when Nicole first started working for her, but Carla had ended that over a year ago, saying he was too needy. Her elderly parents were in Houston, cared for by her sister. No. Carla knew little of family ties and obligations; she threw herself into work.

'Maybe you need something more?' Carla said. 'Something to take your mind off things?'

'That's just it. There has been more. So much more. I hardly know where to start,' Nicole said.

'Really?'

'I'm not sure, but I think Ethan was having an affair.' As much as she'd tried, she couldn't put the message from Mags out of her mind.

Carla jerked her head back. 'What do you mean, you're not sure?'

She told Carla about the note on the back of the menu, her trip to the restaurant.

'That's it?'

'Isn't it something?'

Carla frowned. 'Not really. There could be a million and one explanations. All perfectly innocent. What do his friends say?'

'You know Ethan. He barely had time for us, let alone friends. Everything was work to him. His colleagues don't know the name.'

'There you are then.'

'What?'

'You're being paranoid. If there was something going on, somebody would know.'

'Do you think so?' Nicole was dubious. 'Perhaps they're trying to save me the upset.'

'Honey.' Carla huffed. 'Look, it's not surprising after what you've been through, but Ethan... having an affair? When? You said yourself, he didn't even have time for friends.' Her brow furrowed. 'Come on. He was a good man. Don't torment yourself.'

Nicole looked down into her glass and swirled the water. The string of emotions since the crash and Ethan's passing had left her wrung out.

Maybe if Carla understood, if she told her everything that had been going on these past few weeks, it would ease the strain. She opened her mouth, hardly knowing where to begin, and was immediately stopped by a long wail from above. Finlay.

'Excuse me a minute,' she said and rushed off towards the stairs.

–

'Is he okay?' Carla asked when Nicole walked back into the front room.

It had taken several minutes to settle Finlay, and, in the end, she'd had to move him into her bed to pacify him. 'I think so. He wasn't fully awake.'

'Poor little mite. It's so tough for them.'

Nicole glanced at the ceiling, her senses on hyper-alert. The children had been through so much, she desperately hoped this wasn't the beginning of night terrors. 'The school have offered counselling,' she said. 'I think we'll try it.'

'Sounds like a good plan.' Carla took another sip of wine as Nicole regained her place on the sofa. 'Actually, I have some news.'

'Oh?'

'Yeah. We have a new contract, and it's a juicy one.'

Nicole sat forward. As much as she wanted to share her woes with her friend, it was lovely to talk about something other than herself for a moment. 'Go on, spill the beans. I know you're dying to.'

'Okay, just breathe. I need you to be calm.'

'What is it?'

'We, Jackson's Recruitment, have been asked to fill a position at Harrison Dunbar.'

Nicole felt her mouth drop. 'What? Not Ethan's...'

'No, not Ethan's. I wouldn't do that. And, in any case, I don't think David's looking to fill it just yet. He wants to give everyone time. They do need help though. So, he's asked us to find the partners an assistant, someone with a financial background to support them.'

Nicole was dumbstruck. 'Why us? We're not finance specialists.'

'We can place anyone,' Carla said. 'We're good at what we do. And we're small, personal. You know how David likes to keep his circle close.'

Chapter 29

The following day, a chaffinch was singing its heart out on the apple tree, the mellifluous sound of its voice filtering through the open window as Nicole sat at the kitchen table and cradled her second coffee of the morning. It was 6.15 a.m.

All night, Carla's words had rattled around her head. Why would David Harrison hire them to fill a position in his company? He hadn't approached them to source a new analyst last year when Sarah left. No, on that occasion he chose Spicks, specialist city recruiters for the finance industry. Nicole hadn't thought anything of it at the time. It made sense: it was Spicks' area of expertise. What didn't make sense was choosing Jackson's now.

David likes to keep his circle close. Was David trying to make up for something? Or was he trying to give Nicole a new focus? She was reminded of her visit to Harrison Dunbar and his pressing offer to go through Ethan's home office. What had he been intent on searching for? What didn't he want her to find? Whichever way she looked at this, the decision didn't sit right.

She stared at the half-full mug in front of her. She had heaps to do. Clean the house, finalise the preparations for Ethan's memorial service. The kids needed waking for school in an hour. And she was dog-tired, the endless nights of patchy sleep catching up with her. But she couldn't focus.

She had hoped to talk through her concerns with Carla last night. Offload to her level-headed, grounded friend. Put the false theories, the supposition behind her. But the revelation of Jackson's recruiting for her late husband's company reignited her concern and Nicole was chock-full to bursting. She couldn't talk to her parents, not after what they'd been through this last year. Now she couldn't talk to her best friend either – the new contract brought Carla too close, too invested in the Harrisons to remain neutral.

Was it possible Ania was right to be suspicious about David Harrison's dealings? Could David have pulled the wool over Nicole's eyes about the man who'd spoken to her in the cemetery? She didn't know what to think, who to believe.

Another glance at the clock. It was almost half six. Should she tell Ania?

A part of her told her to leave it. Not to get embroiled in more of Ania's investigation. Though after Carla's revelation last night, she couldn't. What if there really was more to all of this? What if something had gone wrong in the company, something that had contributed to Ethan and Conrad losing their lives? She'd never forgive herself if she didn't look into it.

She grabbed her phone, typed out a text to Ania.

> Don't suppose you're free for a coffee this
> morning?

Within seconds, she received a reply.

> I am free, but you'll have to come to the house. I
> have a delivery. How about 10ish?

Nicole chewed the side of her mouth and fired off another text.

> See you there.

Ania was still in bed when Nicole's text came through. Morning sunshine seeping through the thin curtains lighting the room to a dusky grey.

She eyed her phone warily. What could Nicole possibly want now?

The door to Ania's room creaked as it swung open. 'You awake?' It was Blanka.

Ania hastily reached across to place her phone back on the bedside table before her friend saw it, but she was too late.

'Who are you talking to?' Blanka asked, eyeing the phone. She was wearing her auxiliary nurse's uniform, her blonde hair pulled tightly back into a bun accentuating her thick brows.

'Nicole Jameson.'

'At this time in the morning?' She cursed in Polish under her breath.

Ania shrugged. 'She wants to meet for coffee later.'

Blanka pulled a face. 'Why? It's not like you're friends.'

Ania understood her concern. Blanka was her oldest friend, the person who'd listened to years of her moaning about the people connected to Conrad's work. A situation only exacerbated by the plane crash. To Blanka, the Jamesons and the Harrisons, and the whole of the cagey Harrison Dunbar crew for that matter, were trouble. Trouble that manifested itself in frustration and sadness. She didn't trust them. Ania didn't either, but she couldn't let this lie. There had to be a reason why Nicole kept contacting her.

She smiled casually, as if it was nothing. 'It's only a coffee.'

'Be careful.'

'Nicole's okay,' she found herself saying by way of explanation. 'She's not like the others.'

'I hope not. How's your neck today?'

Ania reached up, rubbed it. 'Better.'

'Good, those pills must be working. I'm just off to work now. Don't forget to take them later.' She reached down, gave Ania a hug and left the room, closing the door behind her.

Ania sighed and pulled back the bedclothes. She still hadn't told Blanka she'd stopped taking the tablets. She meant to, but there never seemed to be a good time and she knew her friend was just trying to help. She didn't want to hurt her feelings.

Yesterday's meeting with Sarah was playing on her mind. The ethical dilemma was interesting. But what fascinated Ania more was her focus on Olivia Harrison. Ania had been so consumed with David, she hadn't considered his wife. The woman by his side at company gatherings, charity events, parties. She pictured the tall, demure Olivia, sweeping through the last garden party Ania had attended like the Queen of Sheba in her flowing dress. The high cheekbones, the piercingly striking eyes. Sitting on the leather sofa in her London flat, unflinching as David indicated to Ania that they would write off the outstanding loan for Conrad's pilot training.

Conrad maintained Olivia had little to do with the daily running of the company. Was that true? Or was she really the dominant force, behind the scenes? If she was, then Nicole would know.

Ania pulled on a T-shirt and her jeans, then reached for the cardigan she had on yesterday. Just as she was slipping it around her shoulders, something slid out of the pocket and floated to the floor. Ania bent down and retrieved the business card. *Ben Anstill, Waltham News.* The journalist. He must have slipped it in her pocket before he left the cafe. *The cheek of the man!*

She went to put it in the bin, but at the last minute paused. She'd been so incensed by the prospect of him approaching her that she hadn't listened to what he wanted to talk to her about. He said he was working on an article about the company. What sort of article? What if he'd been investigating the company and found irregularities, or questionable dealings?

Ania sat on the end of the bed and turned the card over in her hands. *Waltham News.* It wasn't exactly *The Times* or the *Evening Standard*… But whatever it was, it wouldn't do any harm to find out more.

Chapter 30

The pavements of Leytonstone were busier than usual that morning, a slur of voices mingling with the passing traffic. As Nicole climbed out of her car, she was reminded of Sharon's visit and Ania's alleged stalker. Vehicles were parked nose to tail kerbside; she'd had to drive almost to the end of Ania's road to park. She pulled her cardigan across her chest and tucked in tightly behind a group of young women.

But as she drew closer to Ania's house, she couldn't shake the heat on her neck, the feeling of being watched. She thought of the car whizzing off the other day. The man in the baseball cap standing at the end of her drive. The warmth of passing vehicles and surrounding pedestrians leached into her. Even the clouds felt heavy, pressing down hard. So much so, Nicole was grateful when she arrived at Ania's pathway to find her on the doorstep, waiting.

Ania welcomed her inside and closed the door, taking care to pull the chain across. A long-sleeved navy dress hung off her shrunken frame and with her hair loosely tied back, she looked younger today.

'How are you?' Ania asked as she led Nicole into the front room.

Nicole said she was all right, though in truth she felt a bit light-headed. Whether that was due to the pregnancy or the crowds, she was unsure. She was certainly eating more frequently with this child. She'd had her breakfast and eaten an apple and a banana in the car, but her insides were still growling.

Goodness, if this continued, she'd be the size of a house when she reached full term. 'How about you?' she asked.

'I'm not sure.' Ania told her about the reporter in the cafe yesterday and Nicole's stomach flipped afresh.

'Oh, I rather hoped they'd given up.'

'Doesn't seem so.' Ania checked her drink choice.

'I don't suppose you have a biscuit, do you?' Nicole said. 'I didn't manage to get breakfast.' She rolled her eyes, faked a laugh.

She waited for Ania to disappear into the kitchen, then gathered her breath, desperately trying to quell her ragged nerves. With the condolence cards now taken down, and the bright-coloured cushions and a pink throw over the back of the pale grey sofa, the room looked cosy and homely. A photo of the family on the mantel caught Nicole's eye. She walked over to it. It was one of those snapshots, taken on a whim – Conrad sitting at one end of the sofa, Ania the other, the children sandwiched in between. They looked happy, at ease: arms and legs draped across each other, gaze averted. As if they were relaxing on a Sunday afternoon, watching a film together. An ordinary family moment captured for eternity. She picked it up, turned it over. A date was scrawled in pencil on the back. Ten days before the crash...

'Blanka gave it to me.'

Nicole jumped – she hadn't heard Ania re-enter the room. She cursed her nerves again. The news from Carla had unsettled her more than she'd realised.

'She took it a few weeks ago on her phone,' Ania said, handing her a steaming mug.

'It's lovely.' Nicole replaced the photo. She didn't have any pictures like that in her house. All her photos were organised. Framed portraits of them standing awkwardly with false smiles, staged and Photoshopped. Ethan preferred them that way. But there was something natural about this one that was particularly touching.

Ania retreated to the kitchen, returned with a plate of digestives and handed them over. 'You look pale,' she said to Nicole.

'Oh, it's nothing. I'm just a bit tired.'

'So, what did you want to see me about?' she asked as they sat down.

Nicole chewed the edge of a biscuit and felt a little better. 'It's probably nothing.'

'Go on.'

'I just wondered if you'd seen your stalker again. Only someone's been hanging around my street. A driver in a black saloon.' She told Ania about them watching the house, then zooming off. The guy who paused at the end of her driveway.

'That's interesting. No, I haven't seen him since I called the police. But then, like I said, it wouldn't be difficult to go unseen out there.'

Nicole followed her gaze across to the window. A car passed, and another. A group of men walked on the other side of the road. 'I don't know,' she said. 'Something about the incidents make me uneasy.'

'I told you. Something about all of this makes me uneasy.' Ania rubbed the back of her neck.

'Perhaps we should call the police.'

'*I* did, remember. And they did nothing. The police are only interested if people actually approach or threaten you.'

Silence hung between them, long and hollow.

'Have you met Sarah yet?' Nicole asked eventually.

'Yesterday.'

'And how was she?'

'Fine.' Ania told Nicole about Sarah's application to join the Co-op. 'She said some interesting stuff about her time at Harrison Dunbar too.'

'Like?'

'Like why she left.' She talked Nicole through Sarah's ethical dilemma, the questionable interests of some of their clients.

Nicole exhaled dismissively. The ethical decisions of customers didn't necessarily mean the company was involved in anything illegal. 'Harrison Dunbar's job is to maximise customers' investments, not judge them on their interests.'

'She also talked about Olivia's involvement in the company.'

'She's a sleeping partner.'

'It's possible she's not as sleeping as it appears. How well do you know her?'

'As well as anyone connected with the firm, I guess.' Nicole really couldn't see where this was going.

'Sarah said nothing goes on in that company without her say-so.' Ania paused, pressing her lips together before she continued. 'It made me think. The Harrisons said something strange to me. They said I didn't need to continue repaying the loan for Conrad's pilot course. There must be well over twenty grand outstanding. Why would they write that off?'

It did seem a lot of money. But the Harrisons were known for their generous gestures. She'd had to have a word with them herself when they'd gone overboard and bought Finlay a child's ride-on Mercedes to drive around their garden. 'Perhaps they were being kind,' she said. 'They don't have children of their own. I've never heard them talk about family apart from Olivia having a brother in Australia. The company, their staff, are everything to them, and they were close to Conrad.'

'But *I* hardly know them.'

Nicole munched through another biscuit and considered Olivia, David's tall wife with the striking grey-blue eyes. Ethan had been wary of her. But he had never mentioned her being involved in the running of the company and she couldn't imagine her pulling David's strings. What did she have to gain? 'I caught up with Carla, my boss, last night,' she said, changing the subject. 'David Harrison has asked our recruitment company to find them an assistant.'

Ania turned down the corners of her mouth. 'I suppose they are going to have to replace our husbands sooner or later.'

Nicole filled her in on the details. 'It's just feels like an odd decision,' she said. 'We're not financial recruitment experts.'

Ania's eyes widened. 'As if he's trying to buy you.'

'I wouldn't go that far.'

'Think about it. If there was something awry, some insider dealing, or dodgy clients, they wouldn't want you looking into things, would they? What's that old adage about keeping your enemies close?'

'I'm not an enemy.'

'You might be if you dig deep enough.'

If. There it was again, that single little word. Though Nicole couldn't deny, she did feel distinctly uncomfortable about the arrangement.

'I'm thinking of talking to the reporter I met at the cafe,' Ania said. 'Sounding him out, seeing what he knows. Possibly even helping with a piece.'

No! Nicole's hand went to her stomach. Heightened media interest was the last thing she needed. Waiting outside her house, following her. Especially when she had an appointment with the midwife looming. She didn't want the pregnancy coming out before she'd had her scan and told her parents and her children the news herself. 'Why? I mean, the investigation—'

'I'm not waiting months for an air investigation to play out. I want people to look at the company, ask questions. They're hiding something, I'm sure of it.'

Nicole bit her lip. She still hadn't told Ania about the exchange with the intelligence agent in the cemetery and David's explanation. She'd thought it was for the best – Ania was making herself ill with all this speculation – but now she was beginning to wonder.

'It might just rattle enough cages for the authorities to take a deeper look,' Ania added.

Nicole wriggled in her seat. 'I still think you should leave it, until you find something substantial. Listen, why don't I ask some of the employees?' What was she saying? But she had no choice now. She had to get involved. She couldn't see how the press would help and, in any case, she needed to put Ania off, delay her contacting them. Perhaps this was her opportunity to delve deeper. 'Most of them are coming to the service on Thursday.'

Ania baulked. 'At Ethan's memorial. You can't be serious?'

'Not at the service, no. At the wake and afterwards. Leave it with me. At least for a while. I'll see what I can find out.'

Chapter 31

The following evening, Nicole wandered into her kitchen, flicked the switch on the kettle and leaned up against the work surface. Since her meeting with Ania yesterday, she'd been computing their conversation, over and over. What the hell possessed her to agree to this? She, the grieving widow, questioning guests while she was supposed to be saying a final farewell to her husband. She'd had to agree to something, it was the only way to prevent Ania contacting the press and reigniting their interest, and she did want to probe more. But... the idea of doing that at Ethan's wake churned her insides. Why couldn't she have come up with something else?

She made herself a hot chocolate and sat at the table stirring it around and around with a teaspoon. In less than fourteen hours, she needed to stand at the front of the church for Ethan's memorial service, and already her nerves were shredded. She needed a distraction. Something easy. Something to calm her. She placed the spoon down, raked a hand through her hair and clicked onto Instagram.

Nicole rarely checked Twitter or Facebook, but she loved Instagram. Idly scrolling through other people's photos: pictures of their homes, their gardens, their families, their holidays. A little window into their life. She especially liked the travel posts. Nosing around where other people had visited. After a long day, it was an antidote to the troubles of everyday life, a wonderful irrelevance. And, right now, an irrelevance was just what she needed.

A Notification of a private message came up: @Appletree-208. Accompanied by a photo of an autumnal tree. She didn't recognise the sender. Nicole sighed. Probably just another guy, a sleazy hoper, trying to hit on her. Someone she didn't follow, chancing their arm. She'd had similar messages in the past, even though there were photos of Ethan and her on her timeline. *Hello beautiful! You look lovely, fancy connecting?* Or, *You're just what I'm looking for.* God, it was sad, desperate. How many times did they try this before someone answered?

She clicked accept on the message, wondering what inventive words they'd come up with this time, poised to block the sender, and gasped.

> Hello, Nicci. It's me. I know this will be a shock,
> but please… please don't ignore this message.
> This is important. I need to speak with you
> urgently. You must tell NO ONE.

Nicole couldn't breathe. Only one person had ever called her Nicci, and he hadn't used the name in years.

Ethan.

But Ethan was dead.

No. No. No.

Someone was playing tricks on her. Terrible, cruel tricks. Ethan had only been gone a few weeks, his body barely cold. How could anyone be so barbaric? And on the night before his memorial service too.

She should block the sender. Block them, shut down her phone. Ignore.

But something about the message reached deep inside. *Nicci.* Ethan had called her that in the early days of their relationship when they shared the same halls of residence at uni. The name had petered out in the second year. These days, if he did deviate, he called her Nic, at best, and that was rare – Nicole had never been one for shortened names.

Who would possibly know that name now? She racked her brains. Charlie, the friend she'd shared with during that first year, had moved to Canada after graduation. They hadn't spoken in years. Mel and Tim, their dear friends, the couple they spent most of their time with through uni, had emigrated to Auckland a couple of years ago. She'd spoken with them days after the crash. A sombre call as they expressed their condolences.

There was something else about the message too. *It's me.* Ethan had taken to saying that when he called on the work phone. *Hello, it's me. Hey, it's me.* Even though Harrison Dunbar's number was saved on her phone and popped up on her screen. She used to tease him about it, an in-joke between the two of them, which only made him do it more.

This wasn't happening. She should call the police, alert someone. It was harassment, wasn't it? She jumped up, her chest tight as she filled a glass with water and drank it down, then refilled it. The cold fluid trickled through her insides.

It was someone messing about. It had to be.

But the message drew her back to her phone screen like a magnet. She slid into her chair, the same question ricocheting around her mind like a barrage of bullets: why? Why would anyone do this?

Suddenly, she realised she was holding her breath, fingers hovering over her phone. She exhaled, long and hard. They had to be after something. She thought of David's explanation for the so-called 'intelligence agent' in the cemetery. A competitor. Yes, that was it. Maybe it was another competitor, fishing for information. Impersonating Ethan to get her attention. Where was their humanity? How could they possibly think that impersonating her late husband would encourage her to speak with them?

Again, she thought about contacting the police. But what could they do? The message wasn't threatening.

Nicole took another sip of her water and stared at the blank screen of her phone, clutching her stomach with her other hand. The only sound that of the ticking clock on the wall. She should delete the message. Ignore it. That would make it clear to the sender, whoever they were, that she wasn't prepared to put up with this.

But, still, it piqued her curiosity.

A huge shock. Tell no one.

The authorities hadn't found his body…

Surely not? No. If Ethan was alive, he would have been in touch before now. And she'd never known him use Instagram. Though she couldn't temper the hope bubbling up in her chest. She couldn't leave it, couldn't delete it. Because if she didn't respond, she'd never know.

Nicole brought the message back up, tears filling her eyes as she typed back:

> Who is this?

She pressed send before she had a chance to reconsider.

The reply was almost instantaneous.

> Kojak.

Nicole's hand flew to her mouth. No! She'd called Ethan *Kojak* just after they'd moved into this house, when he'd shaved his head for Children in Need. A stupid nickname, after a seventies detective drama her dad used to watch reruns of when she was a child. It was a one-off, meant as a joke, but he'd taken umbrage and they'd argued over it.

No one else knew that.

She didn't know how to respond, a million questions swimming around her head. If it was Ethan, where was he? Had he swum to safety, been sheltered, recovering in a remote location? Images of films of castaways on desert islands sprang to mind.

Why hadn't he alerted the emergency services? And why hadn't he contacted her before now?

Minutes ticked past. She needed to say something. She'd opened the lines of communication now, scratched the surface. She couldn't ignore it. She typed:

Where are you?

Clicked send and waited.

Nothing. Her phone faded. She pressed the screen to refresh, every muscle of her body tense. Every tick of the clock ringing like a chime in her head.

Her doorbell sounded. Nicole jumped, her heart in her mouth. Her thighs trembling as she navigated the hallway.

She pulled open the door. Stared at the young man with the crew cut standing on her doorstep in dark coveralls.

'I've come to collect a parcel,' he said. A strong cockney accent. Checking his watch, as if he was approaching the end of his shift. Home beckoning.

Nicole stared at his watch, then him, mouth agape.

He tilted his head. 'You okay, love? You look like you've seen a ghost.'

'Sorry.' She blinked, a thin recollection of arranging a parcel collection yesterday dawning in her mind. A dress she'd ordered for Katie that was too snug. She'd had it since before the crash; she needed to order the next size. But none of that mattered now. 'Yes, a parcel. I've got it here.'

Nicole riffled through the hallway cupboard, pulled out the parcel and passed it over. The man scanned it and gave her a card.

'You sure you're okay?' he said. 'You don't look well.'

She wasn't well. She didn't think she'd ever be well again. But she wasn't about to talk to someone she didn't know from Adam. 'I'm fine.'

The man gave an uncertain tip of the head.

She watched him walk down the drive and climb into a red van. The engine roared as she closed the door. She leaned up against the cold plastic, took a moment to regulate her breaths.

Nicole re-entered the kitchen to find her phone screen lit brightly. @Appletree-208 had replied.

Chapter 32

Nicole's knees tensed as she slid into the chair. She clicked on the message.

> Go to the airing cupboard. Second shelf. In the right-hand corner, behind the orange towels, there's a phone taped to the wall. I'll call you in ten minutes.

Orange towels. The ones they'd brought from their last house. The ones Nicole had refused to throw away, even though they didn't match the new colour scheme because 'they'd come in handy for something'.

He was alive...

She looked behind her, out of the window into the garden, her mind racing. She had so many questions, but now was not the time. She needed to do what he was asking. She checked the lock on the back door. Double-checked the front, then dashed up the stairs. The airing cupboard was in the family bathroom, at the back of the house, beside Ethan's study. Her hands trembled as she opened the cupboard and pushed aside the duvet covers. They were heavy, bulky. Below them a pile of sheets – more old linen she barely used anymore. Why, oh why, did she have to keep everything?

The old towels were in the middle. She tipped them out onto the floor. Insides hollowing when there was nothing behind. Nothing obvious, anyway. Three minutes had passed since the message arrived.

She started tipping everything out. Pulling and tugging haphazardly. Tea towels, more duvet covers, an old throw falling to the floor in a messy heap. And then she glimpsed it. A small black phone attached to the wall with two strips of duct tape.

Nicole checked over her shoulder. Her hands were shaking so hard, she struggled to peel away the tape. *Tell no one.* This was the sort of thing you read in books or watched on the television. It didn't happen to real folk, like them.

Back downstairs, she closed the kitchen door, then drew the curtains.

Little flutters began in her chest as she switched on the phone. The screen lit. *In emergency, call 999.* Other than that, it was empty. No numbers stored on it.

Another minute passed. And another. It was time. She picked up the phone, stared imploringly at the screen. *Come on!* And then it rang, a jaunty tune like something that accompanied the credits to a children's television programme.

Nicole's hand trembled as she clicked to answer.

'Nicole, darling. Is that you?'

A sob escaped. Nicole's heart lurched, tears springing from her eyes. It was him! It was definitely him. The same intonation, that same musical tone she thought she'd never hear again.

Ethan was alive.

She was crying now, in full flow. Tears streaming down her face like an overflowing drainage pipe. A series of sniffs. So overcome with emotion, she couldn't speak.

'Don't cry, darling.'

But she couldn't stop. More tears came, then more, until her shoulders juddered, and she was sobbing. When she tried to speak, the words caught in her throat. All she could do was sit there and listen to the ebb and flow of his breaths at the end of the line. The same comforting melodious sound she'd lain beside, night after night, for so many years.

'I've missed you,' he said eventually.

His words induced fresh tears, hot and sticky. Her nose was running, her top lip wet, but she didn't care. She said nothing, revelling in the moment, as if she was on borrowed time.

'Are you still there?' he asked.

'Yes.' She sounded like a strangled bird.

'Look, I can't talk for long. We have to be careful.'

'Where are you?'

'Not far away.'

Her gaze flew to the door. 'Where?'

'You mustn't tell anyone. It's important, Nic.'

Why the secrecy? But she didn't ask. She'd do anything to hold on to this moment, to keep it with her for eternity. 'I won't.'

'I'm in Ashford, Kent.'

Who did they know in Kent? 'They searched. Said you couldn't survive in the water for that long.'

'I know. I'm sorry.'

Another sob escaped.

'You need to stay calm. It's all going to be okay.'

Gentle, consoling words. She held on to them, to every one, as if they were tiny gems of happiness, of hope, that she might return to her old life. She rubbed her palm across her stomach, their child beneath.

'I've missed you so much,' he said.

'I thought you were gone forever. I thought you were...' She couldn't bring herself to say *dead*. 'We've arranged a memorial service. Christ, I'll need to cancel!' It was like living inside a dream. At any moment, she might wake and reality would slap her in the face.

'You can't.'

'What?' Her heart thumped her chest.

'Listen, we don't have long. How are the children?'

'Oh, God, the children. They'll be so relieved.' She could tell Ethan. She could actually tell him about the baby now. But... A swirl of confusion. What did he mean she couldn't cancel the memorial service? Surely, he didn't expect her to go through with it knowing he was still alive.

'Nicole, listen. You can't tell them about me, not yet. You can't tell anyone. It's important.'

'W-what do you mean?' She didn't like the sound of this.

'Look, it's risky, talking like this. Can you meet me tomorrow?'

'Tomorrow is your memorial service.' This was so bizarre!

He paused. 'Okay, Friday?'

'Where?'

'Here, in Ashford.'

'I don't understand. Why don't you just come home?' She imagined him walking through the front door. Eyes glistening as he bent down, embraced his children. Their long-lost father returning to his family.

But, almost as soon as they arrived, fear threaded its bony fingers through the images. Thoughts of the party they would throw for him, everyone celebrating his miraculous escape, slipping through her fingers. Something was wrong.

'I can't. Not yet. Can you come here on Friday? I'll explain everything then.'

Nicole's mind bounced. She didn't know what to say.

'Drop the children off as normal and get the train from St Pancras to Ashford International. It's direct, takes about forty minutes. Make sure nobody follows you. Then take a cab to Victoria Park, the entrance near the junction of Jemmett Road and Chichester Close.' Nicole rubbed her forehead and glanced about for a piece of paper, a pen, anything – struggling to keep up. 'There's a red water fountain there, a row of benches,' Ethan continued. 'I'll meet you on the bench beside the lock-up shed, at eleven. Come alone. You'll be home before the children finish school.'

Eventually, Nicole found a pen, the back of an envelope and jotted down the details. 'What about the memorial service?' she said. 'What do I tell everyone?'

'You need to go ahead with that as normal. It's important, Nic. Vital you don't tell anyone. People need to believe I'm dead.'

Nicole couldn't get her head around it. 'Why?'

'Like I said, I'll explain everything when I see you. Can you do this?'

'Yes.' The word sounded feeble, a squeak from a mouse. How could she ignore him? But something must be terribly wrong…

'Good.' His voice dropped an octave. 'I can't wait to see you.'

Her veins were full to bursting. Blood rushing through her insides at breakneck speed. 'Me too.' It was true. She couldn't wait to see him. To lay her hands on him. To hold him in her arms. Something precious she'd thought she'd lost forever.

'Nic, this is important.' The tightness returned to his tone. 'You must hide this phone. Make sure you're not followed. And remember, tell no one. I'll see you on Friday. I love you.' He ended the call.

The screen faded. 'Ethan. Ethan!'

Why didn't he want to come back here? And why was he so particular about no one knowing, about her not being followed to meet him?

Dread crept up her back. Long spindly arachnid legs. She stared at the phone, sitting blank on the table beside her iPhone. When did he put it upstairs? Had he been back in the house? Or had it been there all along? If so, why did he need it?

She rolled her shoulders and looked down at the cold mug of chocolate sitting on the table in front of her. How she longed for something stronger! Ethan was alive, yet… he didn't want anyone else to know. Which could only mean one thing – he was in trouble. And what's more, tomorrow he wanted her to host a memorial service for their closest friends and family to show she believed he was dead.

Her head felt light, dizzy. She took a gulp of chocolate, swallowed it down, then took another. Sugar. She needed sugar. She couldn't process it. Blood rushed to her head. Bile to her throat. Nicole jumped up. Clamping her hand to her mouth, she bolted through the hallway and into the downstairs cloak-room. Reaching the toilet just in time before she vomited.

Chapter 33

Nicole stood on her lawn and surveyed the groups of people sipping wine around her. Cerys, her next-door-neighbour, with her family beside the garden gate. Irene from across the road, sitting on the patio with Carla. A huddle of Ethan's associates from the golf club. Endless Harrison Dunbar employees. Catering staff floated around, offering canapés on round trays. This wasn't how she'd imagined the day of Ethan's memorial would unfold.

Two hours ago, they were in a stone-cold church listening to a vicar eulogise about what a devoted husband and father Ethan was and how he was committed to his work, his clients. People dabbing their eyes with tissues. Now, hats and sunglasses protecting them from the blistering sunshine, the congregation looked like they were at a garden party.

It didn't help that her mother kept referring to the day as a celebration of life. A celebration of life for someone that had passed in a tragic accident. Only he hadn't passed. He was still very much alive. And all Nicole could think was, she was carrying a secret. A secret none of them knew. And it was so big, so cumbersome, that it was crushing her from within.

Ethan was in danger. He had to be. It was the only explanation for this mess. And, as she glanced around again at his colleagues, she was reminded of Ania's concerns. Had something happened at the company? The intelligence agent in the churchyard, the man outside her house, the contract given to Carla. Put together, it did sound dubious. Not to mention Conrad and the sleeping pills...

She'd seen Ania, standing at the back of the church earlier, but the woman hadn't come to the house afterwards. Was that because of the Harrisons, the company employees, or for another reason?

A hand on her forearm. Nicole blinked, jolted back.

'Oh, I'm sorry. I didn't mean to surprise you.' It was Ellen, David's receptionist. 'You looked lost there for a minute. Are you okay?'

Nicole quickly recovered herself. 'Yes, how are you?'

'Fine,' Ellen said. She smoothed down her black shift dress. 'It was a lovely service, the eulogy was beautiful. So Ethan.'

Nicole cleared her throat, sharp and dry, and thanked her. Ellen rambled on about the weather, the garden and how pretty the house was. Nicole tried to nod politely, the words washing over her. *Ask her about the company, Ethan's clients.* If Ethan's situation was connected to the company, she owed it to him, more than ever, to try to find out more.

Nicole cleared her throat. 'How are things at the office?' she asked.

Ellen looked surprised by the question. 'Okay,' she replied, patting her French plait with her free hand. 'It's difficult.'

'It must be hard, reallocating Ethan's workload.'

'That's not really my department. David's been organising it.'

'Difficult for you though,' Nicole said. Heat crept up her neckline. God, she hoped she looked more casual than she felt. 'Having to work out who's doing what. Especially with that new client Ethan was working with. I feel sorry for whoever inherits that file. So much work.'

Ellen stared at her blankly. 'The other partners don't mind.'

'Oh, I'm sure. Still, tough when someone's so demanding. You know...' She stared at Ellen, but the woman just looked back at her, impassive.

'Like I say, I don't really get involved.'

'No. It'll be easier when they get an assistant, I'm sure.'

A bee buzzed around their heads. Ellen looked up at it and then at Nicole, as if something had just occurred to her. 'That woman you asked about… Mags.' Her eyes scrunched, as if she was recalling a memory. 'I think I might have spoken to her.'

Nicole started. She hadn't been expecting this. 'Oh.'

'Yes. It didn't come to me until after you left the other day. I had to call someone for Ethan last month and cancel an engagement. She wasn't a client, just someone he was helping out. I think her name was Mags.'

Someone he was helping out. 'Right. Do you have any contact details for her?'

'No,' Ellen said. 'I got the impression they didn't know each other well, to be honest. It was just a quick call.'

Nicole's heart contracted. *Distant acquaintances don't write notes on the back of restaurant menus.*

'I rang her at work. A milliner's called Bonner's in Southwest London.' Ellen rolled her eyes. 'Took me ages to get through their damn menu systems. I remember thinking it odd he didn't give me her mobile number.'

–

The afternoon pressed forward. Nicole forced herself to shut out all thoughts of Mags from her mind. She couldn't deal with that today. She had to focus, to play the role of the bereaved widow while finding a way of furtively questioning Ethan's colleagues about his work. Ethan was frightened. She'd detected fear in his voice last night and she needed to find out why.

Time passed as she moved from one group to another, desperately searching for an opportunity. Eventually, she spotted Henry, the company accountant, with Will, another partner, beside the trampoline. Nicole dithered. Will was pretty easy-going, but Henry was stiff and low on chat. She'd been stuck on the end of a table beside him at the last Christmas dinner, trying to prise conversation out of him – the longest night of her life. It was unlikely she'd get anything out of them both together.

But she needn't have worried. Just at that moment, Henry touched Will's shoulder, excused himself and moved across to the patio. Nicole took her chance, sweat gathering between her shoulder blades as she sauntered over and greeted Will, who was now standing alone, sipping his wine beside the hollyhocks. She thanked him for coming and listened, nodding appropriately, desperately trying not to recoil while he talked about the service and what a wonderful guy Ethan was. How they missed him. How sorry he was, for her, for the children. It was touching. Heartfelt.

'Thank you,' Nicole said. 'It's tough for you all too.' She took a tentative breath. 'And with Ethan's workload…'

He said he hadn't looked at any of Ethan's files yet. They were with David.

Interesting, Nicole thought. 'Hopefully, we'll be able to find you all an assistant to help out soon,' she said. 'My boss and I are searching.'

Will lifted a brow, shocked to find she was involved in filling a position her dead husband had created. 'I'm sorry, I didn't realise…'

'It's okay. I think David is just trying to keep me busy.' She desperately hoped her smile appeared more convincing than she sounded. A butterfly looped around their heads. Nicole watched it go. The beads of sweat between her shoulder blades were bursting now, perspiration trickling down her back. Thank goodness she was wearing a loose dress. 'So,' she said, fighting to keep her voice level, 'any tips I can pass along to potential recruits?'

Will's forehead arched. He loosened his tie.

'I just mean, anything in particular you are looking for?' Nicole said, faltering. She inadvertently brushed her stomach. Thought about the baby inside. *Get a grip!* She could only imagine the effect this stress was having on her unborn child. 'We'll have a brief, but it's always good to have the inside track, to know what sort of character would fit.'

He switched his weight from one leg to another. 'Enthusiasm and stamina wouldn't go amiss,' he said eventually. 'Investment finance isn't filled with days of nailing those big clients. They're important, of course, but the day-to-day grind of watching, monitoring, predicting the next trend is hard, laborious.'

Nicole's heart sank. This wasn't what she'd been looking for. 'I imagine some clients can be tricky too,' she said, looking up at him enquiringly. 'I know Ethan was having a particular problem with one of his.'

'Some are more demanding than others, I'll give you that.' Will took another sip of wine and looked down the garden.

'That's what Ethan used to say. I bet you've got some great stories to tell. I mean—'

'Salmon and dill puff?' A waiter paused, thrusting a plate in their direction.

'No, thank you,' Will said.

Nicole shook her head.

Will took advantage of the interruption to excuse himself.

She watched him stride across the lawn, the relief clear in his measured gait. She hadn't expected an easy ride, but gaining any information on the company's clients or business was proving practically impossible. Which only made her more suspicious.

A cackle of laughter wafted down from the patio. Carla. She was surrounded by a ring of men, telling one of her infamous anecdotes, no doubt.

The afternoon crawled past. Eventually, guests started to bid their farewells.

Nicole was at the front door, seeing out a group from the golf club, when she heard voices upstairs.

She closed the door. All was quiet. Most of the guests were in the garden. There was no reason for anyone to be upstairs. She shrugged it off, about to make her way back outside, when she heard a soft thud.

'Hello?' she called.

No answer.

She grabbed the banister, angling her head as she swept up the stairs. Only to find David Harrison on the landing, outside the open door of Ethan's study. The door she kept firmly closed. He looked flustered.

'What's going on?' she asked, her gaze passing from David to the study.

David straightened his tie. 'Finlay wanted a few quiet minutes,' he said. 'So, we came up here and he showed me his flag collection.'

At that moment, the toilet flushed, and Finlay emerged from the bathroom, a tiny flag of America in his hand. He smiled at his mother, then took his godfather's hand.

'Come on, mate,' David said. 'Better get back and join the others. Why don't you bring that one with you?'

Nicole returned her son's smile and watched them go, then cast a quick glance into Ethan's study. Nothing appeared to have been moved, but it didn't stop the anxiety ballooning in her chest as she descended the stairs.

She recalled David pressing her in his office about sorting through Ethan's study. Had he been in there? What was he hoping to find?

Back in the kitchen, she was accosted by Olivia. 'Can I have a word?' the woman said, closing the back door, so that the two of them couldn't be heard.

'What is it?'

'The position we've asked Jackson's to fill.' Olivia cleared her throat uncomfortably. 'Look, darling, I know you mean well, but I'm not sure you should be involved in the contract.'

Nicole didn't answer. Ellen or Will had clearly mentioned that Nicole had been asking questions. But that wasn't what really bothered her. *We've* asked Jackson's to fill. Was Ania right? Did Olivia play a bigger part in the company than people realised? And why shouldn't Nicole be involved?

'We wouldn't have asked Carla if we'd have known you were back at work,' Olivia added.

'I wasn't,' Nicole said. 'I'm not.'

Olivia's eyebrows squished together, as if she wasn't making sense. And she wasn't.

'I haven't spoken to Carla yet, but I was thinking about helping. I know the company well. I'm sure I can find the right person for the position. And it would be nice to have a diversion.'

Olivia's face softened. 'I'm just worried about you. It's a lot to take on.'

Before Nicole could respond, the back door opened, and Nicole's mother entered. 'Ah, there you are,' she said. 'And the two of you together, how fortuitous! Olivia's kindly invited us all to Cirencester for the weekend,' she said to Nicole, sporting a wide smile. 'Isn't that nice of her?'

Nicole looked from one to another. She didn't need this. Not now. 'I'm not sure,' she said as diplomatically as she could. 'The children...' She looked out of the window and down the lawn at Katie, who was sitting on the grass picking daisies, gathering them together in her skirt. 'They're just getting settled.'

'The break would take their minds off things,' Olivia said. 'There's a kids' paddle boarding competition on Saturday at Bradford on Avon – it's only a short drive away – they'd love it.'

'Come on.' Nicole's mother patted her daughter's arm encouragingly, looking past her and out of the window. 'The break would do us all good.'

Nicole followed her gaze to her father, in his patio chair. Head lolling to the side, eyes gently closed. He looked exhausted.

She was beginning to feel cornered. But how could she possibly go? She was meeting Ethan tomorrow. She had no idea what that would bring, or what it meant, or even what had happened to him.

'You don't have to do anything,' Olivia said. 'Just pack a few clothes.'

Nicole's head was fit to burst with Ethan's secret. Perhaps a weekend with the Harrisons would afford the opportunity to delve deeper, to help her find out what had been going on.

Her mother squeezed her arm imploringly. 'I know your father would love it.'

She felt torn, outnumbered, swamped. Her head thick with worry. 'Okay. That would be lovely,' she said. 'Thank you.' She only hoped she hadn't made a grave mistake.

—

Ania sat in her courtyard out back and watched a row of sparrows sitting on the telegraph wire in the distance. It was 8.30 p.m.

She pictured Nicole at the church service earlier. How well she'd carried herself. Circulating afterwards, thanking people for attending at the door. So much better than Ania had managed last week. Climbing into the car with her parents, ready for Ethan's celebration of life back at home.

A twinge of guilt. It had been unfair of her to encourage Nicole to quiz Harrison Dunbar employees at Ethan's wake. Immoral. But this wasn't about morality. This was about their husbands, about finding out what was going on in the lead-up to the plane crash. What better chance would they have with so many being in one place together?

The sparrows took flight. She watched them glide gracefully into the air above. She'd gleaned nothing conclusive from Sarah and she was running out of ideas. As much as she hated to admit it – and Ania hated relying on anyone – she needed Nicole's help here. She just hoped that the woman had finally unearthed something. Otherwise, she was going to have to re-examine her options.

Chapter 34

Nicole watched the man sitting opposite her on the Tube scratch his beard, head bent as he stared at his phone screen. The crusty sound of his fingers raking back and forth over the wiry hair carried in the enclosed space. Her gaze slid to a woman two seats away rocking a listless toddler with pink cheeks on her lap. Then to the young man with dreadlocks standing beside the door, fingers curled around the grab rail. None of them paid any attention to her. They were going about their morning business, oblivious to the fact that she, Nicole Jameson, widow of Ethan Jameson, was going to meet her dead husband.

She checked her phone. Two missed calls from Ania. Checking how she'd got on at the memorial service yesterday, no doubt. Thank goodness she'd switched her phone to silent. She had no idea what to say to Ania and, frankly, she didn't have the headspace to consider it amidst the tornado of other thoughts filling her mind.

Over the last twenty-four hours, Nicole's heart had doubled in size. Her emotions vacillating between the joy of getting her husband back, the prospect of reuniting her children with their father, of sharing the news about another child with Ethan – a new son or maybe a daughter – and trepidation at the situation he found himself in. And the threads of emotion wound around each other, tangling, knotting, until they formed a hard lump in her chest.

She should be celebrating having her husband back. Telling her children, her friends, her family. Them all revelling in the blessing that their loved one had ostensibly returned from the grave. They could support Ania's family together.

But something was wrong.

It had to be, otherwise Ethan wouldn't be hiding out in Kent, wanting the world to believe he was dead, and any elation she felt was tempered by the secrecy surrounding his position.

The man opposite crossed one leg over another, catching her toe as he did so. Their eyes fleetingly met. Nicole moved her foot, gave a thin smile of apology, even though it wasn't her fault, and looked away. Waiting a few seconds. Staring at the floor. When she looked back at him, his head was down again, eyes focused on his phone. For a split second, she'd wondered if that was a sign. A signal. Some sort of surreptitious message to make contact. A sigh of relief. He wasn't interested in her. Thank goodness. She'd been careful not to draw attention to herself. Moved down the platform at the Tube station, deliberately selected a quiet carriage.

She arrived at St Pancras to find the station comfortingly busy. Travellers wandering about, queuing at the cafes, checking the screens for train times. A young woman was playing Elton John's 'Your Song' on the piano, the rich notes muffling the background station noise. A group of teenagers in school uniform huddled together near the toilets. Nobody would notice the woman in faded jeans and dark hoody, hair tied back beneath Ethan's old baseball cap, sunglasses masking her face, striding casually through the station. Would they?

She found her platform, checked her watch, and slowly walked up and down. Careful not to catch the eye of other passengers. Relieved when the train finally pulled in, and she climbed into an empty carriage. Keeping her sunglasses on as it left the station, despite the rainclouds, billowing in the sky like balloons about to burst. She stared out of the window inconspicuously, watching the urban landscape change to rural as the train chugged out of London.

A man and a woman entered her carriage at Stratford International. Two women with suitcases climbed aboard at

Ebbsfleet. One of the women struggled to fit her case in the requisite compartment and then whinged about the space available. She was still moaning when they took seats diagonally opposite Nicole. The other woman looked across at Nicole and rolled her eyes. Nicole turned away and instantly felt rude.

This wasn't her. She was one of those people who struck up conversation with the supermarket assistant at the till, or the next person in the queue at the taxi rank. Everyday conversation about the weather, the traffic. The kind of chat that leaves you going on your way with a smile on your face. Creeping around, ignoring people, this was her worst nightmare.

They were almost at Ashford International when a man entered their carriage. Short chestnut hair. Sharp tailored suit. He glanced at her and sat across the aisle, in front of the other women, then turned back again. Nicole looked down at her feet. She made a play of lifting her bag onto her lap, going through it as if she was searching for something. When she looked up again, he was facing forward. But... there was something uncomfortable about his gaze. An icy chill skittered down her spine.

Make sure you are not followed.

Nicole jumped up and made her way down the carriage, bag in hand, as if she needed the loo. She walked through the next carriage, then the next. Checked over her shoulder. Relieved to find the walkway behind empty. The train was pulling into the station now. Passengers rose from their seats. The brakes squealed. The train came to a halt.

Nicole alighted and quickly made for the exit. It wasn't until she was at the ticket machines, that she saw him. The man with the chestnut hair. He caught her eye, his gaze lingering.

She quickened her pace. Breaking into a jog as she passed through the exit. Relief palpable as she spotted the line of taxis outside the station. Nicole jumped into the first taxi. Just in time to see the man with chestnut hair step out of the doors. He checked both ways. As if he was looking for someone. Her? She couldn't be sure. Nicole ducked down and shouted to the driver. 'Victoria Park please, quick as you can!'

Chapter 35

It was quarter to eleven when Nicole entered Victoria Park. The clouds had darkened, the promise of rain imminent. She pulled her baseball cap lower over her brows. *Please, don't rain*, she prayed. Rain was the last thing she needed on top of everything else.

An expanse of green spread out before her, edged by thick shrubbery. She could see a man in the distance throwing a stick for his spaniel. The dog fetching it back, dropping it at his feet. A woman pushing a buggy. A cycle way. The red water fountain in the distance.

By the time she reached the fountain, the area had emptied apart from a young couple sitting opposite each other in the picnic area nearby, hands entwined across the table. Nicole walked around the fountain, found the small lock-up shed, nestled in front of an arrangement of bushes and shrubs, and took the bench nearby. The metal felt icy cold through her denims.

10.55, 11.00 passed. At 11.03, Nicole pulled out her iPhone and checked her messages. Nothing new. Another glance around. Carefully, she pulled out the phone Ethan had left for her. No messages there either.

Where was he? Admittedly, Ethan hadn't been known for his timekeeping. But that was due to his work, in his past life. What could possibly be holding him up today?

Tell no one. Had he changed his mind, or been spooked? She was pretty convinced she hadn't been followed. No one had tailed the cab – she'd checked out of the back window. Her gaze landed on the bushes beside the lock-up. Was she imagining it, or did something just move in there? She watched them for several seconds. Yes… A slight judder. Her mouth dried. She sat forward. Just as a squirrel skipped out.

Nicole let out a long breath. This was ridiculous. Surely if Ethan couldn't make it, he'd message her. Unless something had happened to him. He hadn't told her why he was hiding out, what he was running from. Maybe whoever it was had finally caught up with him…

She couldn't think like that. She mustn't.

It was cold out here in the wind. She wrapped her arms around herself.

A snap. A crackle of twigs. She turned. The couple in the picnic area were brushing themselves down, making off. She watched them walk towards the cycle route, hand in hand. She finally stood. About to go herself, when…

'Nicole, it's me.' The whisper made her jump afresh, every organ in her body jangling. She spun round. She knew that voice.

Nicole watched Ethan check the area as he approached from behind.

Only it wasn't *her* Ethan. The man she married had always been particular about his appearance: every shirt freshly pressed, never leaving the house without groomed hair or clean clothes, even if he was only popping to the post box, or the deli around the corner. Today, he wore a long overcoat she'd never seen before. Tweed and crumpled, as if he'd slept in it. Nothing like the Crombie or the Savile Row raincoat that still hung in their wardrobe. A flat cap covered his blond hair. And, her eyes widened, for the first time he sported a beard and moustache.

He looked like – dare she think it – a tramp. *What the hell has he been through?*

'I'm so glad you came,' he said.

She reached towards him, an automatic gesture, but he froze rigid, shook his head.

'It's too risky,' he said. 'I'm sorry.'

Too risky to hug. What, in case they were seen? There was no one nearby. No one she could see anyway.

'You look...' Tears glittered his fair lashes. 'You look amazing.'

Nicole was lost for words as he sat beside her. A musty, unfamiliar smell curled her nose. This wasn't how she'd imagined things to unfold – the clandestine meeting between a dead husband and his wife.

Except he wasn't dead. He was quite definitely alive.

'How are the children?' he asked.

'They're happier now they're back at school, with their friends.' She should tell him about the baby. But... A little voice inside cautioned her to keep it to herself for the moment. So many questions buzzed around her head. She didn't know where to begin. 'Ethan, where have you been? The coastguard... They searched and searched.'

'I wasn't on the plane.'

'What?' Nicole blinked. Dazed, as though she'd just received a sudden blow to the side of her head.

'I wasn't on the plane. Something came up at the last minute, a critical issue with a client. Something I've been working on recently. Conrad needed to get back; he'd promised Ania. I told him to go ahead without me.'

So, Ania was right. There was an issue at work. 'What was so important? It was my father's birthday.' It seemed ludicrous talking about her father's birthday when she hadn't seen him in almost a month. When he was supposed to be dead.

His eyes were soft, sad. 'I know, and I'm sorry. I was going to call you. I intended to. But then I heard about the crash, and I don't know... I panicked. How is your dad?'

'He's fine.' Nicole blinked again. None of this was making sense. 'What was the issue?'

'Pardon?'

'The issue with the client.'

'It was a big investment. High risk. There's always a chance of losses. This one had been wavering awhile. While I was in Nantes, the value plummeted overnight.'

She narrowed her eyes. 'Why didn't you speak with David? He could have helped you.'

'It hasn't got anything to do with David.'

Confusion washed through her. 'I don't understand.'

'The work was for a private client.'

'You were moonlighting?' Nicole let her jaw hang. She thought of the awkward questions she'd asked at the memorial service. The suspicions about Harrison Dunbar. Her own furtive trip into Ethan's office, looking for clues. 'Does David know?'

'No, I don't think so. And you can't tell anyone.' His eyes widened, desperate. 'Please, Nic… It's important.'

She stared at him a moment. 'I still don't understand why you didn't come back. After the crash.'

'It's complicated.'

Nicole huffed. 'You're telling me. You'd better start talking, Ethan. Because, right now, you're not making any sense.'

'Shush!' She'd raised her voice a decibel. 'I'm sorry. The client wanted a solution, and quick.' His eyes darted from side to side. 'I was in Nantes seeing someone else – a Harrison customer. But these people, they were plaguing me with phone calls, emails. Then they started making threats.'

Nicole could hardly believe what she was hearing. 'What sort of threats?'

'They said I wouldn't make it home if I didn't sort it out.'

'Oh my God! Are you serious? Who the hell are they?'

'People you don't get on the wrong side of.'

She raised a brow.

'I can't tell you.'

'I'm not having that, Ethan. I deserve to know.'

'Honestly, Nic, it's better you don't. Suffice to say, they are people who conduct some of their business outside the law.'

'Criminals? Ethan!'

'It's not what you think. These people are highly organised. I didn't take the threats seriously. Not at first. I thought I could move a few things around, find a solution. They needed me. My knowledge of the markets. It wasn't until I heard about the plane crash that I realised they were serious.'

'I'm not with you.' Nicole frowned, and then it hit her. 'Are you saying you think they tried to kill you in the crash?'

'I couldn't be sure at first. I was terrified when I heard about it, kept my head down, watched the news unfold. But then when I read about the sleeping drug in Conrad's system, I knew. Conrad would never take anything like that before a flight. They must have had someone in place at the hotel when we had breakfast, tampered with his drink. And that's when I was sure… They'd lost confidence in me, their reputation was at risk. They decided to show their associates, all the many people they do business with, that they weren't to be messed with.'

Nicole looked out across the empty expanse of grass, the pathway lined with trees. This was crazy. 'Conrad died in the crash.'

Ethan's face folded. 'I know. If I could change anything… You have to believe me. I had no idea.' He shook his head. 'How is Ania holding up, and the boys?'

'The boys are doing their best. Ania is… going crazy.'

'Oh, God. Poor woman.'

'How could you do this?' Nicole said. 'To Ania's family? How could you jeopardise our happiness, everything we had? You were making good money with Harrison Dunbar.'

'I'm sorry. You have to believe me. I had no idea it would end like this.'

'Why didn't you contact the authorities? They could have protected you.'

'They couldn't.'

'How do you know that? You let us all think you were dead. Not to mention making Ania think the crash was caused by her husband!' She recalled Ania's pursed lips, her tight resolve, convinced something was amiss. And she was right.

'It seemed the safest option. For now.' His voice caught. 'I knew you and the children would be looked after by friends and family. Provided for by life insurance. This way, the client thinks they've won. It's over.'

'We should go to the police.'

'We can't.'

'Ethan, these people are criminals, murderers.'

'And they're not stupid. They have senior officers in the Met on their payroll.'

This would be unbelievable if it hadn't been so real. 'What do you mean?'

'You have to trust me on this. We *can't* go to the police. Not under any circumstances. I won't be safe.'

'So, why come back?'

'For you, and the children… I can't bear to be without you.' He looked down, cleared his throat. 'Nic, I have to ask. Has anyone approached you? Have you noticed anything unusual?'

He looked frightened. Vulnerable. She told him about the intelligence agent in the cemetery, the man outside her home. The delivery driver the other day. Ania's alleged stalker. The sun found a brief crack in the clouds, beaming onto their backs, warming their necks, before it disappeared.

When she'd finished, Ethan scraped a hand down the front of his face. 'This is what I was afraid of.'

'What?'

'They're checking up. Making sure I'm gone.'

An icy chill slipped down the back of her head, spiralling through her shoulders. She squinted at him. 'Does that mean we're in danger?'

'No, it's me they're after. As long as they think I'm dead, you'll be fine. Touching you or the kids would attract too much attention. You just need to concentrate on behaving normally.

Don't do anything out of the ordinary. Nothing to spark suspicion.'

'Like today.'

He looked at her, closed his eyes. 'Just be careful, all right.'

'And if I'm not?'

'What do you mean?'

'If they suspect you are not dead. What then?'

'It won't come to that. It can't.'

Chapter 36

Nicole sat back against the bench, the metal slats digging into her back. Anger burned in her chest. Anger and frustration. All those times she'd made excuses for Ethan because she'd thought he was putting extra hours in at work, doing a normal job, above board. When, in fact, he wasn't putting in extra hours at the day job, he was moonlighting for criminals. *They...*

Nicole didn't know much about the criminal underworld, but she'd gleaned enough from watching the news and television documentaries to know 'they' must be an organised-crime gang, especially if they had enough to invest in the levels Ethan worked.

Shit, shit, shit.

'How could you get yourself mixed up in something like this?' she said.

'I didn't have a choice. These people, they seek you out. They know you are successful, good at what you do. If the investment had worked, it would have been fine for all of us. I could have broken away, we could have moved, made a fresh start.'

'But it didn't.'

'You have to believe me, Nic. Once I'd been approached, recruited, I had to follow it through. I was doing this for us. For our family's future. It's the only thing that has kept me going. I never thought it would come to this.'

They paused as a cyclist passed on the route nearby.

'Why didn't you contact me earlier?' Nicole said. 'Just one phone call...'

'I wanted to. There's nothing I wanted more than to ring you, to hear your voice. But I was scared. I didn't know what to do. I'm a dead man walking.'

She looked into his swarthy face. He was so ungroomed, so different. As if he'd aged ten years in the past month. 'And the phone?'

'I was worried about you, so I made my way back to London, planted it in the house.'

That day when she'd returned home and felt a presence. 'It was you…' She told him about the photo that had been moved in the front room.

'I can't believe I did that.' A muscle flexed in his jaw. 'Someone knocked at the door. I had to hide until they'd gone, leave quickly. It was so hard being back there.'

'Somebody could have seen you.'

'They didn't.'

The note from Mags jumped into Nicole's mind. So many questions… She looked at the branches of the bushes nearby, rippling in the wind. 'Who's Mags?'

'What?'

She talked him through her finding the restaurant menu.

'She's a friend of a client,' he said. 'She had a legacy to invest. It wasn't much, not in the leagues we work. I put her in touch with people who could help her.'

'The message said, "Looking forward to next time."'

He snorted. 'She'd never been to a classy restaurant. Never eaten haute cuisine. She said I changed her life.' The edge of his mouth lifted, his usual lopsided smile, softening his features. He rounded on her. 'You didn't think I was having an affair?' He pulled back, eyes wide. 'You did! Christ, where would I find the time?'

'That's what Carla said.'

'And she was right. Come on, love. There's only ever been you. You and the kids. You're everything to me.'

A helicopter passed overhead, the drone of its engine filling the air.

'Where the hell have you been staying?' Nicole asked.

'It's better you don't know.'

'Well, what are you doing for money? I mean, someone must be helping you. How did you even get back from France, for Christ's sake?'

'A friend *is* helping me.'

'Who?'

'I can't talk about it.'

She turned away, shook her head.

'They're taking a huge risk looking after me. I can't put them in any more danger.'

Anger seared her chest. The vague hazy answers were starting to grate. 'So, when are you coming home?'

'I'm going to have to relocate.'

'What? To where?'

'I don't know yet.'

'No!' Christ, she'd just got him back. She thought about her façade at the memorial yesterday, her stomach roiling as she listened to stories, anecdotes, jokes about Ethan from people who believed he had passed. She'd done it, kept up the pretence, for them. Because she thought it was a temporary measure, a few days at most. He couldn't leave now; the kids hadn't even seen him yet. 'We can sort this out,' she said. 'We'll go to the police together, a different force, somewhere unconnected. They'll help us track these people down.'

He shook his head. 'I'll never be safe.'

'What are you saying?'

'I need to go away, make a new life elsewhere.'

'That's absurd. Then these people… they'll have won!'

Ethan gave a hopeless shrug. 'I'm so sorry, Nic. I really am. I wanted us to have it all, the house in the country, together. We still could!'

'Where will you go?' she asked, ignoring his hopeful gaze.

His face fell. 'I don't know yet.'

'What about us?'

'As long as they think I'm dead, you're safe,' he said again. 'You need to act normal. Don't let anyone think something is awry. They'll soon give up.'

Fear travelled down her back. The guy on the train. Chestnut hair. Staring at her. Alighting at Ashford International. But she had no proof he was watching *her*.

'But the money they've lost,' she said. 'Surely they'll want it back.'

'This isn't about money. It's about respect. Respect and their reputation. They need to show that those who let them down face consequences. That's why I can't emerge, the hero of the moment.' He turned to her, his eyes soft, deep. Suddenly she was transported back to their halcyon days at university, and he was the old Ethan again: slouching on the lumpy sofa in his digs, daydreaming about the children they'd have, the life they'd share, together. 'Come away with me, Nic. When this all dies down. Bring the kids.'

She closed her eyes, shook her head. 'That's madness.'

'Is it? There are loads of places we could go. Start afresh. A new life. Just the four of us.'

The five of us. She pushed the thought aside. 'The children think you are dead.'

He winced, her words clearly stinging him to the core. 'We can do anything, you and I,' he said. 'You know that, don't you? We're the dream team. We always were.'

'You're asking us to leave our lives behind, everything we know. What would we do for money? It's not like you could get a job.'

He sat back, forlorn. 'I'm sorry. I just... I miss us.'

A dog walker approached, a Jack Russell at his side.

Ethan tossed them a fleeting glance and stiffened.

'Is there anything you need from the house?' she asked, desperately trying to be practical. 'Clothes maybe?' She looked him up and down and he half-smiled at her attempt at humour.

'There is one thing. There's a loose skirting board behind the bookshelf in my study,' he said. 'A USB stick is hidden behind there. It contains all our bank details, all my investments. A security policy.'

'But you're dead to the banks. I took your death certificate in.'

'There are offshore accounts. Panama, the Bahamas. I kept them as a backup for us.'

She stared at him, aghast. 'I can't believe you did that.'

'I work in finance, Nicole. I didn't want all our income swallowed away in tax. This was supposed to support our pensions, put the kids through uni, look after us in old age.'

Supposed to... Her heart tumbled in her chest. 'How will you even access the accounts?'

'I'll find a way.'

Illegally, she supposed. Through his dead persona.

'So, that's why you brought me here. To get your money.'

'No, Nic. *You* asked me if I wanted anything, remember? Look, I do need the USB, I need something to live on. But I wanted to see you. To make sure you were okay. To ask you to come with me.'

She stared at the weeds poking through the broken concrete beneath their feet. 'Ethan, I can't. What would I say to everyone?'

'Tell them you're going on holiday. Pick anywhere. We can work out the rest later.'

'You're asking too much.'

'I'm sorry. I just miss you. I miss us.'

She missed him too, but how could he ask her to do this? It was insane. They fell silent as a couple walked along the path and rounded the water fountain.

'I have to go,' he said. 'Think about it, that's all I ask. It'll take a while to sort everything out. I'll contact you on the burner phone, arrange to meet you again.'

The burner phone. A phone that was unregistered and couldn't be traced. It was like something out of a detective drama. Nicole cringed. 'How long?'

'A few days. A week at most.'

A week. The thought of pretending like this for another week, of constantly looking over her shoulder, made her nauseous.

'I'll meet you again, collect the memory stick. You can give me your answer then.' He gave her knee a gentle squeeze. 'Make sure you keep the phone with you. And, Nicole, this is important. You must behave normally and keep this to yourself. The fewer people that know I'm still out there, the better.'

Chapter 37

Nicole pressed the side of her head against the cold window as the train chugged back to London. A patchwork of open fields passed her by, but she didn't see them. She was looking up at the iron-grey sky. The same sky she'd seen that morning. The same sky she would see later when she was back at home with her children.

All that time, all that energy Ania had wasted on suspecting David, and then Olivia, convinced that the plane crash was something to do with the company, when the deal, the cause of Conrad's death, came from elsewhere. Somewhere illicit. And it was connected to Ethan.

Nicole was picking at the side of her fingernail. Tearing away at the flesh. She hadn't done this in years. Not since that agonising night at the hospital with Ethan and Conrad, when Finlay had been rushed in with meningitis. Her son had recovered, thankfully, but not before she'd picked and pulled so much, she'd made her fingers bleed.

Her chest burned at Ethan. Conrad had died because of his dodgy dealing, and now he'd asked her to make the biggest decision of her life.

How could she leave everything behind: her parents, her friends, her work, everything she knew, everyone she loved, and start again with him? It wasn't merely a matter of leaving them either. There'd be no farewell party, no good-luck wishes. No FaceTime catch-ups, no visits, at least for a while. And she wouldn't be able to tell anyone why or where she was going.

The kids! How could she take them away from their school, their friends, their grandparents? She couldn't sit them down and prepare them just in case they let anything slip. Even the slightest comment would make people suspicious. How could they expect two little children to keep such a huge secret?

And what about the child growing inside her? Where would she receive her maternity care?

How could Ethan even think of asking her to do this? The idea was insane.

A voice bellowed over the public address system announcing Ebbsfleet as the next station. A man at the end of the carriage stood and pulled a briefcase from the overhead rack. Nicole cast him a fleeting glance, then turned back to the window. And picked and picked and picked.

How could Ethan have been so stupid?

She thought of Conrad, his broken body buried in the ground. The people Ethan was involved with didn't go about things lightly. He would never be safe. Always looking over his shoulder, jumping at the doorbell, the telephone, no matter where he chose to settle. It was no way to live.

And yet... Could she deny her children their father? She knew he was alive now. Could she raise them encouraging them to believe he was dead, knowing he was indeed still out there somewhere?

But surely that would be preferable to life on the run?

She hadn't told Ethan about the baby. She couldn't. She hugged herself. Pressing her warm palms to her stomach. Her mind buffering.

The train pulled into the station. Nicole was vaguely aware of the passenger with the briefcase alighting. A young woman in jeans and a sweatshirt boarding. The wheels of her suitcase rattling against the floor as she pulled it through the carriage.

You're safe, as long as they think I'm dead. But he wasn't dead. She knew he wasn't dead and now she couldn't ignore the fact.

Ethan had made a mistake. A stupid mistake. He'd over-stretched, got himself mixed up with the wrong people in pursuance of his heady ambitions. But he'd done it for them, his family. He didn't deserve to be hunted down.

She should contact the police. They couldn't all be corrupt. Although, even if she did manage to find a reliable officer, she didn't know anything about this 'client'. Would there be paperwork, an audit trail? She doubted it. If they had organised the crash, they'd be unlikely to leave anything behind to connect them. Were the investments even legitimate? The police might not be able to trace them. And then there was the possibility that Ethan might face charges. Wasting police time, or even perverting the course of justice, fraud. People went to prison for less.

And would the police protect him? She imagined a decision like that would need to move up the chain of command, be made by someone of senior rank. How could she be sure it wouldn't reach someone connected to the very group they were trying to avoid? The client had already tried to kill him once. If his location was exposed... Her back tensed. She'd be putting his life in danger. Putting herself and her children in danger.

Her hand felt wet. She looked down to find a line of blood trickling in the fold between her forefinger and nail, the cuticle in ragged pieces.

She sucked the blood away. A whirlpool of thoughts rushing around her head as the train pushed on. She couldn't make any sense, couldn't find any clarity.

Eventually, the driver announced St Pancras as the next station. A woman nearby snapped her laptop shut. Nicole went through the motions of pulling on her hoody, retrieving her bag. People were walking through the carriage, preparing to disembark when her mobile rang. She retrieved it from her bag. It was Ania.

Had she found out about Ethan?

The phone trilled in Nicole's clammy hand. Instinctively, she glanced up and down the aisle to check she wasn't being followed. The woman with the laptop threw her an annoying *Are you going to get that?* look.

The train juddered to a halt. Passengers bustled towards the door. Nicole waited for the woman to move off, then clicked to answer, her chest constricting.

'Hello?'

'Hey. How are you?' Ania's voice was smooth, seamless.

She doesn't know. Nicole gripped the headrest. A rush of air expelling from her lungs like a burst balloon.

'Hi,' she said. 'Sorry, I've been meaning to ring you. It's been a busy day.' Her step lightened as she moved off the train.

'That's okay. You sound out of breath.'

Behave normally. People darted around Nicole, boarding the train. Nicole shuffled to the side of the platform near the stairs, pressing her free hand against her other ear to block out the noise. 'I'm fine. Just sorting a few things out.'

'Ah. It was a nice service yesterday.'

It wasn't nice. It was anything but nice, laying the memory of your husband to rest, especially when he wasn't dead, but there was no point in getting into that now. 'Thanks.'

'Are you free to meet for coffee later?'

Nicole gripped the balustrade. She couldn't face Ania. Not today. 'I can't, I'm afraid, I'm stacked out.'

'What about at the weekend? We could get the kids together again.'

'I'm away, I'm afraid. Until Monday.'

'Oh.'

Nicole marshalled her thoughts and talked Ania through her attempts at questioning Ethan's colleagues yesterday, the invitation from Olivia. 'This could be a good opportunity,' she said. If Ethan was right, his situation had nothing to do with the Harrisons and the idea of spending a weekend in their company, harbouring this secret, made her queasy. But she had to play along.

The line crackled. 'I doubt it.'

'Oh, come on,' she said. She couldn't afford to lose Ania's trust now. Not when there was so much to sort out. She needed time… 'Look, yesterday was a struggle. Perhaps if I get the Harrisons on home turf, I might be able to dig deeper.'

'Okay,' Ania said dismissively. 'If that's what you want. I guess I'll speak to you on Monday.'

What would Ania think if she knew her secret? That Ethan hadn't died in the plane crash, and she'd just visited him. That Conrad wasn't responsible for his own death, after all.

It was a relief when the call cut. Nicole leaned against the stairwell for some time, the rush of air from passing travellers clearing her head.

Forty-eight hours ago, she would have given anything to have her husband back, restore the life they had together. But not like this. She couldn't get mixed up in Ethan's sordid mess. And she wasn't about to get her children involved either.

His face, earlier, tugged at her. Soft blue pleading eyes. '*I didn't have a choice.*' If that was true, then this could happen to anyone. He didn't deserve to be hunted down, to lose his liberty. The injustice ripped through her. She needed to help him. And if she couldn't enlist the assistance of the police, she needed to do it alone. She'd find his memory stick, wait for his contact. Meet him one last time and pass it on. Then, as much as it pained her, she needed to force herself to let him go, forever. To forget him. It was the only way to keep them all safe.

She could do that. Couldn't she?

Chapter 38

Ania placed a hand on the tall iron gate of the cemetery, cracked and blistered paint catching her fingers as she pushed it open. The sun had broken through the clouds and was warm and gentle on her skin. She wandered down the path and walked among the graves. Short stubby stones, covered in lichen and ivy. Wonky headplates. Tall tombs in a blend of greys, blacks and whites. Marble glinting in the sunlight.

She walked along the concrete path, where weeds grew between the cracks, down Church Avenue and veered off to the left, where lines of heaped earth covered the most recent burials. Halting at the familiar wooden cross with a brass plate and the mound of earth that marked Conrad's grave.

A new grave had appeared beside him since her last visit. The marker read Luke Oliver Simms. She looked at the dates, did the maths in her head. Twenty-one years old. So young. The cross on the other side of Conrad was engraved, Edna Mary Tiverton. Edna was eighty-three. Conrad would be stuck between Edna and Luke for the whole of eternity. It was odd to think that in life people clung to those dear to them, yet in death their remains were sandwiched between strangers. The idea left her cold.

She looked back at Conrad's grave marker, tears filming her eyes as her thoughts cascaded like an avalanche. She'd been wrong about Nicole. She'd hoped she was different, but she was just the same as the others. Under the Harrison spell, enjoying her plush lifestyle far too much to upset the status quo by asking uncomfortable questions. And now she'd been distracted, seduced by a weekend away with them.

Ania busied herself with gathering up the dead carnations, replacing them with the fresh miniature rose plant she carried, the yellow flowers dancing in the soft breeze. So much had happened in the short weeks since the crash. The sleeping pill, the resignation, the man hanging around outside her house. Yet she was no closer to finding out exactly what had happened.

She thought about the receipt from South Wood Services, the phone call with the assistant. They weren't prepared to help her. The police hadn't contacted her about it either – they clearly weren't going to follow it up.

The letter from Piotr crept into her mind again. For some reason, her brother was popping into her head, more and more, and she couldn't understand why. She blinked him away. He'd got what he deserved. He'd let her down when she needed him, then cast her aside, ignored her. Her resolve hardened. Well, she wasn't about to let that happen again. She clenched her teeth. She wouldn't be ignored, and she certainly wouldn't be gagged. Not by Nicole Jameson, or anyone else for that matter.

Ania didn't hear the woman sidle up beside her. It wasn't until someone leaned forward and placed a single sunflower on the heap of earth beside Conrad's grave that she realised anyone was there. The woman turned, made eye contact, gave a nod. She was short, her face pinched with anxiety.

Ania glanced at the wooden cross above the single sunflower, marking Luke's passing. She looked back at the woman, found her viewing Conrad's cross, and a silent thought of condolence passed between them. Was she the mother of the poor boy? She considered her own boys. So young. So much growing to do. And her heart bled for this woman. The idea of losing a child incomprehensible. They weren't meant to die before you. That wasn't the natural order.

'You're the wife of the pilot, aren't you?' the woman said, a Scottish lilt softening her voice.

Ania didn't know what to say. She didn't want to strike up conversation with a woman whose dead son was in the next grave, but she didn't want to be impolite either. She pressed her lips together, nodded.

'I'm sorry,' the woman said. 'I read about it in the newspaper. So tragic.'

'Thanks. I'm sorry for you too.'

'Carol,' the woman said, proffering her hand.

Again, Ania didn't know what to do, what to say, so she shook it. 'Was that...' The lump in her throat was so wide, the words squawked out.

'My son.' Carol nodded. 'Killed in a gliding accident.'

'How dreadful.' Two men killed in the air, lying beside each other in the ground.

'It was.' Carol stared at the grave wistfully. 'It is. Every single day. But then, you'll know that.'

Ania gave another nod. Short, sharp. They both focused on the crosses of their loved ones.

'He loved to fly,' Carol said. 'Gliders, aeroplanes, paragliders. There was something about being up there in the sky, looking down on everything. It was like a magnet to him. Just started his pilot's exams, he had. He wanted to fly for the big airlines, Boeing 777s. He's been obsessed with them ever since he was a kid.'

Ania was reminded of the first conversation she'd ever had with Conrad. 'I'm going to be a pilot,' he'd said. 'I'm going to fly people all over the world.'

'He would have been pleased to have been buried beside your husband,' Carol added. 'A good man. Someone who shared his passion. Someone who was at their happiest amongst the clouds.'

Ania's eyes filled afresh. Conrad had been a good man. Yes, he'd worked long hours. Yes, he kowtowed to David Harrison and the gang at Harrison Dunbar. But, ultimately, he was a good father and a kind soul who'd only tried to do his best by everyone. And now, like Carol's poor son, he was dead. It was bad enough that his life had been cut short. But to end this way... She swallowed back the lump in her throat.

Ania made her excuses to Carol and moved off, waiting until she was out of sight before riffling in her bag for the reporter's card. If no one else would help her, maybe the press would. It was time to share her suspicions with the world.

Chapter 39

The carpet crunched under Nicole's feet as she made her way into Ethan's study, screwdriver in hand. It was just after 8 p.m. Her children were sleeping in the next rooms. She should be packing now, sorting out their clothes for the weekend. Instead, she was searching for Ethan's memory stick.

She looked at the desk, with the motivational books stacked atop, Ethan's iPad to the side, and thought of Ethan crawling around the house last Saturday. Imagining the commotion if they had arrived home and happened upon him.

Her mobile buzzed in her pocket, making her jump. She cursed her frayed nerves, checked the message. Olivia. Confirming times for their arrival tomorrow. She was once again reminded of finding David on the landing yesterday, the study door open. She was sure he'd been in here. Did he suspect that Ethan had been up to something? Was he trying to find the details of his secret client?

Nicole gave the bookshelf a gentle shove. It didn't move, didn't budge an inch. She couldn't risk trying to move it like this on her own, not in her condition. She'd have to empty the shelves first.

She collected small piles of books and gently placed them on the ground. One after another. The top shelf was soon emptied. Minutes later, the second shelf was too. By the time she got to the third, her arms were starting to ache. She leaned up against the desk, paused a moment. Then started again. Heart dropping when she noticed a second skin of books behind. Ethan had done a tidy job of hiding this memory stick. He certainly didn't want anyone finding it.

She was on the last pile of the next shelf, the penultimate one, when she turned quickly, catching her elbow on the corner of the desk. And stumbled. Placing a hand out to steady herself, she reached to grab the desk to save her fall. And cursed again as Ethan's motivational books thudded to the floor.

At the same time, her mobile rang. It was her mother calling. She let it ring out, go to voicemail, then opened the door and peered out onto the landing. Shoulders dropping when all was quiet. The secret was eating away at her, slowly, in bite-size chunks. Ethan had said it would take a while to sort things out, a week or so. She'd bought time with Ania, but only until after the weekend. What would she say to her then? Ania was fighting for justice; she wasn't going to let this go easily.

Nicole's heart skipped a beat as her phone sounded again – her calendar reminding her about her father's upcoming oncology appointment on Wednesday.

She forced herself to take long breaths. In and out. In and out.

The last shelf was cleared and the bookshelf, now a fraction of the weight, slid away easily from the wall. She knelt behind it, examining the thin gap between the wooden board and the wall. She retrieved the screwdriver, wedged it into the gap. The skirting was loose, it only took a little unscrewing, then wiggling, to pop it off. And, sure enough, a black memory stick with a red cap toppled to the floor.

Nicole picked it up and turned it over in her hand, a mixture of relief and angst rushing through her. Offshore accounts. Accounts she hadn't known about. Though that was nothing unusual, she tended to leave the financial planning to Ethan – that was his job, after all.

She rose and made her way downstairs, leaving the bookshelf jutting out at an angle, books scattered across the floor. She fired up her laptop, plugged in the memory stick and waited. If she was to help him, she should know what was on there.

A password box came up. She should have guessed it wouldn't be easily accessible. He wouldn't go this far to hide it and then leave it open. She tried a few combinations, then pushed the laptop aside, frustrated.

Perhaps she was being over-cautious. If they were to separate – she paused as the very word sent a shooting pain through her chest – Ethan needed something to live on. She had the life insurance, after all.

Oh, God... the insurance claim. She should cancel. She couldn't possibly claim it, she'd be committing fraud. But... to do that, she would have to tell them Ethan was alive. Which meant, one way or another, she'd be signing his death warrant. And then, what would she and the kids live on? Oh, what a mess!

A tear trickled down the side of her nose. Ethan wasn't a bad man. He'd been a fool, wronged, and now he was trying to make the best of a bad situation. Trying to keep them safe.

She crossed to the front room, memory stick in hand. Checking the road outside as she drew the curtains. It was empty. No BMW. No black car. Nobody hanging around. Not that she could see anyway.

Shit, she could do with a glass of wine. She swept a hand across her stomach and sighed. Another thing she couldn't do. Another secret she was keeping.

She couldn't go with Ethan, couldn't subject her children to a life of looking over their shoulders, but could she stay here? Was it safe? Her chest sparked with anxiety. Stay. Leave. Call the police. Don't call the police. The dilemma of what to do pressed on her.

Tell no one. Ethan couldn't have been clearer in his instruction. But why shouldn't she? He'd admitted someone was helping him. Of course they were – how would he manage for money, clothes, food, accommodation, otherwise? Why shouldn't she share the load?

And if there was anyone she could trust, anyone out there, it was her father.

She couldn't tell her mother. Alice would panic, call the police immediately. Her father was different. Grounded. If she explained the situation properly, once he'd got over the initial shock, he might appreciate her predicament, give her honest advice. He used to work in IT. He might be able to break into the files on the memory stick.

Though… she looked back at the appointment in her diary. After what he'd been through recently, she didn't want to pile any more stress onto his shoulders, and he'd looked so tired yesterday. But she had to confide in someone.

Perhaps he'd be better, fresher, after the weekend. Nothing was happening with Ethan for a few days, at least. Next week's oncology appointment was a review. If it was positive, she could take her father aside afterwards, talk things through.

The burner phone bleeped, slicing through her thoughts: Ethan. She pulled it out of her pocket.

> How are you, lovely?

She texted back.

> All okay.

It wasn't okay. It was anything but okay, but how could she subject him to more worry?

Seconds later, the phone bleeped with his reply.

> Good. Can't tell you how great it was to see you today. I've missed you so much. Will be in touch soon x

Was it great? Her heart said it was. Her heart sang with joy at the prospect. But her head cautioned her. The lies, the secrets, the threat... She couldn't see how this was going to end well for any of them.

Chapter 40

'That really is a beautiful view,' Nicole's father said, resting back in his chair and exhaling loudly.

Nicole looked out at the rolling countryside, unfolding into a patchwork of fields as far as the eye could see, and nodded. They were sitting on the Harrisons' decking enjoying a mid-morning coffee, the sun beaming high in the sky.

Katie shrieked as she ran across the lawn with a football under her arm. David Harrison on her heels, Finlay coming up at the rear.

'You're supposed to kick the ball, not carry it,' Nicole's father shouted at her, laughing.

Nicole looked past them at her mother at the bottom of the garden, deep in discussion with Olivia about the water lilies in the pond. She couldn't deny, it was encouraging to see her parents so relaxed. Her mother's cheeks were glowing, the years falling away from her father's face with every passing hour, only to be replaced by a spray of freckles. The pressures and angst of the past few weeks brushed away like leaves in the light breeze.

It had been a lovely family weekend. The children had enjoyed the paddle board race in Bradford on Avon yesterday, and the lavish picnic Olivia had prepared in Barton Farm Country Park afterwards had been second to none, with champagne and strawberries, and chocolate cake for the kids.

Lovely in so many ways... But – she clenched her jaw – heart-wrenching too. Watching the Harrisons, two people whom she had doubted, whom Ania had suspected of being involved in their husbands' demise, at pains to ensure they all had a good time. Yesterday evening, sitting with them, listening to them chatter about their holiday last year on the Amalfi Coast, then a theatre show they'd recently been to. Happy, shallow conversation. Conversation that Nicole couldn't indulge in because she was periodically retreating to her room to receive secret texts from the man they all thought was dead. The man who'd gone behind their backs.

The worst thing about it was the knowing. When David touched her shoulder, or Olivia passed her a warm encouraging comment. *It will all be okay. We'll get through this together.* All the time wondering if her fragile secret would break and expose her. If Ethan would be spotted, discovered. Constantly on edge for some news. It was like walking around in a bomb vest that might explode at any minute.

Her knees tensed. After the clarity of Friday, her brain had descended to mush and all weekend she'd wandered about in a semi-zombie state. Almost numb. Unable to contemplate what the future held or make sense of the surge of thoughts racing around her head.

David's phone rang, the trill filling the garden. He disentangled himself from the children, moved to the side of lawn to take the call.

'Are you okay?' her father asked. 'I mean, I know you're not okay, but—'

'I'm fine.'

'You're so quiet. I wish there was something I could do.'

His sincerity was excruciating. 'I'm good, Dad. Really. You have to stop asking me.'

'I'm sorry.'

His forehead crumpled and her knees tensed afresh. She didn't want to upset him. 'It's all right. Ignore me,' she said. 'I've just got a lot on.' She averted her gaze, towards the view, the tumbling fields beyond, and swallowed. Maybe she should tell him now. Spill it all out, while the others were out of earshot. He could clearly see she was struggling.

'Nicole, darling!' She looked up and shielded her face from the sun as David crossed the grass to join them. 'Can I borrow her for a moment?' he said to her father.

'Only if you can make her smile. I'm not having much luck here.'

David snorted. 'Oh, I think I can do more than that!' He motioned for her to follow him.

Nicole's legs were leaden. She rose warily. The ground was hard beneath her feet. She walked through the French doors and into their spacious kitchen.

David paused at the centre station and reached for his laptop.

'I want to talk to you about money,' David said.

'Oh!' Relief whooshed out of Nicole like a burst balloon. She pressed a hand to her stomach, the heat of her touch seeping through the thin linen of her shirt.

'Listen.' His brows met in the middle. 'You're going through so much and if we can do anything to alleviate your worries, we want to help.'

Tears brimmed in Nicole's eyes. He had no idea.

'I messaged Henry on Friday, chased up the life insurance. You'll be pleased to know it's finally all sorted.' He flipped open his laptop, clicked a few buttons. 'This has been transferred to your personal account today.' He turned the screen to face her.

Nicole felt her jaw drop as she stared at the six-figure sum in front of her. She had no idea it would be that much. She looked at David and then back at the screen. Ordinarily, she would be elated. Relieved. It was far more than she'd anticipated, definitely enough to pay off the mortgage and then some. She might even be able to move to that house in the country, after all. Maybe even get a granny flat for her parents… Though, she wasn't entitled to a penny of it.

She moved her hand, clamped it over her mouth.

'Ethan was like family to us,' David said. 'You all are. I want you to be secure. For my godchild to be comfortable.' He rambled on about a quarterly bonus Ethan was still due which they would be honouring too.

A strangled sob. A sob followed by tears, spilling out, rolling down her cheeks. How was she ever going to resolve all of this?

'Oh, my dear.' David pulled her close and, despite herself, she buried her face in his shoulder. 'It's all going to be okay. It'll get easier.'

He didn't understand. He had no idea of the straitjacket of guilt tightening around her. Because, whichever way things turned out, it was never going to be okay again.

Chapter 41

Nicole moved out to her patio, a fresh cup of coffee in one hand, her iPad in the other. It was Monday morning. The kids were at school. The company was arriving to collect the gazebo in an hour. Her brain still felt like cotton wool, her thoughts incoherent, but finally she was home and alone, away from the watchful eyes of her parents and the Harrisons. She no longer had to hide the burner phone in her clothes, disappear off to rooms to check for messages. She no longer had to act out the part of grieving widow to the Harrisons, of keeping-it-all-together mother to her parents. She sat back, closed her eyes.

Her mobile rang. Ania. She watched the phone dance across the table before it rang out and went to voicemail. She should call Ania back. Check in on her. But so much had happened and she had no idea what to say to the woman.

She pulled the burner phone out of her pocket and read back the last message from Ethan, sent yesterday evening, 8.11 p.m. *Glad you had a good weekend, you needed the rest. Give the kids a hug for me. Will be in touch soon x* It was almost as if he was away on a business trip.

Wednesday, he'd said. He was hoping to resolve everything, secure the passage to wherever he was going, then arrange to meet her on Wednesday. She wished she could go to sleep and wake up on Wednesday, and then this would all be over. Although, in truth, she had no idea exactly what *over* meant.

Ellen's report about Ethan's acquaintance with Mags drifted into her thoughts. It was bad enough with Ethan's predicament picking away at her, but something about Mags, about Ethan's explanation on Friday, sat uncomfortably. They sounded like associates, yet she hadn't come forward, hadn't introduced herself.

Nicole was picking at the skin around her thumbnail again.

Ellen said Mags worked at a milliner's called Bonner's in Southwest London. Nicole fired up her iPad and searched for Bonner's. A host of results popped up: a furniture maker, a bakery, an estate agent. She typed 'milliner' beside her search, tried again. *Felicity Bonner Millinery – award-winning milliners of the finest bespoke hats since 1969.* Bingo! She clicked the link to the website. Coloured photographs of classy hats sat beneath the banner – *Luxury Couture Millinery.* There was a page about the history of the company. Another on quality, examples of designs. She clicked on the *Contact us* page and found the postal address. A phone number below.

They were only on the other side of London. She imagined Ethan cruising across town to meet her.

It was 8.50 a.m. Opening hours were listed from 9. Mags would probably be arriving for work soon, possibly brewing her first coffee of the day. What would she look like? Slim probably, Ethan liked his women slender. Fair hair, or dark like Nicole? Dark, possibly, small and petite. Dressed in a trouser suit if she worked in the offices. One of those with a jacket that nips in at the waist, a crisp white shirt beneath. Or perhaps she was on the shop floor in overalls.

Oh, God, she was getting carried away with herself. After all, Ethan had denied any notion of an affair… but then he would.

Maybe if she just called the company, spoke with Mags, determined the nature of her relationship with Ethan, she'd feel better. Though… she didn't even have a surname.

Nicole sat back and looked down the garden, her thoughts threading together. Her phone pinged on the table. A text from Ania.

Ignoring Ania's text, Nicole punched the number for Bonner's into her phone and pressed call. The phone rang out twice, then connected to a recorded message. She sighed, recalling Ellen's disparaging comments about their menu system and listened as the voice asked if she wanted sales, accounts, numerous other choices. She moved through to another menu, and finally selected the option to be on hold for the next available representative. Trepidation eating away at her as she held the line. She was beginning to wonder if this was such a good idea when a crisp voice filled the line.

'Felicity Bonner Millinery. Thank you for holding.' A pause. Warm, fresh, friendly. 'How can I help you?' the voice said.

'Ah, yes. I need to speak to Mags, please,' Nicole said, with as much conviction as she could muster.

A brief silence. She half expected the call handler to say, *Mags, who?* But she simply replied, 'Just one moment.'

Nicole held her breath. Seconds flitted past. Eventually, the same woman came back on the line. 'I'm afraid she's on holiday. Would you like to leave a message?'

A message. Nicole hadn't bargained on a message. 'Um, yes… It's Nicole Jameson here. I need to speak with her about a personal matter. Could you ask her to call me when she's next in the office please? It's not urgent, I just need to reach her.' She passed over her mobile number and ended the call.

Chapter 42

Ania stirred and glanced at the clock. Almost 12 p.m. She remembered arriving back from the school run, curling up on the sofa, checking her phone. She must have dozed off. She hauled herself forward, grabbed her phone and googled *Waltham News* for the umpteenth time since she'd risen that morning. The press piece should have been posted by now. The reporter said first thing.

She pictured the journalist sitting on the armchair opposite her in this very front room on Friday. He'd sounded eager when she'd telephoned. Arrived within half an hour, armed with his notepad and pen, fresh-faced and earnest. Two hours they'd spent together. Talking things through. She'd been thorough, open. Told him all her fears.

He'd said he couldn't discuss his research on Harrison Dunbar, but he'd include as much as he could in the article.

Her phone buffered. An icon at the top said it was updating apps in the background. She placed it on the sofa beside her and rolled her shoulders. Her neck ached like crazy from being curled up for so long. She refreshed her phone – *come on!* – placed her hands behind her head and reached her elbows back, stretching out her shoulders. A row of searches flashed up on her screen. And there it was – *Wife of Airline Pilot Speaks Out*.

A bolt of adrenaline. Ania clicked on the link and faced a photo of Conrad, his two boys beside him, sitting on the bench in their back yard. The photo she'd supplied to the journalist.

Two weeks ago, former teaching assistant Ania Gilbert lost husband and father of two, Conrad

Gilbert, when the company plane he was piloting crashed into the English Channel…

The next paragraph talked about the journey from Nantes to London. Where the plane went down. How it was too dangerous to attempt recovery.

Ania scrolled down to a picture of her and Conrad on their wedding day, a paragraph about her loss, the ensuing grief, her boys. She moved on, further down. And then she was at the end. Wait! They'd missed stuff out.

She flicked back up to the top, reread the article, word for word. It was a heart-wrenching piece about the loss of a husband, a father, in tragic circumstances. That was what she'd wanted – to keep the story alive. There was a line about her querying the sleeping tablets. Another mentioning Conrad had been planning to leave the company. But barely anything about Harrison Dunbar. In fact, the company was only mentioned once in the whole piece, as owners of the plane and the firm that Ethan and Conrad had worked for. Nothing about clients and unethical interests. And nothing about what the reporter had uncovered about Harrison Dunbar. He'd only conveyed her dissatisfaction vaguely in the final paragraph in the form of quotes:

'I just want answers now, to find out what happened to our husbands, and why. I cannot understand why the investigation is taking so long.' Air Investigation said the inquiry is ongoing.

It sounded like she was having a pop at the Aviation Authority more than anything else. Ania chucked her phone aside. This was her chance. To prick consciences, pose questions. Why hadn't he printed what she'd told him? And what about *his* interest in the company?

No…

Bile rose in her throat. He'd played her. Lured her in, pretending to be investigating the company when he was actually after a personal piece. Anger rose in her chest. Anger and frustration fusing together. And Nicole was now ignoring her calls, her texts.

Tears spilled down her cheeks. She felt suffocated. Suffocated by the red tape of a prolonged investigation. Suffocated by the silence. How dare they gag her?

She jumped up, grabbed her car keys and the receipt from South Wood Services, resting on the mantel. She could bear it no longer. It was time to take control.

—

Ania's frustration built as she crawled through the stop/start streets of Leytonstone. She glanced at the brake lights ahead, ground her teeth. Two men in suits walked past. A woman stood in a shop doorway, vaping. The lights changed and she was off, heading out of the city.

By the time she reached the motorway, Ania was brimming, the weight of her exasperation insurmountable. She needed to get out of London, inhale the fresh country air, clear her head. And there was somewhere very particular she wanted to go.

The motorway, clogged with lorries and cars, like little boxes closing in on her, offered little respite. It wasn't until she turned off at junction 9 that the roads thinned, and she felt an ounce of the tension in her back ease. Being here, taking these roads, she felt Conrad's presence. Almost as if he was sitting beside her.

As she drove around Redbourn, the mist started to clear. She lowered the window, felt the rush of wind in her hair, and continued on her way to St Albans. Before she knew it, the clock on the dash read 1.40 p.m. Shit! Where had the time gone? The boys finished school at 3.15. She ought to make her way back, the traffic heading into London would be heavy, but... She was so close now, only a couple of miles from the service station. If she spoke to the staff face to face, if they realised how important it was, she was sure they'd feel compelled to help her. At least quietly let her view the CCTV footage to see if Conrad was accompanied by anyone. It had to be worth a try.

Ania spotted a lay-by ahead, pulled in behind a Mini and dialled Blanka. She answered on the second ring.

'Hey.' Blanka's voice sounded full of sleep.

'Hi. Sorry to bother you. Can you pick the kids up for me? I've been held up.'

'Sure.' The car rocked as a lorry passed on the road beside. 'Where are you?' she asked.

'Oh, not far away. Shouldn't be late. Thanks for getting the kids. You're a star.'

Ania cut the call before her friend had a chance to probe further and leaned back into the headrest. She hated lying to Blanka, especially when she'd been so kind. But she also knew Blanka was worried about her and telling her she'd driven out here was hardly likely to quash her concerns. No. She'd tell her later. When she was back home, with a clear head and a plan of how to move forward.

She waited for a space in the traffic and pulled back out onto the road. Ania didn't notice the car pull out behind her. Didn't hear them accelerate after her as she sped up. It wasn't until they flashed their lights that she noticed them in the rear-view mirror, and frowned. A black Audi. The driver obscured by a combination of the sun visor pulled down low and dark sunglasses. God, she hoped there wasn't a problem with her Astra. It was old, they'd been meaning to replace it for ages. She slowed. The Audi slowed too. And suddenly she was reminded of Nicole talking about a black saloon outside her house. Heat rose in her chest.

A car overtook them both and zoomed off ahead, leaving the road empty apart from the pair of them.

Ania pressed her foot on the accelerator. If memory served her right, she'd reach a roundabout soon and start climbing into the city. The road opened ahead. The car pulled out, as if they were going to overtake. Ania shot the driver a sideways glance as he drew level. Perhaps she was wrong. Maybe there *was* a problem with her car after all. But... what was that? Instead of driving past, the car was veering towards her. If she didn't move, they would collide.

Ania yanked down the steering wheel, hard. The screech of brakes filled the air as her vehicle's back end snaked, resisting the sudden movement, but the Astra held firm. She accelerated. The Audi snuck back in behind. She pressed on, heart hammering in her chest, trying to make speed. But the Astra couldn't compete. They'd no sooner rounded the next bend when the Audi was at her side again. She flatted her foot to the floor as it veered towards her. Ania braked too late. The car rocked, spun on its axles. And rolled. Bump. Bump. Bump. The jolts tumbling through her body. A crash as the windscreen caved.

Ania didn't notice the other driver accelerate. Didn't see the Audi race off into the distance. All she saw was the world turn black.

Chapter 43

Nicole's mobile buzzed as she pulled up at the school later. She squeezed into a space opposite the gates, unbuckled her seat belt and pulled her phone out of her pocket. A text from Carla. Her stomach grumbled. This incessant hunger was driving her crazy. She grabbed a banana from her bag, clicked to open the message and started unpeeling it:

> Check out the piece in Waltham News. Looks like
> Ania's been talking to the press.

Nicole's heart sank to her toes. This was the last thing she needed. She cast the banana aside, clicked on Google search and watched the wheel on her phone screen spin. As soon as she input *Waltham News* and Ania Gilbert, the article came up. She took her time to read it, working slowly through the paragraphs. A gentle piece, talking about the plane crash and how Ania's family were coping. A short line on her questioning her husband's use of sleeping tablets. A single mention of Nicole, as Ethan's wife, and only a brief line on the inquiry calling off the search for Ethan, reporting his body hadn't been recovered. Nothing new. Relief flooded her. No doubt, Ania had expressed her suspicions about Harrison Dunbar, but clearly, with nothing to substantiate her accusation, the newspaper had been careful with their words. Thank goodness.

Seconds ticked past. She picked up the banana and started to eat it, but the fruit felt hard and dry in her mouth as the guilt of

Ethan's secret simmered inside her. Poor Ania, compelled by her mission to find something, anything, to absolve Conrad from blame. And she was right – Conrad was an innocent party, an innocent man murdered. She hadn't spoken to her since before the weekend, hadn't returned her calls because she didn't know what to say. But she couldn't avoid her forever.

She picked up her phone, selected Ania's number. Pressed the phone to her ear as the call rang out. Parents were arriving at the school gates now, clumping together, ready to pick up their little ones. After five rings, the phone was answered.

'Hello?' Ania's voice sounded chipped, off.

'Hey,' Nicole said.

A cough winged its way down the line.

Nicole frowned. 'Are you okay?'

'It's Blanka.'

'Oh, I'm sorry,' Nicole said. She'd only met Blanka once in town, briefly in passing, when she was getting some school shoes for Finlay. A stern woman, heavy hooded brows. She recalled her following Ania down the aisle at Conrad's funeral. 'I was after Ania.'

'She can't come to the phone.'

'Okay. Could you ask her to ring me? Only—'

'She can't ring. There's been an accident. She's in hospital.'

Nicole jolted forward. 'What?'

'This afternoon. Her car, she ran it off the road near St Albans.'

Ran it off the road? Nicole pressed her free hand to her chest. 'Is she okay?'

'She's in a coma.'

'Oh my God!' A coma sounded serious, possibly life-threatening. 'How bad is it?'

'We don't know yet.' Voices filled the background. All speaking at once. 'I have to go.'

The kids were lining up at the school gate. Nicole could see Finlay with his book bag in her rear-view mirror. Ania's boys had just lost their father, and now their mother was in hospital, fighting for her life. 'Can I do anything to help?' she said. 'Pick up the children or—'

'No. We're fine.'

'Okay.' Nicole was in a fix. She didn't know what to do. 'Where is she now?'

'Luton and Dunstable Hospital. It's the only place that had room. I have to go.'

The line went dead. The children were spilling out of the school gates. Finlay fourth in the queue.

Nicole almost fell out of the car. How could this happen? She stumbled across the road, focusing on putting one foot in front of the other. *Ran it off the road.* On her own, or with help? She needed to collect her children and hug them hard, then she needed to get to Ania. She needed to find out what the hell had happened.

Chapter 44

It was nearly 6 p.m. by the time Nicole had settled the children with her parents, navigated through the late-afternoon traffic and made her way to Luton and Dunstable Hospital.

Blanka was sitting on a row of plastic chairs in the corridor near Accident and Emergency. She looked taken aback as Nicole approached.

'I'm Nicole,' Nicole said, holding out her hand, in case the woman didn't remember her.

Blanka looked at her hand and then at her. 'I know who you are. You didn't need to come.'

'I couldn't not.' Nicole lowered her unshaken hand. 'How is she?'

'No change.' Blanka's voice was thick with emotion. 'She's broken her leg in two places, but it's her head they're concerned about. The CT scan didn't show up any fractures. They're going deeper with an MRI now.'

Adrenaline thumped in Nicole's gut. 'What exactly happened?'

'They're not completely sure. A passing motorist found her car upside down at the side of the road, she was inside.'

'Oh my God!'

'Her car's a write-off.' Blanka slumped back into her seat.

Nicole dropped her bag at her feet and sat beside her. 'What was she doing in St Albans?'

'She wasn't actually in St Albans. The police said she was on the A5183, the road heading into the city. Looks like she rounded a bend and lost control of the vehicle.'

Nicole opened her mouth and closed it again, flabbergasted.

'St Albans was her and Conrad's special place,' Blanka said. 'They used to go there a lot when they were first seeing each other. It's where he proposed.'

Their special place. The words tightened the vice on her chest. 'I didn't realise.'

'I don't think it was a planned trip.'

'What do you mean?'

'She didn't tell me she was leaving London. She called me early afternoon, said she was held up and asked me to collect the children from school.' She drew a long breath, spoke through her exhalation. 'The police are looking into it, but they don't believe anyone else was involved.'

No one else involved. For a split second, the relief inside Nicole was overwhelming. But any trace of comfort was quickly consumed by the guilt of the secret she carried on her shoulders. The secret she hadn't shared with Ania.

'What are you saying?' she said. 'Was she driving too fast, was there something on the road?'

'I don't know. She hasn't been thinking straight.'

'What?'

'She hasn't been well. She's been acting very erratically.'

No, no, no. 'You're not suggesting she meant to crash…' The thought was incomprehensible. 'She wouldn't.'

'Maybe she was going too fast, wasn't paying attention.' Blanka's face clouded. 'How would *you* know anyway?' The question was rhetorical. 'You don't know her. Not really. You barely bothered with her until your husbands died.'

Nicole recoiled. It was true. But that was hardly her fault. She thought about Ania at the funeral, their meeting at the park. Ania had looked pallid, brittle. She'd been worried about her. But when they met again at her home last week, she'd seemed stronger. Militant about clearing her husband's name. 'I can't believe it,' she said. And she couldn't.

Blanka huffed a sigh. 'She hasn't been herself since Conrad died. Forgetful around the house. Taking to her bed, preferring to be alone.'

'We're all in shock.'

'This wasn't only shock.'

Nicole recalled her first visit to the house when Ania was resting upstairs. Ania's voice when she'd called the other day, full of sleep, as if she'd woken her.

'I encouraged her to go to the doctor, but she refused anti-depressants. And she's been lying.'

'What?'

'I had to persuade her to get painkillers for her neck. The doctor gave her amitriptyline, to treat the pain, calm her down. I've been giving them to her. I thought she was taking them. Today, I found a pile of them in her bedside drawer. It looks like she put them in her mouth, then took them out when I left the room.' Blanka's eyes filled. 'She wouldn't admit she had a problem. She wouldn't accept help.'

Ania had talked about the pills making her woozy. How could Nicole not have realised things were this bad? 'I'm so sorry.'

They hushed as a nurse walked past.

'How are the children?' Nicole asked.

'I haven't said much to them. I don't want to until we know what's going on.'

'I can pick them up, take them to mine if it would help?'

Blanka shook her head. 'They're sleeping over with a neighbour. I'll take some time off work, look after them.'

They were interrupted by the trill of Nicole's phone. 'Olivia' flashed up on the screen as she pulled it out of her pocket.

Blanka noticed it and immediately stiffened. 'I don't want the Harrisons anywhere near here,' she said. 'They've done enough damage already.'

The words drove deep beneath the skin. 'I'm sure they just mean to help.'

'Keep. Them. Away,' Blanka said. 'If she has any chance of recovering from this, Ania needs to rest. I don't want her upset.'

Nicole declined the call.

Time ticked past. Nurses strode up and down the corridor. Nicole got them both coffees and they drank them down, twiddling the empty Styrofoam cups nervously in their hands. 6.30 p.m. passed, then 7. Nicole thought of her parents putting the children to bed. 7.30 p.m....

'You should go home,' Blanka said eventually. 'Visiting hours are almost over. It's family only afterwards.' She heaved a sigh. 'I'll tell them I'm her sister. I'm the closest thing she has to family anyway.'

Nicole dithered. She didn't want to leave, but they could be there all night and she had her children to consider. 'Okay. Will you call me if you hear anything? I presume you've still got Ania's phone?'

'I have, but I'm not using it. I was just looking through the contacts for her family.' She looked away, sighed. 'Not that she'll want them involved,' she muttered as she retrieved her own phone and asked for Nicole's number.

Nicole was intrigued about Ania's family, it seemed an odd thing to say. She passed over her number and watched Blanka punch it into her phone. She was about to ask more when another nurse approached. Blanka stood and stopped her to ask if there was any news and they moved down the corridor together, out of earshot. That was a conversation for another day.

Chapter 45

Later that evening, Nicole stood at her kitchen window, hot mug of coffee in her hands, replaying her conversation with Blanka. Stricken, depressed, ill. Yes, Ania was probably all of those things. She could understand why she might take a trip out to St Albans, especially if it was a place that brought her closer to her late husband. But she struggled to believe Ania would drive recklessly on purpose; she had her children to think of.

Maybe there was something in the road...

Blanka had said Ania wasn't thinking straight. Whenever Nicole met her, she was certainly focused on the plane crash. Focused to the point of obsession.

Nicole dragged a hand down the front of her face. If only she'd picked up on the desperation. If only she hadn't gone away for the weekend. If only she'd supported Ania properly instead of brushing her off on Friday. If only...

Her phone rang. Olivia. She hadn't returned her call from earlier. She placed the mug on the counter and answered, her insides still swirling.

'Nicole, are you all right? I've been trying to reach you. Have you heard about Ania?'

'Yes, I've been at the hospital with Blanka.'

'Oh.' Surprise filled her voice. 'How is she?'

'In a coma. I wasn't able to see her. They're running tests, checking for brain damage.'

'Oh, my goodness! Do you know what happened?'

She told her what she knew. 'The police are looking into it.'

'That's what they said on the news. How awful.'

On the news. So, it had already appeared in the media. 'I can't believe something like this could happen. Especially after...' Her words trailed off.

'Mental illness,' Olivia said. 'It's such a terrible thing. I mean, you only had to read that newspaper article this morning to see she was suffering. Poor thing. And she looked so ill at the funeral.' A beat passed. 'I thought I'd go down there tomorrow. Speak to Blanka, see if she needs any help.'

'It's family only at the hospital,' Nicole said, reminded of Blanka's vehement comments about keeping the Harrisons away. She didn't tell Olivia that only applied outside visiting hours. 'Blanka has told them she is her sister. She's taking care of the boys.'

'Ah...' A note of silence. When Olivia spoke again, her tone was formal. 'Well, give Blanka my best, won't you, when you see her next? Naturally, if there's anything we can do, anything at all, tell her not to hesitate to ask.'

Nicole doubted Blanka would relish that offer. She said she would pass it on and then fabricated another incoming call so she could ring off. She wasn't about to dissect Ania's life with Olivia.

Word of Ania's accident had got out surprisingly quickly. Nicole googled Ania Gilbert accident. Her piece with *Waltham News* came up. Then another piece: *Breaking News – Pilot's Widow involved in Car Accident* – written by the same reporter.

> Days after she'd spoken of her grief, Ania Gilbert, the widow of pilot Conrad Gilbert, is in a coma this evening after being pulled from her car which was found upside down beside the edge of the A5183 outside St Albans. She is now in a critical condition. Hertfordshire police are not treating the incident as suspicious...

Nicole pictured Patryk and Robert, their innocent faces. So young…

Her phone screen faded. What must have been going through Ania's head?

She picked up her phone again. No messages from Blanka. No news.

Oh, God. Please let her be okay.

Without thinking, Nicole dug deep into her pocket, pulled out the burner phone and dialled. Ethan had said the burner phone was for emergencies only. Well, as far as she was concerned, this was an emergency.

Ethan answered on the third ring. 'What is it? Are you all okay?' No preamble. No niceties.

'We're fine. It's not us.' She walked into the front room as she gave him a brief rundown on Ania's accident.

'Shit! What happened?' His voice was tight, frightened.

She relayed the information Blanka had given her. 'Doesn't it seem weird to you? The timing…'

'I don't know what you're saying.'

'Could this be the people that are after you?'

'No.'

'Why not? People have been watching Ania too.' She told him again about the alleged stalker.

'Sounds like a reporter,' Ethan said. 'Look, they've no reason to stalk Ania. It's me they're after.'

'But—'

'It's a coincidence, love. The police aren't looking for anyone. You said yourself, she was going crazy. Maybe she wasn't thinking straight.'

She had said that, and she'd meant it too. Oh, poor Ania!

'How are things there?' he asked.

Nicole looked out of the window at the empty road outside. 'The same.'

He asked about Ania's boys, and she told him Blanka had arranged for a neighbour to look after them. 'I'm scared.'

'I'm so sorry, darling. I wish I could be there with you. Are the children all right?'

'They're fine.'

A breath of what could only be relief whooshed down the line. 'Look, it's good to be vigilant. Make sure you keep the doors locked and stay close to crowds when you go out. It'll all be over soon.'

'Okay,' Nicole squawked.

'I have to go. Message me. Let me know how Ania is, will you?'

'Of course.'

They said their goodbyes and the call ended. She wished he was here too.

She moved out to the hall, checked the front door and lowered herself onto the bottom stair. Blanka's passing comment about Ania's family snuck into her mind. *Not that she'll want them involved.* What did she mean? Conrad had never spoken about Ania's family in Poland. As far as she was aware, they hadn't come over for the funeral. Had something happened there?

Chapter 46

The following morning, Nicole was in the kitchen, sorting out the ironing – anything to keep occupied – when her mobile bleeped with an email. The memorial engravers – a final confirmation of the wording for Ethan's memorial plaque. *Ethan George Jameson. Dear father of Finlay and Katie. Beloved husband of Nicole. Taken too soon.* Her throat hollowed. How she'd agonised over those little details. What to have – a tree, or a plaque. Where to put it in the crematorium. They needed somewhere, a place where they could remember him. To mark his passing. But that was before he'd come back.

She was gazing at the screen, unsure of how to respond when the phone erupted in her hand. An unknown number. She stared at it a second, swallowed tightly and swiped to answer.

'Nicole, it's Blanka.'

Nicole let out a long breath. Of course it was Blanka. What other strangers had her mobile number? The paranoia of Ethan's situation was really getting to her now.

'What's the news?' she asked.

'Ania still hasn't woken, but she's stable. No brain damage, as far as they can see.'

Nicole moved towards the table and collapsed into a chair. 'Oh, I'm so relieved!'

'So am I.'

Blanka gave her details of Ania's hospital ward, the visiting times.

Nicole thanked her and rang off. It was almost midday. Her kids had a French class after school. There was plenty of time to visit Ania this afternoon and still be back to pick them up. Ania might even have woken by then. She dearly hoped so.

–

Two hours later, Nicole stepped into the empty hospital lift and glanced over her shoulder. This was her life now. Checking the area around her. Ensuring she wasn't being followed. Nerves on a knife-edge.

It was only 2.15. Visiting time didn't start until 2.30 p.m. She'd made good time on her drive from Highgate to Luton, arrived early. If she was going to beat the traffic back into London, she didn't have long. The lift juddered and cranked into gear. Within seconds, she'd reached the sixth floor.

It took Nicole a while to find Ania. She was tucked away in a side room on her own at the end of Carrington Ward. And when she did finally step into the room, her heartstrings stretched to a single line. Ania looked so small, so thin with the blue blanket tucked tightly around her, even with the enlarged right leg – the plaster cast hidden beneath the covers. Eyes closed, dark hair brushed away from her gaunt face. A cut on her right temple, a swollen bruise distending her left cheek, the only facial signs of the accident. An IV line ran from her hand to the drip beside her. The bleep of machines filled the room. A sickly-faint clinical aroma infused the air. It was a pitiful sight.

Nicole was reminded of a television documentary she'd watched about unconscious people. They said people in comas could sometimes hear what was going on around them. 'Hello!' she said brightly. Grabbing a chair from the side of the room, dragging it closer to the bed, lowering herself into it. But she had no idea what to say next… She watched the rise and fall of Ania's chest, her eyes filling. She'd let Ania down. She was supposed to be looking out for her.

A tear escaped, meandering down her cheek.

And now, sitting here, she was letting her down again. Because Ethan wasn't dead, he wasn't even on the plane. And the crash wasn't an accident. It was murder...

Nicole shuddered. She knew all this. And she was keeping it secret. From Ania, from the Harrisons, from her family. From the police. God, she hadn't thought about the police. It was probably a criminal offence she was committing.

A tear dripped off the edge of her chin, plopping on the floor below. The secret wound itself around her, a noose around her neck.

She reached out and held Ania's limp hand. It was cold and bony in her own. 'I'm so sorry,' she said. Her words echoed in the room. 'I didn't know.' She squeezed Ania's hand. Apologised again.

'Sorry for what?'

Nicole jumped back at the voice. Blanka. The woman was standing in the doorway, frowning at her. How long had she been there?

Nicole let go of Ania's hand and wiped her eyes. 'Oh, nothing.' *Everything, this whole situation.*

Blanka shuffled into the room carrying a steaming cup of coffee in her hand. It didn't look like the first cup either, going by the dried stain down the front of her sweatshirt. 'Sorry for what?' she repeated, her face taut, eyebrows drawn together.

Nicole shook her head. 'For not noticing how bad things were,' she fudged. 'For not helping more.'

Blanka blinked dismissively and placed her cup down on Ania's bedside table.

'Is there any more news?' Nicole asked, desperate to change the subject.

Blanka shook her head. She smoothed the blanket at Ania's side. 'We've been listening to Coldplay together,' she said. 'It's her favourite band. We used to joke that Chris Martin was the only man you'd leave Conrad for, didn't we, darling?' She pushed a stray strand of hair away from Ania's forehead.

The gesture, the tender heartfelt words, brought a lump to Nicole's throat.

Time ticked by. The two women exchanging light conversation. Nicole desperately trying to keep it together by asking about the boys. Blanka responding, then talking about her job at the hospital. Asking Nicole about her work at the recruitment agency. Blanka was surprisingly easy to talk to, effortless compared to Ania, and the more they talked, the more she opened up.

A nurse wandered in, took Ania's blood pressure and disappeared. Quiet fell upon them. Allowing time for the finer details of Ethan's situation to crawl back into Nicole's head. Where was he living? What was he doing for money? So many unanswered questions. So many unresolved issues. But the one thing that embedded itself in the side of her brain was, who was helping him? Feeding, clothing, housing him. He couldn't do this alone. And, after the phone call to Mags's company yesterday, only to be told she was on leave, she felt a strong sense of unease.

–

Nicole's head throbbed as she navigated home through the traffic later. It had been awful trying to behave normally. Making small talk with Blanka at Ania's bedside, the crushing guilt of the secret almost splitting her in two.

Who was helping Ethan? A colleague? It seemed doubtful, under the circumstances. Someone from the golf club? The elusive Mags, coincidentally on leave. Or Tamsin? Ethan did used to say, Tamsin would always be there if he needed her.

Nicole thought of Tamsin's phone call last week, her decision not to fly over for the memorial service. Did she really hurt her back or did she know Ethan was still alive? She'd phoned again, while Nicole was away at the weekend, asking how the service had gone and sending her love, but cut the call short because someone was at her front door, promising to ring again soon. Was Tamsin helping him? It would have to be somebody he trusted implicitly, and his sister would surely come under that category.

There was only one way to find out.

Nicole was back in London now. She pulled off the main drag, turned into the next side road, parked up and dialled Tamsin. The phone rang out, again and again, until the voice-mail kicked in. It was just after four. This time of year, Cape Town was an hour ahead of London. She should be around, especially if she was laid up with her back.

I'm sorry I can't take your call at the moment...

Can't or won't, Nicole thought as she listened to the answerphone play out. She left a message, asking her sister-in-law to phone her. Was she even in Cape Town? She needed to know what was going on. If Tamsin knew something, she needed to speak to her. And soon.

Chapter 47

Sweat beaded on the back of Nicole's neck as she sat in the hospital waiting area, sandwiched between her mother and father. It was 10 a.m., Wednesday. The burner phone in her pocket pressed against her thigh. She hadn't spoken with Ethan since Monday evening. She'd messaged to update him on Ania yesterday and he'd responded to say thank you, but nothing else. He was being careful, she knew that. But it didn't stop her reeling. Today was the day everything was supposed to be resolved. Yet Ania was still in a coma and Ethan was... Well, she had no idea where Ethan was. She wasn't sure how much more of this she could bear.

Maybe she should sort out Ethan, then take her children away somewhere, until everything settled down. At least then she wouldn't have to face her friends and family, day in, day out, on tenterhooks. A secret the size of a football wedged in her chest.

The oncology reception was busy. Every seat occupied. A child sat beside a toy box in the corner, pressing buttons on a toy phone, the intermittent chimes breaking the silence. A tired-looking man in an anorak opposite cast the child an annoyed glance. But Nicole barely heard them. She was battling a permanent hum in her own head.

A hand on her wrist. Her mother. Nicole was picking again. Peeling away at the flesh beside her thumbnail. She met her mother's gaze, stilled herself.

Her father held her other hand and gave it a squeeze, his fingers stone cold. It wasn't supposed to be like this. She'd come here to support them, not them support her.

A lady in uniform came out. 'Mike Saunders?'

They all rose. The three of them followed the nurse down the corridor and into a room at the end.

The consultant, Mr Andrews, was a small man with a wizened face and glasses that slipped down his nose. He was sitting behind his desk when they entered, sporting his usual gentle smile. The smile that gave nothing away.

Nicole indicated for her parents to take the two seats in front of the consultant's desk and moved behind her father, resting her hand on his shoulder.

Andrews leaned forward, lacing his hands together on the desk. 'How are you feeling?' he said to Mike.

'All right.' Her father tilted his head to the side. 'Unless you're going to tell me otherwise?'

'Not at all,' Andrews said. 'Your latest test results are back and all as expected. No sign of the cancer returning. Things are looking good.'

The room suddenly felt brighter, as if someone had switched on a light. Her mother reached across and grabbed her father's arm, pressing her lips together as she looked from her husband to Andrews.

'Thank you,' her father said. He reached up with his free hand and took Nicole's, holding it tightly. Nicole found herself looking down, watching the skin around his knuckles whiten.

Andrews went on to talk about ongoing medication, his voice fading to a drone in the background.

She should be elated, on top of the world. Her father was well. Continuing to respond to the treatment. The future looked bright. Clear. Paving the way for... A tear of sadness escaped. Her parents were rising, thanking the consultant again as she quickly swiped the tear away.

She followed them out of the room and down the corridor. Nicole's father gushing over Andrews' knowledge. His deft of hand in surgery. Praising his openness, his personal manner. It was both joyful and crushing. The best news he could have hoped for. Completely unaware that Nicole was about to drop a bomb that would plummet his excitement to the ground.

They were almost at the lift when Alice halted in the middle of the corridor. Tears swelling in her eyes. Streaming down her face. As soon as she wiped them away, fresh ones springing up. She started to tremble, shoulders quaking as a sob escaped. Nicole helped her father manoeuvre her to the side, out of the way of a passing patient, and lower her into a chair.

'My darling,' her father said, crouching in front of his wife. Embracing her in a rare show of public affection. Nicole could only look on as her mother sobbed. The stress and anguish of the past year, as raw as a fresh wound, pouring out of her. It was heartbreaking. 'It's going to be okay,' he said, stroking her hair.

Nicole closed her eyes. Because those five little words sealed her fate. She couldn't talk to her father. He already had her mother to manage, her nerves wrung out. They were both still shaken over losing their son-in-law, and Ania's recent accident. It wouldn't be fair to involve him in Ethan's predicament.

Maybe a holiday, for her and the children, *would* be a better solution. At least then she wouldn't have to pretend. She could deliver the memory stick to Ethan, then go away for a while, a month or two. It would give her time to think, to work out what to do next. How to keep her family safe. She dug her hand in her pocket, willing Ethan to call. Because living like this, with the weight of his secret on her shoulders, was purgatory.

—

Half an hour later, Nicole was climbing into the car after dropping off her parents when her iPhone buzzed. *Tamsin.* She pulled it out of her bag. But it wasn't Tamsin, it was Carla.

'Hey,' Carla said, dragging out the word. 'How are you?'

'I'm all right, thanks.'

'You sure? You don't sound it, hun.'

Is it that obvious? Her pulse accelerated. She was going to have to be more careful, more guarded. 'Oh, it's just the usual,' she fluffed. 'Life, you know. I've just come from Dad's oncology appointment.'

'And?'

'Looking good.'

'That's great news!'

Her enthusiasm was touching. 'It is. I think the shock has just hit Mum though.'

'Ah.'

A second's pause. *Talk to Carla.* Carla was her friend. She'd confided in her numerous times.

'Olivia said you had a great time at the weekend,' Carla cut in.

The weekend. Sitting on the lawn in Cirencester, the sun on her back, seemed like an age ago now. Almost from a different life. But that wasn't the only thing that struck Nicole. *Olivia said...* Carla had clearly been spending more time with the Harrisons. And Carla was fiercely ambitious. She'd be out to impress with the new recruitment contract, hoping that David would put in a word for her with his peers, that it would open a new avenue for her company, bring in new business. If Nicole told her, if she emptied her heart, Carla might feel compromised. At the very least, Ethan was working for a private client, somebody who wouldn't cast the company in a good light. No. She couldn't confide in Carla. Not about this. 'We did,' Nicole said weakly.

'That's good. Olivia also mentioned you were thinking of returning to work. You know there's no pressure here, but if you are thinking of coming back, we'd love to have you.'

The last thing Nicole wanted was to be involved with Harrison Dunbar now, to walk around on eggshells around Ethan's colleagues. 'I'm not sure I'm ready yet,' she said. 'In fact, I was thinking of taking a holiday. Possibly taking the children out to see Mel and Tim in New Zealand.' She was surprised at how simply the idea spilled from brain to mouth, and how easily she chose her destination.

'That sounds like a wonderful idea.' If Carla was disappointed, it didn't show in her voice.

'Yeah. Might be the break we all need, you know?'

'I do. Listen, take as long as you want, hun. We'll be here when you're ready. I was only sounding you out, just in case. Let's catch up, have a glass of wine or two before you go. When you finish your antibiotics. If you have time?'

She wouldn't have time, but she wasn't about to say that now. 'Of course. You should think about finding a temporary replacement to help out until I come back.'

'Is that what you want?'

'I think it would be a good idea. You might finally get a weekend off.'

Carla laughed.

Nicole thanked her, rang off, and stared out of the windscreen. The first seed had been planted.

She was about to turn over the engine when she heard a bleep. The burner phone. Finally, Ethan had messaged! A rush of relief flooded her veins as she pulled it out of her pocket.

Hey, beautiful. How are you today?

She stared at the phone a moment, then out the windscreen at the road ahead. In truth, she wasn't sure how she was. She closed her eyes, pressing her eyelids together. Should she mention her dad's news? She decided against it, better to keep things simple. She took a breath, opened her eyes and typed back.

All okay, thanks. You?

The reply seemed to take an age. She watched the clock on the dash. A minute passed, then another before the screen lit again and two messages came in together.

> Yes, all fine.

> Any more news on Ania?

She messaged back that there was nothing new, Ania was stable but still in a coma.

> Okay. Good that's she's stable. Listen, there's been a slight change of plan. I have to go away for a couple of days. Making arrangements is proving trickier than I expected. I could be out of signal for a while, but don't worry, I'll be in touch as soon as I'm back. x

Go away. Where? He'd talked above moving, setting up a new life. If he decided to go abroad, he'd need a passport. Obtaining a passport illegally wasn't likely to be straightforward. But the notion of waiting longer, of not hearing from him, of being left in limbo to deal with all of this alone, was crushing. And why would he be out of signal? She wanted to ask where he was going, but he wasn't likely to tell her that. He'd been cagey enough about his address in Ashford.

She typed back:

> Why?

Just to put things in place, prepare. There's
nothing to worry about, I promise.

How long?

Should be sorted by the weekend. Be strong, my
love. Take care of the little ones x

By the weekend. It was Wednesday. Another couple of days and
this would finally be over. Wouldn't it?

Chapter 48

As soon as she turned the corner into Swain's Lane later, Nicole knew something was wrong. A liveried police car was parked outside her house, an ambulance on the opposite side of the road. Nicole depressed the brake, slowing as she passed the bewildered faces of her neighbours, gathered on the pavement.

Surely the police haven't found out about Ethan. How could they?

Her heart walloped in her chest as she pulled into her driveway. But there was no one at her door. And suddenly she realised that her neighbours weren't looking towards her house. They were staring across the road. At Irene's.

Nicole climbed out of the car and moved down the drive to join them. She nodded at Cerys from next door, tipped her head to the chap in the plaid shirt from further down the road that she only ever smiled at in passing.

'What's going on?' she said to Cerys.

'Irene's had a break-in.'

'Oh no!' A police officer was walking down Irene's driveway, talking into a radio handset. He switched it off and turned back towards the old woman's front door. 'Is she okay?' Nicole asked.

'I don't know. That officer' – Cerys nodded towards the man on the drive – 'told me. She must have phoned them herself.'

Nicole crossed the road, ignoring the calls from Cerys telling her they'd been asked to wait there to be questioned. The officer had opened the front door, was stepping inside when she called out.

'Hey!' she said, quickening her step as she hit the driveway.

The officer turned, pulling the door behind him so that she couldn't see inside. 'Can I help you?' he asked. He was short and broad, his polo shirt stretched across a muscular chest. His cropped silvery hair lifting in the light breeze.

'Is Irene all right?' Nicole asked.

'And you are?' He looked her up and down.

'Nicole, I'm her—' She was just about to say 'neighbour' when a voice interjected from inside.

'Let her in. She's family,' Irene's raspy voice called.

Nicole let out a sudden breath. She sounded okay, thank goodness.

Another distant voice. Male. 'I thought you said you had no family around here.'

'I don't. Well… not blood anyway. Let Nicole in.'

The officer at the door stood aside, leaving enough room for Nicole to enter the hallway.

In the front room, Irene was sitting in her usual chair beside the window, her pink fringe pushed aside. She was holding a compress to her cheek. A paramedic in green overalls knelt beside her. Another paramedic stood the other side of her chair.

'You're hurt!' Nicole said, rushing towards the old woman.

Irene waved her away, her usual stand-offish manner. 'It's just a bruise,' she said. But her voice quavered, her eyes were rheumy, and she looked shaken.

'What happened?' Nicole said, hovering awkwardly in front of her. It didn't seem appropriate to sit.

'Some blasted kids tried to break in,' Irene said. 'One knocked on the front door saying they were making a charity collection. When I answered, the other came in the back.' She flinched as she nudged the compress. 'You need to watch out, my girl. We leave our back doors open, think we are safe. Those bastards scaled my gate.'

Nicole tensed. She'd heard about break-ins in the area, they all had. Irene's garden was secured by high fencing, mirroring Nicole's. They both had six-foot side gates they kept locked.

And Nicole's French doors at the back were always flung open in the warm weather, especially when the children were playing in the garden. She was going to have to be more careful.

'Was anything taken?' she asked, breathless.

'They didn't get a chance,' Irene muttered. 'I just wish I'd managed to catch one of the bleeders.'

'Do you have any idea who it was?' Nicole said to the officer.

'We've just started our enquiries here,' he replied. 'But I'm sure you've heard, there have been a number of burglaries nearby. They're usually after credit cards, bank cards, cash, car keys. Anything they can make off with quickly. We're investigating a few leads.'

Not particularly reassuring.

The officer squinted at Nicole. 'I take it you live locally?'

'Just across the road.' Nicole looked out of the window. The crowd on the pavement had grown now, blocking the entrance to her drive. 'Is there anything I can get for you?' she asked Irene.

'A proper cup of tea would be nice,' Irene said. She cast a disparaging glance at the mug on the coffee table beside her. 'There's far too much sugar in that one.'

'Have you seen anyone acting suspiciously?' the officer asked Nicole. 'Perhaps kids hanging around?'

Nicole scooped up the mug and shook her head. She hadn't seen any kids lingering. Though… She had seen a man at the end of her drive. The car outside that had sped off. Then there was the delivery driver in the BMW with the parcel she'd never received. The driver had spoken to Irene. Could it have been the same people, checking out her home for future reference? She'd convinced herself they were something to do with Ethan, but what if they weren't? She opened her mouth, about to pass on the information when Irene dropped her hand to her lap. Exposing a deep-purple bruise the shape of Australia on her cheekbone.

Nicole gasped. 'How did you get that?'

'I fell chasing after the bleeders,' she said. A small cut ran underneath her eye.

'That looks like it needs a stitch.'

The paramedic kneeling beside the old woman tucked a stray strand of hair behind her ear and looked up at Nicole. 'It's borderline. We want to take her in, get it checked, but she's resisting.'

Irene's eyes turned fiery. 'I'm not going anywhere. I just need to rest awhile.'

'Maybe you should listen to them,' Nicole said gently. 'It would only take a couple of hours. I'll come with you.' She checked her watch. She'd have to call her parents, get them to pick up the kids.

Irene huffed.

'Head injuries can be dangerous,' the paramedic continued.

'It's not my head, it's my cheek,' Irene said. 'And I told *him* not to call you people.' She looked up at the police officer, pursing her lips. 'That's it. I want you all to go. Now.'

The paramedic traded a look of despair with her colleague. Nicole had the feeling this argument had been going on for some time. There was no reasoning with the old woman, not in this mood.

'I can stay with her for a bit if it'll help,' Nicole said.

The paramedics rose uncomfortably. They couldn't force her to go with them.

Irene shifted in her chair. Her hand shook as she indicated for Nicole to pass her stick, which was resting against the side of the sofa. She did look incredibly frail.

'It's all right, she always uses a stick,' Nicole said reassuringly to the paramedics. She turned to Irene, taking care not to spill the cold tea still in her hand. 'I'll see everyone out and make you a nice cuppa.'

Nicole looked at the police officer, motioned to the door and guided them all into the hallway, pulling the door to the front room closed behind her. She let out the paramedics, turned to the policeman and passed on her concerns.

'That's interesting,' the officer said when she mentioned the driver that had rushed off. 'What make was the car?'

'I don't know. I didn't notice.'

'Did you manage to catch any of the number plate?'

She shook her head, suddenly feeling very inept. 'No. I'm sorry. Do you think it's the same people?'

'Hard to say. But we'll certainly look into it. Anything else?'

Nicole guided him out into the kitchen and flicked the switch on the kettle. 'Oh, there's a lot more. You might want to write this down.'

Chapter 49

Later that evening, Nicole leaned her back against the kitchen counter and swilled the milk in her glass. It had started raining outside, an intermittent tap at her window. The kids had returned from her parents' overtired. At bedtime, they'd bickered: Finlay hid Katie's toothbrush; Katie pinched the dragon he slept with. It was as much as she could do to coax them into bed and, even then, as she read Finlay a story, Katie was shouting at him through the wall that divided their bedrooms. In the end, she'd moved him into her room at the other end of the landing – he would wander through in the night anyway. Was she pushing them too hard? The permanence of losing their father was kicking in now. They'd only been back at school a short while and what with all the trips to the hospital to visit Ania, and then Irene's fall, she hadn't been around as much as she wanted.

And she was distracted. Distracted by Ethan. Distracted by her father's oncology appointment. And now she was distracted by the incident at Irene's. She'd sat with the old woman for several hours after the police had gone. Helped her into bed. Phoned numerous times to check on her. She seemed fine, but was she? Really?

Nicole took another sip of milk, relishing the thick fluid slipping through her insides. She placed the glass down and checked her iPhone. No new messages. Irene must have settled down for the night. The weight of responsibility pressed down on her, she hoped she was okay. She was just turning this over when a nasty thought crept in. Who would look after Irene if she left? Most of the old woman's friends were dead. She always seemed to be getting a taxi to some funeral or other. Who would do her shopping, or pick up the pieces if she had another fall?

But it wasn't just the thought of Irene that was plaguing Nicole, it was everything.

The rain picked up. Growing heavier, drumming the window. Globules of water running down the glass, blurring her view of the garden.

She checked the doors again: the back, the front, the French doors in the sitting room. All were locked. The house was secure. But she couldn't sit still, couldn't settle.

The officer's eyes had narrowed earlier when she'd mentioned Irene's account of the BMW. He'd taken down the details and said he'd return tomorrow to take a statement from the old woman. He clearly thought the BMW was connected to the distraction burglaries.

Was that true? If so, perhaps the other car was as well. And the baseball cap wearer at the end of her driveway. They could be nothing to do with Ethan.

Nicole worked through the list of incidents, one by one. Ania's alleged stalker – which could be explained as a rogue reporter, someone who didn't want to be identified or vilified in the press for hounding a bereaved widow. The people outside the house – now possibly connected to the burglaries in the area. The intelligence agent in the cemetery who David Harrison had dismissed as a competitor. Even the man at the railway station… He hadn't followed her cab, had he? Was it possible this was all paranoia, and that the people Ethan had been working with did believe he was dead, after all?

The notion marched around her mind like an army of restless ants, searching for a way out. If this was all true, Nicole and the children weren't being watched. They didn't need to go away.

Come with me.

Her heart wrenched as she recalled Ethan's pleading face. A month ago, they had a nice life, a promising future. Two healthy children. A new baby on the way to complete their little unit.

If only Ethan had discussed things with her. They could have worked it out. Sold the house. He could have changed jobs. At least then they'd all be together. Now the only way they could be safe was to navigate their lives apart.

The events at Irene's had changed things though. She didn't need to go away, didn't need to run. She could be there for her parents, for Irene, for Ania. She didn't need to disrupt her children. And – she caressed her stomach – she could stay here, in this house, to prepare for her baby's arrival.

Suddenly she felt lighter, as if the knot of worry was uncoiling within. Ethan was safe. They were safe. As long as they stayed apart.

She needed to speak with Ethan. She pulled the burner phone out of her pocket. The screen lit. It was time to reach out to Ethan. She only hoped he was there to listen.

Chapter 50

The following morning, Nicole checked her phone for the tenth time as she stood outside the garage at the end of her street. Desperately trying to keep to her routine, she'd taken her car in for its annual service and was waiting for her father to pick her up so that she could borrow his vehicle to visit Ania this afternoon.

Ethan still hadn't been in touch. He hadn't replied to yesterday's text either, despite her sending a long missive in three separate notes, explaining what had happened at Irene's. She'd even tried phoning, hoping that a call would spur him into action, but there was no answer. Where was he? Out of signal? A shiver. Oh, God. Was he even alive?

Why, oh why, hadn't she asked him where he was going?

Her father waved as he pulled up alongside. 'You okay, love?' he said as she climbed into his shiny Volvo.

'I'm fine.' She fought to keep her voice even. 'How's Mum today?'

'She'll be okay.'

She'll be okay. His way of saying she was still struggling.

'Why don't you guys come over for dinner tomorrow evening?' Nicole said. 'We could eat in the garden if the weather's nice.' *It's important to keep things normal.* For the children. For everyone. For the sake of her own sanity.

'That sounds lovely.' He reached across and patted her hand, his face brightening. 'I'll check with your mum, but I don't think we have anything on. Thanks.' The engine hummed as he continued down the road.

'Are you sure you don't mind me borrowing your car for the day?' she asked. She relied so much on her parents. Possibly too much.

'Of course not.' Another smile. He kept his eyes on the road. 'You know we're here to help.'

The words clawed at Nicole. She turned away, sharp tears pricking her eyes. *Here to help*. If only they knew how much help she needed right now.

—

Later that day, Nicole was surprised to find Blanka sitting outside Ania's room when she arrived at the hospital. 'Everything all right?' she asked.

Blanka rubbed the back of her neck and nodded. 'The nurses are just changing Ania's bed.'

'Ah.' Nicole pulled up a chair and sat beside her. 'You look beat.' She'd never have dreamed of saying that to Blanka a week ago. The woman had looked so severe and unapproachable. It was extraordinary how a couple of hours around a quiet hospital bed had eased things between them.

Blanka snorted. 'We couldn't find Patryk's football shorts this morning,' she said, gazing into space. 'Do you know where they were? Behind the sofa. The boys had been playing catch with them last Saturday and forgotten all about it.'

Nicole laughed. 'You're doing a wonderful job, you do know that?'

Blanka shrugged. 'They're family.' She looked away. 'As good as.'

A nurse wandered past. The doors at the end of the corridor flapped as she disappeared.

Blanka turned to Nicole. 'Thank you,' she said.

Nicole was taken aback. 'For what?'

'For coming in, supporting us. I wasn't sure about you at first. Conrad's job, the people around him, the hours he worked, have given Ania so much grief over the years. She said you weren't like the others, and she was right.'

Nicole stared at her, speechless. She hadn't been expecting this. Ania seemed to tolerate her presence, at best.

'Ania finds it hard to let people in,' Blanka said, as if she guessed her thoughts. 'Few people get to know the real her.' She looked down at her hands clasped together on her lap, her eyes dewy. 'Conrad, me and the kids. We're her world.' Her voice broke. 'Or we were.'

The sentiment was touching. 'You must have been friends a long time,' Nicole said.

'Since we were in nappies. We lived in the same street, played together when we were little. Ania didn't know her father, he left before she started school. Her mother raised the kids alone, working two jobs to keep everything together. They used to come to our house before and after school.'

Nicole was reminded of Blanka searching Ania's phone, the mutterings under her breath. 'Did you manage to get hold of her family?' she asked.

Blanka shook her head. 'I couldn't find anything on her phone. Not surprising really, she blocked all her extended family after she fell out with her brother.'

'Oh, I'm sorry. I didn't know.'

'Why would you? She doesn't talk about it. She rarely speaks about her old life back in Poland.'

Nicole's heart wept for Ania. She had always longed for a sibling and the grief of having one you never saw, never spoke to, seemed torturous. 'Were they ever close?' she asked.

'Who?'

'Ania and her brother.'

Blanka looked at the ceiling awhile, a faraway look spreading across her face. 'She idolised him when they were kids. We all did. He was a great character, a real daredevil, the one who used to get into all the scrapes. But such charm! He could talk his way out of anything.' Her mouth curved into a forlorn smile.

'They had it tough though. He was three years older than us. Their mother fell sick with leukaemia when Ania was fourteen, and those kids...' She shook her head. 'They pulled together to care for her at home. Ania cooked, cleaned. Woke up in the night when her mother was bad. I lost count of the times she fell asleep at school, because she'd been up at all hours. When he left school, Piotr got a job as a builder's labourer, to bring in the money. My mother helped, of course, we all did, but they did most of the caring themselves.'

'Wow.' Nicole couldn't imagine how difficult it must have been to care for a mother, then lose her, and so young. The notion cut her to the bone. 'I had no idea.'

Blanka lifted a single shoulder, let it drop. 'Like I say, she doesn't talk about it. Keeps it all buried inside. Conrad was one of the few good things to happen to her.'

A porter with an empty trolley trundled past, the wheels intermittently squeaking against the polished flooring.

'It was sad what happened between her and Piotr though,' Blanka continued. 'They promised their mother on her deathbed they'd take care of each other. Such a shame it all turned sour.'

'What do you mean?'

'We all planned to come to England together after their mother died, a new start. We spent months saving, planning, booking our passage.' She huffed, eyes glazing, as if she was back there, the three of them sitting around her mother's shiny dining room table, chatting. All talking at once, blooming with excitement at the possibility of travelling to a new country, making a new life. 'He waited until the night before we left to pull out, tell us he wasn't coming. He'd been offered a new job with another building company, too good an opportunity to miss. But the guy he was to work for was bad news.' She turned to face Nicole. 'He was well known in our community. Fingers in all the wrong pies, if you know what I mean. Ania was gutted. She tried and failed to talk him out of it. They didn't speak for ten years after we arrived here. She tried to reach out to him when she married Conrad. I think she wanted him to give her away at the wedding, but we couldn't trace him. Folks at home told us he'd moved away. Then, about a year ago, he turned up on her doorstep, out of the blue. Claimed to have turned his life around, was working for a luxury car dealership. Decided to surprise her with a visit.'

Nicole pressed her lips together. This story didn't sound like it was going to have a happy ending. 'Did they sort out their differences?'

'Sadly, no. He only stayed a few days. She discovered the company he worked with was involved in sourcing cars over here. Stealing them to order, then shipping them to Europe, replating them and selling them on illegally. He hadn't changed at all. If anything, he'd branched out. Ania exploded, threw him out. She didn't want him near Conrad or her boys.'

'Has she heard from him since?'

'No. And she won't now. His body was found in a supermarket dumpster, six months ago. He'd been stabbed to death.'

'Oh, my goodness!'

'I know. It was awful. The police never found out who did it, but he'd been running with the wrong crowd for years. I guess it's a case of, if you live by the sword, you die by the sword.'

Chapter 51

Nicole drove home in silence that afternoon. No radio, no music, no podcasts blabbering in the background. The doctors were pleased with Ania's progress. They thought she might wake any day. Blanka was hoping to take the boys in at the weekend. But Nicole couldn't get Blanka's account of Ania's family out of her mind. It was unimaginable to lose a mother at such an early age, then to fall out with her only sibling. A family splintered. Broken apart. Then for her brother to be killed in such tragic circumstances. And then her husband...

She considered her own parents, how much she relied on them. *The poor woman.*

Ania had finally found happiness with Conrad and the boys. No wonder she resented anyone who threatened to take that away from her, or that she was so passionate about fighting to clear Conrad's name. Problem was, she was pointing the finger at the wrong people.

You live by the sword... She recalled Blanka's words, thought of Ethan's predicament, and recoiled. Oh, God. How she wished he hadn't mixed himself up in this mess. She only hoped she could help him escape before it was too late.

Her car was sitting outside on the forecourt when she arrived at the garage. Stevie, the mechanic, waved her inside. Nicole liked Stevie. He was a short slim man, with thinning grey hair, shiny eyes and a lined face that crinkled into a smile when he greeted customers. He'd been servicing and mending their vehicles for as long as she'd lived here.

'Hey, Nicole,' he said. 'All sorted.'

Nicole thanked him and proffered her credit card as he pressed a few buttons on the computer. The printer spat out a receipt.

'Oh, I didn't know you had a lump on there,' he said, grinning from ear to ear, as if it was an afterthought. 'We nearly knocked it off with the ramp.'

Nicole frowned. 'A lump?'

'A tracker. Underneath the tailgate.'

Nicole suddenly felt white-hot, as if she'd been plunged into a furnace. A tracker. She *was* being followed. 'Ah, yes. I forgot about that,' she said, battling to keep the quake from her voice. 'Take it off, will you? Now.'

—

An hour later, Nicole sat at her kitchen table, willing Ethan to respond. As soon as she'd arrived home, she'd tried to ring him, then sent another text, asking him to call. And still he hadn't replied.

Trying to behave normally at the garage, brushing off the tracker as an aberration, a trial she didn't want to continue, while Stevie removed it, had tested her nerves to the limit.

She had been wrong. Someone was watching her. But they weren't only watching, they were following her every move. How long had the tracker been there? If she hadn't taken her car into the garage, she'd never have known.

You're safe as long as they think I'm dead. Was that true? Because now she was beginning to wonder. And she was fearful for herself, for her children…

She opened the burner phone again, read her text. *Ethan, ignore my message yesterday. We are being watched!!! I need your help. Call me as soon as you get this.*

Still no reply. He couldn't have seen it. If he had, he would respond urgently. He wouldn't put his family in danger.

A thought occurred to her. What if his burner phone had died? Or what if he'd lost it? He wouldn't be able to read her messages or reply.

Tamsin hadn't responded to her either. Were they together somewhere?

She picked up her iPhone and opened Instagram. Clicked to direct messages. No new messages from @Appletree-208. But Ethan hadn't deleted their thread. Not yet. Good. If he lost his phone, he could get another, make contact that way. She typed out quickly:

> Ethan, I'm worried. Message me to confirm you
> are okay. Need to speak.

This was worse than she'd thought. Familiar misgivings crowded her as she switched to Google and searched for flights to Auckland. If she went away, she was abandoning Ania, just when she was gaining Blanka's trust. And Irene when she needed support. And her parents. Not to mention her job, and taking the children away from their friends, their family. Tears burned her eyes. But she couldn't see a way out of it. Whatever happened with Ethan, whatever he did, she needed to keep her children safe. She had no choice now but to leave.

Chapter 52

The following day, Nicole squeezed into the lift with the other visitors and pressed the button for floor six. She'd spent most of the morning packing. Squirrelling the children's clothes into suitcases, tucking them away underneath her bed. And still no message from Ethan. How long should she wait? The earliest flight she could get for her and the kids to Auckland was on Monday. Another three days away.

For some reason, visiting hours at the L&D hospital were busier this Friday afternoon. The lift was rammed, the air thick and sticky. An elderly couple stood in the corner. Three young men at the back. The woman working the controls stared into space, clutching the hand of a young girl. The girl – six or seven, Nicole guessed – looked up at her with unashamed sea-blue eyes. Nicole gave a gentle smile. She reminded her of Katie. Ever since she'd been little, she'd been fascinated by the habits of other people, strangers around her. Nicole was always tugging her hand, telling her to stop staring.

Katie. An ache filled her throat. Out of her two children, Katie was the one who worried her most. Finlay was still young, making his way. He'd had a few chums over to tea, been invited to the odd birthday party, but he seemed content to play with whoever was nearby. Katie was different. A clingy baby, who suffered from separation anxiety as a toddler, she tended to make firm friends and keep them. Even at six, she had a best friend in Jess. Nicole had often encouraged her to play with other children, invite someone else to tea, but Katie refused unless Jess was coming too. The ache spread into her chest. How was she ever to tear Katie away from her best friend, even for a month or two?

The lift pinged at floor four. The little girl stepped out with her mother, glanced back at Nicole, and was gone. Nicole leaned up against the side of the lift, watching the numbers climb. The lift juddered at floor six, the doors cranked open, and she stepped out into the corridor.

The doors to Carrington Ward sat open and welcoming. Nicole sauntered in and continued through the ward and into the corridor beyond with the individual rooms. The door to room six was closed, the blind pulled over the little window. Nicole pushed it open, inadvertently catching her sleeve on the handle, jerking back, and cursing her clumsiness. Only to find the room empty. The bed freshly made. The surfaces clear. A faint clinical smell filled the air. The door of the bedside cupboard, the cupboard that had contained Ania's personal possessions – fresh night clothes, toiletries – hung open.

She turned back to the corridor, craning her neck for a nurse, a doctor, but there was no one nearby. She was just hitching her bag up onto her shoulder, about to backtrack to the nurses' station when she spotted a cleaner moving across the floor with a dry mop.

'Excuse me,' she said.

The woman looked up.

'My friend.' Nicole pointed towards the room.

'Gone.' The woman shook her head as she spoke.

'What?' Nicole suddenly felt hot. The corridor blurred around her. She pressed a hand to the wall. 'What do you mean, gone?' Not dead surely. No. No. She couldn't be dead. She was turning a corner. The doctors were pleased with her progress. *Things were looking up...*

The cleaner widened her eyes at Nicole's response. 'I'll get someone.' She leaned the mop up against the side of the wall and moved off.

Nicole rested against the wall and gasped for air. This was like a bad dream. But it wasn't a dream. She was here, now. And

Ania was… She thought of Patryk and Robert. Still grieving the loss of their father. No. *This can't be happening.* Why hadn't Blanka phoned?

'Can I help you?'

Nicole opened her eyes and blinked to find an Asian nurse in front of her. Her name badge read Kirti.

She peeled herself from the wall and straightened, unable to quell the dropping sensation within. 'My friend,' she said, her voice barely a whisper. She pointed to the room.

'Ania.'

Something about the woman's tone lifted her. 'Yes.'

'She's been moved to Clerkenwell on the fourth floor.'

'Moved?' Nicole's voice cracked. Blanka hadn't said anything about her being moved.

'Yes. She woke this morning. They took her a couple of hours ago.'

Chapter 53

Two floors below, Nicole's heart was still thumping in her chest as she entered Clerkenwell. Ania had woken. How was she? At the nurses' station, an administrator was talking into a phone. A doctor engaged with an agitated visitor. Nurses tied up with other patients. She checked the board behind the desk. Ania was in room one.

It was a large ward, with a walkway up the middle, side wards coming off at intervals. Nicole passed the first two, glancing up and down. Patients and visitors looked up briefly. In the third ward, two of the beds were surrounded by curtains.

She trudged on, moved through double doors, turned a corner and immediately spotted Blanka, sitting in a chair at the side of the corridor, a phone pressed to her ear. She stood as Nicole approached.

'Nicole! I was just trying to call you. I didn't know they'd moved her until I arrived.'

'How is she?'

'The doctors said her vitals are good. I've only spoken to her for a few minutes, but she seems well.'

'That's wonderful!' And to Nicole's utter amazement, Blanka reached out and encased her in a tender embrace. The gesture brought tears to Nicole's eyes. She smiled as they parted. 'When can I see her?'

'Soon, I think. The nurses have been trying to reach me since half ten. Robert was playing with my phone on the school run. He switched it to silent, the little scamp. I missed their calls.'

'The boys will be so pleased.'

'They will.'

A door opened and a nurse emerged. He turned to Blanka. 'You can go in now.'

Nicole followed Blanka into the room. The ward was on the other side of the hospital, facing the road. The low hum of passing traffic filtered through the open window. There were no machines, no drip here.

Ania looked gaunt, her eyes sunken to tiny holes, her skin pallid. She gave a weak smile at Blanka. A smile that faded when she spotted Nicole.

'What's she doing here?' Ania said.

'Ania, don't be like that,' Blanka answered. 'Nicole's been here every day. She's been really supportive.'

Nicole swallowed, desperately trying to appear normal. Although she hadn't been normal in so long, she was beginning to wonder what it was like. 'We've been worried,' she said, tugging at her collar. It was inordinately hot in there. 'How are you feeling?'

'I'll be fine.'

'Are you sure you can't remember anything?' Blanka said to Ania softly.

'I remember calling you from the lay-by. Setting off again. Then nothing.'

'It'll come.' Blanka stroked her hair. 'Don't force it.'

Ania asked Blanka to bring the boys in that evening and Blanka said she would. Finally, she turned to Nicole. 'So, did you find anything out at the weekend?'

'Oh, not this again,' Blanka interjected. 'You need to rest.'

'I am resting. I'm just asking a question.'

A wave of nausea. Nicole tugged on her collar again. She knew this moment was coming, she'd been expecting it. And she had absolutely no idea about what to say, or how to answer. Because whatever she said, she'd be masking the truth. Her peripheral vision blurred as she started to talk about the weekend, how she'd uncovered nothing new.

Ania huffed.

'I don't know,' Nicole said. 'I really think we should leave the inquiry to the authorities. If there's something there, they'll find it.' She shifted from one foot to another. Ethan was alive. Conrad was murdered. And she couldn't even tell his wife the truth.

'No.'

The floor wobbled beneath her. Nicole blinked several times, then rested her hand on Ania's bedside table.

'She's right,' Blanka said to Ania. 'This constant speculation isn't doing anyone any good. I mean—'

Nicole didn't hear any more. Sweat pricked the back of her neck. She watched Blanka's mouth opening and closing, forming the words, but she couldn't hear them. She felt hot and clammy. The room began to spin. And, suddenly, the ground came up to meet her.

'Nicole! Nicole!' Blanka's voice cut through the darkness. Nicole opened her eyes to find herself on the floor of Ania's room.

'I'll call for the nurse,' Ania said.

'No!' Nicole said. She gazed up at Ania, her mouth bone dry. She'd blacked out, fainted. But it was worse than that. As soon as she tried to move, to lever herself up, a pain shot through her side. She'd hit her tummy on the way down. The baby! Panic bubbled up inside her. She gripped the chair leg with her sweaty hands.

'You're not well,' Blanka said.

The room came into focus. 'I'm okay. Just a bit hot.'

'You need help.' Blanka grabbed her arm, helped her up into a chair and touched her clammy head.

'I'm not ill,' Nicole said.

'Well, you're not right.'

And then, to her surprise, Nicole finally broke her cardinal promise to herself. 'I'm not ill,' she repeated. 'I'm pregnant.'

241

Thirty minutes later, Nicole rested back on the bed and flinched as the radiographer squirted cool gel on her bare stomach.

Blanka had insisted on calling for a nurse after she'd fainted. A nurse that had taken her blood pressure, checked her pulse, but didn't like the look of the cloudy bruise on her side and made arrangements for her to be transported to the other side of the hospital for a scan.

The screen beside her lit. The radiographer swept the camera across her tummy. And there it was – a cloudy white image on the screen. Her baby! Nicole's eyes filled.

'Everything looks quite normal,' the radiographer said. She continued to swipe the camera across Nicole's belly, making notes. 'Ooh,' she said, as the child kicked out a leg. 'Looks like you've got a lively one!'

Nicole couldn't speak. She couldn't utter a word, muted by the sheer joy she felt. Eleven weeks. She was eleven weeks by her dates and her baby was fine. She'd lost her last children at eight and ten weeks. This had to be a good sign, didn't it? There was a nasty bruise purpling on the side of her stomach, but she didn't appear to have injured her child. Everything looked normal. It was just a shame Ethan couldn't be there to share it.

Chapter 54

Back at home, Nicole lay on the sofa and looked up at the ceiling. There was still no word from Ethan. Where the hell was he?

The kids were playing with Finlay's Scalextric in the playroom. She could hear the cars whizzing around the track. Her parents were due for dinner shortly, the lasagne she'd cooked that morning was heating in the oven. Which meant she could kick back and take five minutes to make sense of the day.

So many mixed emotions. The panic of fainting and falling. The elation of seeing her baby on the screen for the first time. The relief of Ania waking.

Blanka had still been at Ania's bedside when Nicole left the hospital earlier. She'd phoned, given Blanka and Ania the good news that all was well, then headed directly home. She'd go in and see Ania again tomorrow. Thankfully, the two women had agreed to keep her secret, for another week at least, and hopefully, by tomorrow, she'd have formulated something to say to Ania about the crash, and about Ethan. Because today she didn't have the brain space to deal with it.

The doorbell sounded. Her parents were early. She hauled herself up and moved out to the hallway. Surprised to find that it wasn't her parents standing on her doorstep.

'Hello, Nicole.' It was Sharon, her family liaison officer. She looked fresh and breezy today in a navy T-shirt and one of her jazzy wrap-around skirts, her dark curls pushed to the side of her face.

Nicole looked past her, down the driveway. She appeared to be alone. 'Oh, hi!' she said. 'Is there some news?'

'I wondered if we could have a chat?'

Nicole bit her lip. 'I haven't got long. My parents are coming for dinner.'

'It won't take long,' Sharon said.

Footsteps thundered the stairs as Nicole thrust another frustrated glance down the driveway and let her inside. Finlay and Katie stopped abruptly at the bottom when they realised the guest wasn't their grandparents.

'Hello!' Sharon said to them. She raised a brow at Nicole. A brow that meant what she wanted to discuss wasn't for little ears.

Nicole ushered the children into the front room with instructions to watch for Grandma and Grandad from the window and closed the door. 'Is everything okay?' she said to Sharon. They were still standing in the hallway.

'Well, yes. This is rather awkward,' Sharon said.

'Go on.'

'I need to ask you if you have received any contact from anyone claiming to be Ethan.'

Nicole's heart quaked. *They know.* A second ticked past. The burner phone she kept with her was in the side pocket of her dress. 'I don't know what you mean,' she said, her voice tight.

'We've had a report. A witness who claims to have seen Ethan.'

Nicole placed a hand to her throat. 'What? Where?'

'In Highgate. Around the corner. A week last Saturday.'

Nicole felt her legs start to buckle. She put out a hand, grabbed the hallway table to steady herself. *A week last Saturday.* The day Ethan came to the house. How could he have been so stupid?

'I'm sorry to have to ask you this,' Sharon continued. 'I realise it must be a shock.'

'Of course I haven't!' The roar of a car engine. Her parents were on the drive. Nicole glanced at the door, then back at Sharon. 'Who was this witness?'

'An anonymous caller phoned the front desk.'

Doors slammed, footsteps tapped the tarmac. Nicole opened the door before her parents could ring the bell.

Her father instantly noticed Sharon, then Nicole's expression. 'What's going on?' he said.

Nicole couldn't speak. Her tongue stuck to the top of her mouth.

'I'm sorry to bother you,' Sharon said. 'I was just following up on—'

'They said someone has seen Ethan,' Nicole said, the words spluttering.

'What?' Her mother. 'What do you mean?'

'An anonymous witness called the station,' Sharon explained. 'They believe they saw Ethan, walking through Highgate Cemetery.' She passed on the date.

'You're not serious.' Her father's face clouded.

'This does happen occasionally,' Sharon said. 'Sometimes people are mistaken. I just wanted to check with Nicole that she hadn't seen or heard anything.'

'I haven't.' The words squawked out.

'This is madness!' her father said. 'It was probably someone who looked like him. Or somebody playing a cruel prank. Ethan's been dead a month.' He moved forward, placed an arm around his daughter. 'Don't you think she's been through enough.'

Sharon held up her hands. 'It's my duty to ask the questions, investigate. That's all.'

'Investigate!' Her father's voice lifted a decibel. 'You're not suggesting he's still alive and run off somewhere?'

Nicole felt the hallway sway around her. She forced herself to breathe. She couldn't afford another blackout.

'Wait!' Her father again. 'Did you say a week last Saturday? How come we are only hearing about it now?'

'The information was delayed coming through to me.' Sharon coughed uncomfortably. 'The note was left on a desk while an officer went on leave. I'm sorry.'

Her father cursed under his breath.

'As I say, I'm just here to ask the questions,' Sharon said.

'And you've done that,' her father replied.

At that moment, the children burst out of the front room and hurled themselves at their grandparents. Alice coaxed them into the kitchen, with the promise of gifts in her handbag.

The detective turned to Nicole. 'I'm sorry to have disrupted your evening. You know where I am if you need me.'

'Wait!' Nicole reached out, caught her arm. 'What does this mean?'

'It was only one sighting, but we're obliged to investigate. We'll check cameras in the area. If anything comes to light, we'll be in touch.' Her face slackened. 'If you've heard nothing, my advice would be to put it out of your mind. It was one call. Your father's right, it's probably nothing. Someone messing about, or mistaken. We just have to follow it up.'

Chapter 55

Ania rested her head against the pillow and stared up at the ceiling. Blanka had left half an hour earlier and Ania was tired, weary, but her brain wouldn't switch off. Why hadn't Nicole told her she was pregnant? She'd never have put pressure on her to ask questions at Ethan's wake if she'd known, especially after... She shuddered as she recalled Conrad telling her about the Jamesons' previous miscarriages. She thought about the visit to her house the other day. Nicole looking drawn, asking for a biscuit. And today, passing out at her bedside. It was warm in here but, still... She should take extra care. Children were precious, she needed to think of the baby.

She rewound to before the car accident. The plane crash, Conrad's resignation, the sleeping drug, her meeting with Sarah, the newspaper article. The receipt from St Albans. She still needed to find out more about that.

It was strange. As much as she picked and pulled at her memory, she couldn't remember the car crash. The only flash-back she had was in the lay-by on the A5183, talking to Blanka on the phone, asking her to collect the kids. Nothing after-wards. Almost as if the event was locked away in a tiny box in the vault of her mind, with no access to the key. What had happened? She hadn't been driving particularly fast.

Unless it wasn't an accident at all. If that receipt, that location was crucial, then it made sense that someone would want to thwart her attempt at finding answers.

The more she considered it, the more her resolve hardened. Whatever happened, whatever the cause of her collision, as soon as she was out of hospital, as soon as she was well enough, she needed to take that route again. Visit the petrol station this time, speak with the staff. Find out who had accompanied Conrad when he visited on the fourth of June, and who else visited around the same time. Because, more than ever, she was convinced there was something fishy about that visit.

She couldn't stop investigating now. She couldn't expect Nicole to help her, that would be asking too much. No. She would push on alone, find another way, another route to the truth. Because the truth was out there, it was just a matter of finding it.

Chapter 56

'It's a hoax. It has to be.'

Nicole responded to her father with a nod. Though her heart was squeezed so tight in her chest, it was about to burst. They were standing in her kitchen, the detective now gone.

Nicole really needed to get away. Why, oh why, wasn't there a flight until Monday? And why hadn't Ethan contacted her?

'Don't let this spoil your evening,' her father said, squeezing her arm.

'He's right,' her mother chimed. 'It's just some cruel prank. Or an honest mistake.'

Nicole forced herself to get drinks and move out to the patio. She was growing adept at pouring herself a glass of wine, carrying it about and not drinking it.

'You look tired,' her father said. He was standing against the backdrop of the garden, the sun behind him, casting a glow around his head.

'I'm fine,' Nicole replied. They had no idea that a couple of hours ago she'd fainted in a hospital room, then watched her growing baby on a screen. Oh, how she wanted to tell them! It seemed wrong that Blanka and Ania knew, and they didn't. But she couldn't. She needed to prepare them now. Prepare them for her leaving. It would be so much harder if they knew she was pregnant. No. Her priority was to keep her family safe. At whatever cost. 'Actually, I've got some news,' she said.

Her parents traded a glance.

Nicole took her time to tell them about her plans to take the children away to visit her friends in New Zealand. When she said they were leaving on Monday, her mother pressed her hand to her chest. 'So soon! What about school? The children are just settling.'

'It seems right to go now. The holidays start in a couple of weeks anyway.'

'Why not wait?'

'The school holidays are only for six weeks. If we leave now, we can take a couple of months before they go back in September. A proper break, for all of us.' Mel and Tim had been so excited when she'd phoned that morning and told them they were coming.

'Do you really need to go for so long?' her mother said.

'It's a long flight, we might as well make the most of it. And it's only eight weeks.' Nicole's chest tightened as the lie deepened. She'd rehearsed this in her head so many times, yet now as she spoke the words aloud, the gravity of them felt like a lead weight. 'It'll soon pass.'

'What about your job?'

'Carla's keeping it open.'

'I don't know what to say,' her mother said. 'Have you really thought about this? About going away, leaving your loved ones behind after... Well—'

'I've thought about nothing else.' That part was true. Her heart ached. A permanent pain rang like a telephone in her head.

'We'll drive you to the airport,' her dad said. 'Wave you off.'

Before she could answer, Finlay shouted from the lawn. 'Look, Grandad, no hands!' He was balancing precariously on the top of the climbing frame.

'Come down now, darling,' Alice said. 'Your dinner will be ready soon.'

Nicole placed her glass of wine down on the table and lowered her voice. 'I need to ask you not to mention this to the children.'

'You haven't told them?' Alice's jaw dropped. The shock traversed to her father's face too.

'No. They'll get too excited. I'm not telling them until the last minute.'

'Is that wise?'

It was too late to answer. The children descended on them, laughing and giggling. Nicole, grateful for the interruption, took them inside to wash their hands. And the moment passed.

–

Later, the cool evening air nipped at Nicole's arms as she walked her parents to their car.

Dinner had been a raucous affair. Katie had been learning about apes at school and was at pains to tell her grandparents about them, while Finlay annoyed her with chimp noises. It wasn't until Nicole served pudding – apple pie and ice cream – that everyone quietened, and she had the chance to survey her family, soak up their last minutes together.

And now, the children were in bed, and her parents were leaving. It had gone too quickly.

She hugged her mother and watched her climb into their gleaming white Volvo.

Her father opened the driver's door and hesitated. 'Are you sure about this holiday?' he said.

Nicole wrapped her arms around him, squeezing him tight, relishing the familiar smell of Brut aftershave in the crook of his neck, the same aftershave he'd worn for years. His chest didn't feel bony today. She knew it was impossible for him to gain weight so quickly, it was only a couple of days since the consultant's appointment, but he already felt plumper, rounder somehow, as if his body was celebrating the diminished threat of disease. 'I am,' she said as she released him. 'It'll only be for a couple of months.'

Nicole wasn't sure what made her glance down the driveway as he climbed into the car. It was a brief second, only just enough to take in the red Fiesta parked kerbside opposite. The woman sitting inside, fiddling with her phone, as if she was waiting for someone.

Her father closed the door and turned over the engine, pulling her back to him. The electrics droned as he wound down the window. 'We'll see you soon,' he said, mournfully. 'Take care.'

Nicole said she would, gave a half-smile and watched the car crawl down the driveway. The red lights of the brakes flashed up as her father stopped at the bottom in his usual cautious manner. She raised a hand to wave, just as she always did. And suddenly her heart ached so hard it felt as though it had broken into pieces. When, if ever, would she be doing this again? The ache spread across her chest as she watched them pull out onto the street, savouring every moment until they disappeared.

Her hand fell gently to her side. She turned and walked back to the house with heavy legs, feet scuffing the tarmac. She was almost at the door when she heard someone call out her name.

Nicole paused and spun round. It was the woman from the Fiesta. She was climbing out, crossing the road, walking up Nicole's drive. She hadn't been waiting for someone to come out of the houses nearby. She had been waiting for Nicole.

Nicole frowned. *Not another bloody journalist.* 'Sorry, do I know you?' she said. She didn't have the energy for this.

'No, not really.' An Eastern European accent coated her words. But… different to Ania's or Blanka's. Stronger.

Nicole blinked. She was frowning so hard now she was giving herself a fresh headache.

'But you do want to speak to me,' the woman continued. She lifted a hand, combed it through her short spiky hair. 'I'm Mags.'

Chapter 57

Nicole stared at the woman in front of her. Mags didn't look at all how she expected. She'd imagined someone older. Yet Mags was young, barely out of her twenties – short and dark-haired, like her.

Nicole clutched the door frame. She wasn't prepared for this. She'd expected them to meet in a cafe or a pub, on neutral ground. Not at her home, with her children sleeping upstairs. 'How did you know where to find me?' she asked.

'I dropped Ethan off here once.'

Dropped him off. From what? A date?

'Look, I can see this isn't a good time,' Mags said, stepping back. 'I can come back.' She curled her mouth into an empathetic smile, but her gaze was dark, heavy.

'No, it's okay.' Nicole pulled herself together. This was what she wanted, wasn't it? To bottom out Ethan's connection with Mags, another tick on her list. Though now they were together, there was something about the woman that made Nicole uncomfortable. She hadn't expected her to be so attractive, so demure in skinny jeans, a white linen shirt with the sleeves rolled up, kitten heels.

And that intense gaze. Did she know about Ethan?

'I didn't mean to surprise you,' Mags said. There it was again, that strong accent.

Nicole indicated for her to enter and followed on behind.

'You have a lovely house,' Mags said, running her finger along the bottom of the mirror as she looked around the hallway. The action, so personal in a stranger's home, was oddly disconcerting.

Nicole thanked her uncomfortably, then led her through to the front room, checked her drink preference and disappeared into the kitchen. Leaning against the kitchen worktop, gulping deep breaths. Did Mags know Ethan was still alive? Is that why she'd come here, to her home? To deliver a message from him.

Nicole flicked the switch on the kettle and retrieved the burner phone from her pocket. The screen was blank. Ethan had said he would make contact by the weekend. Was this his idea of contact?

She took her time making the drinks, regulating her breathing, calming her nerves. By the time she was finished she felt stronger. She inhaled deeply and lifted the mugs, gripping their handles hard. She could do this.

She walked into the front room, expecting to find the woman settled on the sofa. But Mags was at the dresser, examining their array of family photos – of Katie and Finlay at various stages of growth. Nicole's parents. Ethan and her in mortar boards on graduation day. Their wedding photo…

Nicole stiffened.

'These are lovely,' Mags purred. 'Such beautiful memories.' She looked up and met Nicole's eye. 'You must miss him.'

'I do,' she said. 'We all do.'

She passed over a coffee and motioned for them to move across to the large sofa, where they sat at either end. Awkward silence hanging in the void between them.

'You wanted to speak with me,' Mags said eventually.

'Yes. I found your details in Ethan's things. It sounded like you were friends. I just wanted to reach out to everyone he knew.'

Mags narrowed her eyes. 'My details?'

'Well, a note actually. On the back of a restaurant menu.'

The woman frowned, as if she didn't remember.

'I asked around. Ellen, the receptionist at Harrison Dunbar, recalled phoning you on behalf of Ethan. She told me where you worked.'

'Ah.'

The air thickened between them. Mags clearly wasn't about to offer more.

'I understand Ethan helped you with an investment,' Nicole probed when she could bear the atmosphere no longer.

'Yes. Just after I lost my father. He visited my work a couple of times, to go through paperwork. Put me in touch with people who could help. I treated him to a dinner at a restaurant of his choice to say thank you.'

'So, you were business associates.'

'I suppose we were for a while. My dad died suddenly, and I was struggling. Ethan was kind. It was easier, you know, talking to someone else who had also lost a parent.'

Nicole shifted in her seat. Counselling wasn't exactly Ethan's style. Though Ethan *had* lost his mother in his twenties too. 'I see.' But something about the arrangement niggled her.

Mags drew a long breath and cast another glance at the photos on the dresser. 'I can feel him here,' she said. 'It's almost like he never left.'

Nicole tensed. Here it was. The message...

'How are your children coping?'

The question almost knocked Nicole sideways. 'They're doing okay. Up and down.'

'They must miss him.'

It seemed an odd thing to say. Of course they missed him. He was their father. The criss-cross statements were making her dizzy. Did Mags really know about Ethan? Or was she fishing? 'They do, terribly,' she said. 'When did you last see him?'

'I don't know exactly. A few months ago.' She shrugged.

'Did you know Conrad too?'

Mags stared at her. 'The pilot who died with him. No.'

She doesn't know. Ethan hadn't reached out to Mags and, if the two were to be believed, they hadn't had an affair either. There was definitely something odd about the woman though, something uncomfortable that Nicole couldn't shake.

She took another sip of her coffee. Tried to play it safe. 'I wish I'd known about you earlier,' she said. 'You could have come to Ethan's memorial service.'

'I'm not good with memorials, or funerals.'

'Ah.' Unsurprising if she'd recently lost her father. It must have been difficult for her to come here, Nicole thought, and face Ethan's wife, a stranger. She'd clearly been fond of him during their short association. Maybe that was why she was so edgy. But, as much as Nicole tried, she couldn't shake the uneasy aura in the room. Was Mags telling the truth? Or saving Nicole more heartache?

'He was good at his work,' Mags said. 'I've never known anyone so dedicated to their clients.'

'He was. Did you meet any of them?'

'Meet?' The woman's brow crinkled as she shook her head. 'No. He was always getting calls though. There was one client who called regularly during our meetings. A man called Andrei... What was his surname?' She gazed at Nicole, eyes darting from side to side. 'Zeglov. Yes, that was it. Andrei Zeglov. Such an unusual name. And so persistent. Do you know him?'

Nicole shook her head. 'No. I only met a handful of his clients.'

They were interrupted by a cry from above. Finlay. 'I'm sorry, I'll have to go,' Nicole said.

'It's okay. I should probably leave anyway.' They placed their drinks down and strode into the hallway. 'I just wanted to pass on my condolences for your loss.'

Finlay wailed again. Louder this time, calling for his mum.

'I'd better go,' Nicole said opening the door. 'Thanks for coming.'

An hour later, Nicole descended the stairs. It had taken an age to get Finlay off to sleep after yet another nightmare. In the front room, she crossed to the window and peered around the edge of the curtain. The light was fading. Dusk drawing in. The road outside clear.

She lowered herself onto the sofa, reflecting on Mags. A strange visit. The woman, looking through her photos, the intensity of her stare. She shuddered.

She thought about the persistent client. Zeglov. She'd seen that name somewhere before... In Ethan's study – his notebook.

Nicole jumped up and took to the stairs. The study was cold inside. She'd pushed the bookcase back up against the wall, but loose books still littered the floor. She stepped over them, moved across to the desk and opened the bottom drawer. And there it was – the notebook. The one that she'd found the restaurant menu loose inside. She flicked through the pages. Through lines of figures and notes she didn't understand. Then, right in the middle, she found it: ZegloV-sw7. It wasn't a code, after all. It was a name. A client name.

Back downstairs, the burner phone was still empty. She fired up her iPad and googled Andrei Zeglov. Surprised to see several articles grace the screen. *Rich Russians in London.* She scrolled down through names she didn't recognise, scanning the piece, but couldn't see Zeglov's name. There were several articles in Russian. Another about Russian oligarchs, digging into the source of their wealth. Still no direct mention of Zeglov in any of the English-language pieces. Frustration gnawed at her. She clicked on another article, of rich Russian kids living in London – only to face a slim dark-haired woman, climbing down the steps of a London house, designer shopping bag in hand. *Tiana Zeglov, daughter of Andrei, flits between their Moscow and London homes...* But there were no addresses, nothing personal, and no photos of Andrei.

She stared at the picture of the young woman for some time. The ornate black iron railing running beside the front steps. The tulips engraved into the glass panels in the front door. ...*their Knightsbridge home*, the article said.

She looked back at the notebook and googled, 'Where is SW7?'. The search result came up instantly. SW7 was the postcode district for South Kensington, Knightsbridge and Brompton. Bingo – it was the same person. It had to be.

Nicole tucked the notebook in her pocket, closed the drawer and checked the burner phone again. Who the hell was Andrei Zeglov and why was he so important to Ethan?

Chapter 58

It was 12.40 on Saturday lunchtime when the burner phone finally buzzed. Nicole was running late. The kids were due at a birthday party at 1 p.m. and they'd spent the last fifteen minutes searching the house for Katie's silver shoes she'd insisted on wearing.

'Come on!' she said, ushering her daughter up the stairs. 'Try your bedroom again. If not, you're going to have to wear your trainers.'

Nicole watched her go, retrieved the burner phone from her pocket and lowered herself onto the bottom step. Her chest burning as she swiped the screen. A different mobile number.

The text was short.

> It's me. Sorry I haven't been in touch. All sorted now. Are you all okay?

Relief washed over her. Ethan was alive and well. She scrutinised the screen: he'd changed his phone number. Which meant he wouldn't have seen her other messages about Irene's break-in or her asking him to call her urgently. No point in mentioning it all now. Her fingers rippled over her screen to reply:

> Yes, you?

Yes. All good. Let's meet at 4 p.m. tomorrow: I'll message you the location in the morning x

Should she call him and tell him about the tracker? Or ask him about Zeglov? She mulled this over a second. No. It wasn't worth it now. Ethan already thought she was being watched. She needed to be cautious, make sure she wasn't followed.

Tomorrow would be the last day she would see her husband. Forever. The hardness of her heart surprised even her. Now it was all about the kids. She had to find the inner strength to keep her family safe.

She switched the burner phone to silent – the last thing she wanted was for it to ring when she was out.

Her iPhone rang. She pulled it out of her other pocket, expecting her mother to be calling with some reminder for something or other. Surprised to see 'Ania' on the screen.

'Hi. How are you?' Nicole said warily.

'I'm fine. Sitting up in bed. Just had a bowl of cornflakes.'

'Oh, great.'

'Not really. They were only cheap ones. Anyway, more to the point, how are you?' She lowered her voice. 'And the little one?'

Ah. She's checking up on the baby. 'Fine, thank you. I just need to take it easy.'

'Good advice. No more fainting?'

'No more fainting.' She thought about the message from Ethan, the burner phone still in her hand. The guilt was stronger now Ania was awake. A molten rod driving through her.

'Okay, I just wanted to check how you are doing. Are you coming in later?'

'Yes. This evening. The kids have a birthday party this afternoon.'

'Right. I'll see you then.'

The line went dead.

'Found them!' It was Katie, at the top of the stairs, waving a silver shoe.

Nicole quickly tucked both phones out of sight as her daughter descended the stairs. 'Oh, well done,' she said. She didn't have the energy to ask where the shoes had been. 'Come on then, let's get going. If we take the car, we might still get there in time.'

As she hauled herself up, she felt something slip around in her other pocket. Ethan's notebook. With Andrei Zeglov's name in it. And she couldn't help wondering, if Zeglov was such a persistent client, why had she never heard his name before?

–

The traffic was heaving through Highgate. Jess's house, near the end of Chester Road, was less than half a mile away. Ordinarily, they would have walked. It was almost five past one by the time Nicole arrived, only to find cars parked kerbside, nose to tail. She had to drive past Jess's, and nearly fifty yards up the road to find a space. Then turf the kids out of the car and jog them along the pavement. Katie tripping over the hem of her Cinderella dress. Finlay roaring at every passer-by in his bear outfit.

A cacophony of children's voices filled the air as they approached Jess's house, a mid-Victorian terrace.

'We're late,' Finlay said glumly, pulling the hood of his bear costume off his head as they climbed the steps.

'Only by a few minutes,' Nicole said. She rang the doorbell. No answer. And again. It wasn't until she banged the door with her fist that it was pulled open.

Jess's mum looked flustered. No wonder. According to Katie, she'd invited the whole class and then some. Forty kids running around her house; Nicole didn't envy her.

Jess's mum welcomed the children inside. Nicole thanked her again, hugged the children and said she'd see them later. 'Have fun!' She lifted a hand and waved as the door closed.

Nicole didn't hear the footsteps behind her as she made her way back to her car. Didn't notice anyone nearby. She was so intent on bringing up the satnav on her phone and searching the postcode SW7 that the first thing she felt was a hand on her forearm. She spun round, and her breath hitched.

'Mrs Jameson.'

It was the man from the cemetery, the intelligence agent. He was wearing the same dark suit, the edge of the jacket lifted where his other hand was in his pocket. The same sunglasses. The same thick hands. Only today his expression was tight, the skin taut across his cheekbones.

They know about Ethan...

Nicole stood back, the burner phone in her pocket pressing against her thigh. 'What is it?' she asked.

'I'm going to have to ask you to come with me.'

They definitely know.

Nicole's heart was in her mouth now. Her phone with Zeglov's postcode in Google Maps still in her hand. She dropped it to her side. 'I'm afraid I can't. I've got things to do.'

'Not today.' He gestured to a car across the road. A black BMW. Took his hand out of his pocket. And that's when she saw the gun.

Chapter 59

The journey through London was surreal. Sitting in the back of the BMW, watching the world go by through the blackened windows. The man with impossibly thick hands at her side, unspeaking. Refusing to answer her questions about who they were, or where they were going. The nose of the gun fixed firmly at the side of her ribcage.

The driver glanced at her in his rear-view mirror as he turned a corner. More sunglasses, masking his eyes, even though the sky was the colour of lead outside.

Were they from the security services? She couldn't be sure; they hadn't shown any ID. Why would intelligence agents feel the need to wield a gun? And why would they demand she hand over her iPhone? She couldn't be sure of anything anymore. All she knew was, she still had the burner phone and Ethan's notebook. If they frisked her, they'd find both.

The world continued around them, a blur of bodies. The people of London going about their Saturday business. Yet here she was in a strange car, with two men she didn't know, travelling to an unknown location. And she couldn't even raise the alarm.

No one knew where she was. No one, not even Ethan, was coming to save her.

Katie and Finlay came to mind. Trotting into the birthday party, faces of wonderment. Would she even be there to pick them up?

Time ticked past on the dashboard. They were on Finchley Road now, driving towards St John's Wood. Heading west.

She tried to concentrate, to track the route. Fifteen minutes ticked by, twenty... They moved through the centre of the city, passing Knightsbridge Tube station on their left, the barracks on their right. Hyde Park. The car indicated left on Kensington Road. Nicole lowered her head, craning her neck as it turned into a side road.

Rows of white multistorey terraces were separated from the pavement by a handful of steps, dark iron railings either side. They pulled into a space opposite a house with glass panels in the door. Glass panels with engraved tulips in them. The same tulips she'd seen on the photos accompanying the article she'd read last night. Fear sliced through her. Thick Hands wasn't working for MI5 or MI6. He was working for Andrei Zeglov.

Chapter 60

Nicole was guided into the house through a narrow hallway, her gun-wielding captor beside her. They shuffled through a pair of double doors and into a large white sitting room with high ceilings, complete with cornices and a crystal chandelier. Long windows were edged with pale blue drapes.

Beside the fireplace, a man stood, a glass of what looked like whisky in his hand. He wasn't a tall man, quite the contrary, but his build was stocky and his features dark, though his charcoal hair was threaded with grey. He wore a striped shirt, open at the neck, and black slacks. As Nicole was shoved further into the room, he turned and gave a polite smile. 'Mrs Jameson,' he said, raising a glass. 'Andrei Zeglov. We finally meet.'

Nicole, still flanked by the heavies from the car, flinched at the depth of his Russian accent.

'There's no need for all that,' Zeglov said, waving away the gun with his free hand. 'I think Mrs Jameson and I understand each other.'

He indicated for them to sit on one of the two blue, over-sized sofas curled around the hearthrug. Several easy chairs, in various shades of blue, and small occasional tables were arranged nearby. A painting above the fireplace sported a countryside scene.

'Mrs Jameson, or should I call you Nicole?' Zeglov said.

Nicole couldn't speak. She watched a vein pulse in the temple of Thick Hands as he finally lifted his shades and sat. He returned her gaze. Small squinting eyes, as cold as ice.

A shiver slipped down her spine. They hadn't blindfolded her. It didn't matter that she knew where Zeglov lived, or what he or his heavies looked like. Which could only mean one thing. She had far more to lose than they did.

'Some refreshments perhaps?' Zeglov said, holding his whisky out at an angle.

She shook her head. Short, sharp shakes.

'Come on, you must be thirsty. Daniel, bring her a drink. A stiff whisky. Oh, but you can't, can you?' Zeglov leaned forward and met her eyeline. 'Better get her a glass of water instead.'

They knew about the baby…

The sofa displaced as Thick Hands rose and left the room. Daniel. He didn't look like a Daniel.

'Mrs Jameson.' Zeglov looked at the ceiling briefly, as if he was working through what he was about to say. 'I like to think of myself as a patient man. But there comes a point when even the most patient man is pushed beyond his limit.'

Nicole shrank back. At least Katie and Finlay were with people she knew. Safe. For now…

'I think you know what I want,' Zeglov said. 'So, why don't we get this over with? Where is your husband?'

As long as they think I'm dead. Nicole thought of the memory stick at home. The message on the burner phone, still in her pocket. The meeting with Ethan tomorrow. She'd come this far. She couldn't falter now. She couldn't give up her husband. She wouldn't. 'He's dead.'

'I think we both know that's not true.'

Silence hung menacingly in the room.

'What were you doing in Ashford a week last Friday?' he said eventually.

'How do you know where I was?'

'Oh, I know everything about you. I know where your children go to school. I know you shop at Sainsbury's on your way home from work on a Friday. I know you visited the maternity clinic on the Thursday before the plane crash.'

It was him. Him that planted the tracker. His people that had been following her, watching her. And not only since the plane crash. He'd been learning about them all, for months.

'I've been watching you for a while. And Ania.'

'Why?'

'I make it my business to know what my associates' families get up to. In fact, I know more about you and your marriage than I think you do.'

My marriage? Nicole felt her mouth drop. What did her marriage have to do with anything?

'And I also know that Conrad didn't intend to cause the plane crash. That his drink was spiked with a sleeping drug. Spiked by your husband.'

Panic jolted through her, a sudden electric current. 'No!'

'That's right. You see, your husband took a lot of money from me.'

'He works in investment. Sometimes things go wrong.' She was battling to keep her cool. *Ethan caused the crash.* No. Zeglov was trying to bamboozle her. Trying to trick her into giving him up.

'What went wrong was that he was skimming off me for months. Only investing a percentage of my money.'

'I don't understand.'

'I'm sure you don't. Ethan was building a nice little nest egg for himself. If I hadn't noticed, if I didn't have other people in the field to check, I would never have known. And he'd have become a very rich man.'

Nicole stared at him, desperately trying to process everything. An investment, Ethan had said. An investment that had plummeted.

'When I confronted him, he panicked,' Zeglov added. 'Organised the crash, with his name on the flight schedule. Orchestrated his own death.'

No, it can't be. She recalled Ethan's forlorn face in the park. He'd made a mistake, got involved with the wrong crowd. But he wasn't a bad man. He was just trying to make a better life for his family. Zeglov was lying. 'It's not true.'

Zeglov moved over to a table nearby and tapped it twice.

The door opened. Nicole turned, expecting Daniel to walk through with her drink. But – a sharp intake of breath – it wasn't Daniel. A woman entered, met her eyeline fleetingly, then placed a glass of water on the table beside Nicole. Squares of ice chinked together as it hit the surface. It was Mags.

'I believe you've met Magda,' Zeglov said.

Mags. Magda. Nicole closed her eyes a second.

'Magda works for a milliner,' he said. 'But then you already know that, don't you? What you don't know is that she also works with me.' He leaned forward again, as if he was sharing a secret. 'On the side. Moonlighting, I think they call it.'

Against her better judgement, Nicole grabbed the glass and gulped a mouthful of water. No wonder she'd felt uneasy with Mags last night. The questions, the woman's shiftiness: looking at her photos, implying she could feel Ethan's presence. She was fishing. And when she didn't get answers, she dropped Zeglov's name into the conversation. Was she fishing to see whether Nicole knew about Zeglov, or hoping that she would reach out to her husband? Oh, God! Nicole was entangled so tightly in the spider's web, she had no idea how to even start clawing her way out.

'Your husband couldn't resist her.'

No! She turned to Mags, who had moved over and settled herself in an armchair, one leg crossed over the other, demurely. Her long black dress, split at the side exposing a sleek stockinged calf. She waited for her to say, *not in that way, we were just friends.* Just like she had implied last night. But Mags simply stared back at her, the tip of her tongue poking through her white teeth.

Nicole's heart clenched. 'You told me your father had died,' she said to Mags. 'Ethan supported you.'

'My father did pass away.' Mags' accent sounded even stronger, richer today. 'And Ethan did support me. He just helped with other things too.'

No…

'Not as much as Conrad, it seemed,' Zeglov said. 'He couldn't get enough of her. You see, Mags was the one who seduced Conrad in the first place. And Conrad introduced her, and then us, to your husband. She was Ethan's contact.' His eyes gleamed. 'Wove them all around her little finger, did our Magda.'

Was Nicole hearing this right?

'Come now,' Zeglov said, his tone mocking. 'Don't look so shocked. It's a honey trap. It happens all the time. We needed to work with an experienced financier, someone respected in the business, someone who would consider slightly more varied types of investment, shall we say? It was Mags' job to find them. And find them she did. With a bit of help.'

Chapter 61

The heat of the room was suffocating Nicole. Zeglov was making this all up. He had to be. Fabricating a story to bring her on side. Ethan wasn't a murderer. Conrad was his work colleague, a dear family friend, there was no way he would kill him. She stared up at the Russian defiantly. 'I don't believe you.'

'Then perhaps this will enlighten you.' He picked up a remote control, pressed a button. The painting above the fireplace faded to a blank screen. Zeglov pressed another button. A room filled the screen. Not the one they were in; the sofas were different colours – amber and yellow – but similar. People moving around in various states of undress. Laughing. Joking. Drinking. A party. Her gaze fell on a man in the corner, a naked woman on top of him. The curvature of her waist, the bones of her spine pressing against the skin as she squirmed about, her face in his. She turned. Looked directly at the camera. And Nicole gasped. It was Mags. Conrad beneath her, pulling her back to him.

The camera spanned round. To other couples. On chairs. On the floor.

And there he was. Ethan on the sofa. His naked body entwined with another woman. Openly having sex in front of everyone. Nicole pressed a hand to her chest, turned away, closed her eyes. When she opened them again, the camera had moved to another figure sitting in a chair, a woman's face at his groin. David Harrison. But what bothered Nicole, what chilled her to her core was the woman sitting opposite, watching: it was Olivia.

Nicole placed her hands over her eyes. She couldn't watch anymore. They were all involved. David, Ethan, Conrad... Even Olivia.

The footage flicked off. Slowly the painting returned. And the room quietened.

'So, you see, our tentacles reach far and wide,' Zeglov said.

Nicole thought of Ania's suspicions over the Harrisons. 'How do you know it wasn't David who caused the crash?' she said.

'Why would he? He doesn't work for us. Not yet. Conrad only recently introduced us to David and Olivia. That's a relationship we are nurturing,' he said. 'It's always good to look after your contacts, don't you think?'

Nicole didn't know what to think. Her whole world was a lie. Her marriage was a sham. Conrad wasn't the man he claimed either, having an affair behind Ania's back. Both husbands involved in a secret murky world. And David and Olivia? Them and their 'Harrison family' and 'we look after our own'. Well, if this was the way they looked after their family, Nicole didn't want any part of it.

'Not that it'll be too difficult to recruit them,' Zeglov continued, clearly still talking about the Harrisons. 'My sources tell me they aren't averse to bending the rules, every now and then.'

Nicole started. But she didn't have time to think about David and Olivia's business dealings now. She felt violated, sick. Betrayed, deceived. But that wasn't everything: if Zeglov was to be believed, Ethan caused the plane crash. He murdered Conrad... A drop of sweat trickled down her temple. 'Ethan would never kill Conrad. They were friends!'

'Unless of course he had no choice. He couldn't just disappear, could he? He knew we'd keep searching for him. But an unrecovered body in a plane crash with his name on the flight schedule – it couldn't be more convincing. Some might say, almost the perfect crime.'

Nicole didn't buy it. Ethan wouldn't. And anyway, if he had planned this, if he had meant to murder Conrad that day, he would have prepared more carefully, taken the memory stick with him. 'How do I know it wasn't you?' she said, returning Zeglov's steely stare.

'Because Ethan was seen at the hotel in Nantes that morning having breakfast with Conrad. Daniel watched him tamper with Conrad's drink while he went to the toilet. Think about it. Only someone close to Conrad, someone who'd been in his house or had access to his luggage, would know he'd previously been prescribed sleeping pills. Believe me, Mrs Jameson, if I meant to kill Ethan or Conrad, I could have found far more inventive ways of doing it.'

'But...' *The resignation.* 'Conrad wanted to leave the company.'

'Conrad was using my money to repay the loan for his pilot training. He wanted to leave as the loan reduced, but he was my contact maker. He was far more useful to me there. Which is why I persuaded him to stay. Conrad was the last person I wanted dead.'

This wasn't making any sense. None at all.

'Mrs Jameson,' Zeglov said, hooking her gaze. 'The last time I saw your husband was on the Tuesday before the crash, a meeting I called because my sources had alerted me to a problem with the investment. Do you know where we met that day?' He didn't wait for an answer. 'In a lay-by near St Albans. On the A5183.'

Bile rose in her throat. She swallowed it back. 'Where Ania had her accident.'

Zeglov raised both brows. 'Oh, come now, Mrs Jameson. I think we both know it wasn't an accident.'

'What?' Ania couldn't remember anything leading up to the crash, or so she said.

'Ania gave an interview to the press, raising questions about the crash, then drove to St Albans, where Ethan and I last met.

He was following her, he thought she was onto him. We know that because we were following her too. We arrived just as the crash happened. But your husband gave us the slip.'

Nicole's stomach dropped to the floor. She could still hear the sadness in Ethan's voice as he expressed concern about Ania, asked after the boys… It was too much information to process.

The door clicked open. Daniel entered. He gave Zeglov a nod.

'Why now?' she said, her voice barely a whisper. 'The plane crash was almost a month ago. Why approach me now?'

'We spotted Ethan in Highgate. We weren't able to get close, but we knew then, our suspicions were confirmed.'

When he came back to the house. A risky move on Ethan's part. The irrational actions of a panicked man. A bit like murdering his friend, sacrificing him to save his own skin…

The conversation with Sharon, the liaison officer, the sighting, flashed up in Nicole's mind. 'You were the anonymous caller,' she said, speaking the words aloud.

Zeglov smiled. 'A little heightened police interest didn't do any harm.' He sniffed. 'We had hoped it might move things along, that you would lead us to him. But it seems you like to give us the slip too.'

Nicole recoiled.

'Look, Mrs Jameson. We believe Ethan arranged the trip to France to buy time. When we met, he assured me I was mistaken, and everything was under control. But then he started avoiding my calls, ignoring my messages. He couldn't make back what he'd stolen. He knew I was after him, and he was running scared. Which is why he organised the plane crash to convince the world he was dead. And it almost worked.'

Oh my God. 'Did Conrad know he was fiddling?' Her voice was almost a whisper.

Zeglov shrugged. 'I doubt it.'

She pictured Conrad standing at their kitchen counter, a mug of coffee in his hand, a lopsided smile on his face as he delivered the punchline to one of his many jokes. He stopped by so often. To collect Ethan for a client meeting. To pick him up for a training session at the gym. She'd been so pleased when Conrad had persuaded Ethan to join a gym and work on his fitness. *Conrad. Sent to his death by a man he trusted.* Their dear, dear friend. How could Ethan do this? 'Someone's been helping Ethan,' she blurted.

'Not anymore. We've already got to them.'

'W-what do you mean?'

'Suffice to say, they won't be helping anyone else soon. But that's not something for you to concern yourself with.'

Her mind blurred. Murder. Threats. Violence. How the hell did her life descend into this world? *Oh no – Tamsin!* What if it was Ethan's sister helping him? What had they done to her? She considered the memory stick he wanted so badly from the house – the investments he needed to live on. How he'd disappeared for several days, changed his phone number when he contacted her yesterday. He must have given them such a run-around. But to callously abandon whoever was helping him… Just like he'd callously abandoned Conrad, sent him to his death. A man he'd spent time with, taken into his heart. Where was his humanity? She really didn't know him at all.

But… If Nicole did hand him over, would that make her free? Ethan owed Zeglov money. He might still pursue his debt. Come after her and the children. No matter how far they ran, he would be searching for them, looking for compensation for his loss. Perhaps she could sell the house.

Nicole's chest was tight. Tight and bone dry. 'If this is about money—'

'I don't want your money, Mrs Jameson. This is a matter of principle now. I want your husband.' His gaze was piercing. 'And I think you know where he is.'

She pressed her stomach. She could barely breathe. 'Please! I don't.' And she didn't. Not yet anyway.

'I don't believe you.' A beat passed.

'He's supposed to be contacting me,' she squawked, 'with a location to meet him tomorrow. He wants stuff from the house. That's all I know.'

'I see.' Zeglov's face eased into a nasty smile. 'Then as soon as you hear from him, you message me. Daniel will give you the number.'

'What will you do with him?'

'That's for me to decide. And for you to put behind you.'

This was too much. If Zeglov was to be believed, Ethan instigated the plane crash, murdered his own friend, then tried to murder Ania... 'What about us?' she said, her mind in overdrive.

'If you give me Ethan, you won't be touched. Any of you. Your parents, your children. Ania, her family. I give you my word. If you deliver your husband, you'll never hear from me or my people again. You have twenty-four hours.'

'What if he doesn't reach out by then?'

'Then there will be consequences. Naturally. You and your loved ones would be, shall we say, collateral damage.' His face hardened to granite. He nodded at Daniel, who moved forward.

'Wait!' Nicole said. 'You said help.'

'What?'

'You said Mags recruited Conrad, with some help.'

'Ah, yes. Our friend Piotr. I think you need to ask Ania about him. You see, Ania's not as squeaky clean as you think either.'

Chapter 62

On the motorway later, rage bubbled inside Nicole, burning like a furnace. It was surreal being back in her car, on her own. She was heading to the hospital to see Ania, yet only hours earlier she'd faced the muzzle of a gun, her life hanging in the balance.

The drive back through London after she'd left Zeglov had been charged. Daniel at her side, but he hadn't wielded a weapon this time. He didn't need to. He knew she wouldn't make a fuss, wouldn't go to the police, wouldn't enlist the help of others. They knew where her children went to school, where her parents lived. They'd infiltrated every facet of her life.

She should go to the police. They offered protection in circumstances like this, didn't they? She'd seen a documentary about it once. But… she was reminded of Ethan's comment about his criminal friends, their connection with senior police officers. Was that even true? Oh, God. She'd deal with the consequences, take her punishment, if it meant her family, the people around her, were safe. But how could she be sure they would be?

She recalled the black BMW pulling up alongside her Toyota in Chester Road. The nerve twitching in Daniel's jaw as she climbed out of the car. The kids spilling out of the party, parents waving and smiling and greeting her as she passed them to collect her children. A mother outside Jess's house moaning about all the sweets in the party bag. Oh, wouldn't it be nice if that was all she had to worry about? Instead of life and death.

How could Ethan do this to her? She thought back to their university days. Ethan forever chasing the next big thing. Of their conversation in the park – *I did it for us. For the family.* Why was he stealing from Zeglov? To build up funds to set up his own company earlier than expected? Fuel his heady ambitions of being the next David Harrison, of being a thirty-something dynamo in the financial world?

Come with me. Did he really want her to go with him? He already had blood on his hands, trying to protect his own selfish future. A future fed by ruthless greed. Or was he just buttering her up, to get what he wanted? She'd seen him do it countless times with clients. And she hadn't known about the sex parties, the other women. No, he'd been careful to keep that away from her. More lies. Her insides reeled at the messages, the texts. *How are you, lovely? I've missed you so much.* Where would it end? What would he do next? He lived his days chasing the next big deal, the prospect of a better life. It was all about the prospect for Ethan, she could see that now. He didn't care who got hurt, who lost their lives, along the way. Anything to further his own ends.

She'd fought for him all her adult life. Supported him against her mother, covered for him, had his back. He'd said he worked the long hours because he wanted to make a better life for them, his family, and she had believed him. Pacified everyone, kept everyone happy when he was late or absent at gatherings. And she'd thought they were happy, a tight little unit.

Though it was all a sham. A façade.

As much as it galled her to admit it, her mother had been right. Ethan did walk all over her. All over her and the kids to get what he wanted, scuffing his feet as he went. Going behind her back with other women. Participating in criminal activities. Putting them all at risk.

Nicole thought about the videos of the sex parties. Zeglov's leverage to ensure compliance, his little piece of blackmail. Once they were involved, they couldn't leave. So, Ethan had decided to engineer his own exit at the expense of everyone else. The idea made her sick to the pit of her stomach.

Well, she wasn't having it, she wasn't about to stand for it a moment longer. She would deal with Ethan. But there was someone else she needed to deal with first. She'd barely believed her ears when Zeglov had told her Piotr had been involved. Piotr, Ania's brother! And what did he mean when he said, 'Ania's not as squeaky clean as you think either'?

Chapter 63

Nicole's chest was raw as she moved down the hospital ward to Ania's room. Raw and hard. It was almost 5.30, another half an hour to go until visiting time, but the nurse said Ania was doing well. Eating. Drinking. Chatting. She could go in early.

Ania was sitting up in bed eating a yoghurt, her hair loose around her shoulders, when Nicole entered. The colour had returned to her face, a peachy glow, and she looked stronger. Good job. Because she needed to be Herculean for what Nicole was about to put to her.

'Hey,' Nicole said as she entered. If she was going to get to the bottom of this, to get Ania to open up, she had to keep things pleasant. For now, at least. 'How are you doing?' She reached into her bag and pulled out a large bar of Cadbury's she'd bought from the kiosk on the way in.

Ania's eyes immediately brightened. 'Better now.' She pushed the yoghurt to the side of the table and ripped open the chocolate like a kid at Christmas, offering it to Nicole.

Nicole shook her head. 'What are the doctors saying?'

'Not much. I was hoping to go home tomorrow, but they don't think there will be a doctor on to clear me. The nurses reckon I might have to wait until after the weekend.' She snapped off a square of chocolate and placed it in her mouth. 'Any news?'

Nicole pulled up a chair. She wasn't sure where to begin. 'Nothing from Air Accident. But I do have something to tell you.' She cleared her throat, then launched into the tale of the birthday party, the visit with the Russian. When she talked about being escorted through London at gunpoint, Ania dropped the chocolate bar and pressed a hand to her mouth. 'Wait. You need to hear me out.'

Nicole watched the hand fall, Ania's mouth gape, then her face harden, as she talked about her meeting with Ethan.

'Why didn't you tell me before?'

'You've been in a coma. He's in hiding. Look, you need to listen, there's more.'

Ania pushed the chocolate away, as though her appetite had suddenly waned.

Nicole talked her through the messages at home, the burner phone in the airing cupboard, Ethan's story about being hunted down, the messages afterwards, the dilemma over what to do. His side of the story versus Zeglov's theory about Ethan causing the plane crash.

'Wait! Are you saying Ethan killed Conrad? We need to ring the police!'

'It's not that straightforward.'

Ania's face hardened further, the skin pulling taut across her cheekbones. 'It is from where I'm sitting.'

A nurse entered and smiled at Ania, seemingly oblivious to the tension in the room. 'Nice to have an early visitor. I expect your other friend will be in later.'

'Probably.'

A stony silence pervaded as the nurse bustled around, smoothing bedsheets, taking Ania's blood pressure.

Nicole waited until the nurse left before she skimmed over the video footage of the party, mentioning who was there without going into specifics. There would be plenty of time for that later. Zeglov's account of Ethan pushing Ania off the road outside St Albans. All the while watching Ania's expression. She was making all the right noises: conveying surprise, horror, and still Nicole searched for a flicker of something, some sign of latent guilt. Determined if it was there, if Ania was involved in this in any small way, she would find it.

But all she saw was shock and heartache.

'Zeglov's given me twenty-four hours to deliver Ethan,' she finished up matter-of-factly. As if she was telling a friend about the delivery of a new car. 'Otherwise, we're all in trouble.'

'I don't see why I'm in trouble,' Ania said. 'As far as I'm concerned, this is Ethan's mess. He killed my husband. He should pay.'

'You see, that's the thing,' Nicole said. 'There's something I can't quantify in all of this.'

'What?'

'Zeglov said they had extra help recruiting Conrad. That someone else provided the initial introduction. Someone called Piotr.'

Ania's eyes popped wide. Suddenly, she looked afraid. Very afraid. She dropped her head into her hands. 'Oh my God.'

–

Ania was struggling to breathe. Even before the car crash, she knew. She knew something was wrong, awry, especially when she discovered the petrol receipt from St Albans. And she'd been right. But never in a million years could she have imagined this.

How could Piotr be involved?

When she looked up at Nicole's face, it was thick with anger. Surely, she didn't believe…

Ania coughed, cleared her throat. 'It's not what you think.'

'I don't know what to think,' Nicole said. 'Why don't you tell me about Piotr?'

A pain throbbed in Ania's neck. All she could do was talk Nicole through her history with her brother. His life in Poland. Their argument. The difficult relationship that ensued. 'It can't be anything to do with Piotr—'

'I know he was murdered,' Nicole interrupted. 'Blanka told me.'

'Then you'll know he couldn't have been involved in this. He was already dead.'

'Blanka said he came over to surprise you a year or so ago. What happened during that visit?'

Ania couldn't speak. Her mouth was dry and tight. She took a swig of water from the glass on her bedside table.

'He turned up unannounced.' Her mind switched back to that Monday evening. She'd been expecting a man to come and give her a quote for a new front fence. He was late, she was in the middle of cooking dinner – spaghetti Bolognese – when the doorbell sounded. The boys were arguing over the television. It was a usual fraught evening, rushing through their routine. But instead of the fence man, Piotr was on the doorstep. Piotr! All smiles. That same gleam in his eye. The one she'd always looked up to, the one she'd loved so much when they were young. She blinked the image away. 'We hadn't spoken for years. I was in shock. The boys knew they had an uncle, but they had never met him. And he surprised us all. He looked so well. He'd turned his life around, told us he had a new job, wanted to build some bridges.' A tear pricked Ania's eye as her chin quivered. She looked across at Nicole. 'I thought I'd finally got my brother back.' The tear spilled out. She swiped it away with the back of her hand. 'Anyway, it wasn't to be. He kept taking Conrad off on his own. It was only when Conrad told me why – that Piotr was trying to recruit him into an illegal car business – that I realised. He hadn't changed at all.' A pain stabbed at her chest. 'He'd discovered where Conrad was working, who employed him and thought my husband could find him some fresh pickings. Rich people with luxury cars for him to steal. I threw him out. Six months later, he was dead.'

The room quietened. The only sound Ania's sniffs as she wept.

Nicole handed her a tissue. 'Zeglov's gang had been trying to recruit Conrad,' she said. 'He was resisting. So, they brought in Piotr to help persuade him.'

Ania pressed the tissue to her cheeks. 'I thought it was bad enough when he was stealing cars. But this...'

'They were paying Conrad. Mags worked with them too. Part of the arrangement was to recruit a financier to manage their investments. It sounds as though Conrad was using the money to repay the loan faster so that he could get out, leave the company. I guess that's why you found his draft resignation.'

Ania's eyes blurred again. The idea of Conrad using the opportunity to work towards what they both wanted, what they both needed, was another spear to the soul.

'How do you know it wasn't the Russians who organised the plane crash?' she said. 'For all I know, they could have killed Piotr, too.'

'Conrad had a lot of contacts in the business. He was more valuable to them alive.'

'So, the crash was only down to Ethan?' Ania spat out the words. She had never liked Ethan. Swanning around in his expensive suits, keeping her husband out until all hours. But, right now, she couldn't despise him more.

'It certainly looks that way.'

'What about the Harrisons? You said they were at the parties too.'

'They were. But according to Zeglov, they are innocent in all of this. He's grooming them for future use. They had no idea Ethan was working on the side, although they certainly knew what company our husbands were keeping and said nothing.'

A blast of rage coursed through Ania, searing her insides. She straightened. 'So, what are we going to do about it?'

'Well, it seems to me we have two options. Neither of them particularly favourable.'

We. Ania felt a heaviness in her chest, a sinking feeling in the pit of her stomach. When it came to the crux, could Nicole be trusted to do the right thing? After all, Ethan was her husband, the father of her children. 'We should bring in Blanka,' she said. 'She'll help us.'

'No. We keep this between ourselves. The fewer people who know, the better.'

'I'm not sure.' She ran her eyes over Nicole's tiny frame. And, in her condition, they shouldn't risk putting her in any more danger. 'But—'

Nicole's interruption came through tight teeth. 'He's my husband. *I'm* going to deal with him.'

–

Back home, Nicole sat in silence. Night had drawn in, elongating the shadows in her living room. The hour with Ania had passed almost in the blink of an eye. Trying to come up with a plan. To decide the best way to deal with the situation.

She hadn't told Ania about the orgies, or about Conrad and Mags. It was enough knowing her own brother had drawn her husband into this mess, to lure Ethan in. The poor woman had lost her mother, her brother, and her husband. She and Conrad didn't enjoy as many years together as she'd have liked, but the memories they shared Ania cherished. Nicole couldn't see what there was to be gained from soiling that memory, not if she didn't have to. And, despite what Zeglov had suggested, Nicole felt confident that Ania was telling the truth. She might have had a criminal brother, but she wasn't involved herself. What did she stand to gain?

Nicole sighed. She hadn't heard from Ethan again. And she wasn't about to reach out to him either. Not now. Because she had a crucial decision to make.

Less than twenty-four hours. She had less than twenty-four hours to decide whether to send a man to his death or try to involve the police and deal with the consequences. Thank goodness the children were at her parents' on a sleepover because now, more than ever in her life before, Nicole needed time to think.

Ania had been unequivocal – they should hand Ethan over to Zeglov. But Nicole couldn't decide which path to take. She was complicit in fraud – if she involved the police, if she did find an officer to help her, she faced the possibility of having her baby in prison. If she leaned towards Zeglov, she was feeding the father of her children to the wolves. Sending a man to his death. Because she had no doubt that's what Zeglov had planned.

Nicole sat in the darkness, digging her nail into the flesh around her forefinger.

Less than twenty-four hours. *Please, God, let Ethan text in the morning.*

Chapter 64

Nicole watched the morning light slowly brighten her bedroom. Pick, pick, picking. Five o'clock rolled around to six, then seven. When the clock finally struck eight, she'd picked her fingers raw. She climbed out of bed and checked the burner phone. All was clear.

She glanced at the cases all packed beneath her bed as she pulled on her jeans and shirt. Cases she'd never use. At least she hadn't told the children about the trip – one blessing. She'd have to cancel the flights. They were all in this together; she couldn't abandon Ania. They needed to sort out their husbands' mess, look out for each other, take care of their little ones.

Her iPhone rang out, dancing across her bedside table. 'Tamsin' flashed up on the screen. Nicole stared at the phone for several seconds before answering.

'Hello.'

'Hey!' Tamsin's voice gushed down the phone. 'How are you all?'

'We're okay,' Nicole said warily, taking a seat on the edge of the bed.

'Listen, I'm sorry I missed your messages. My damn phone died and then the phone company delayed sending a replacement. But, good news! My back is on the mend. I'm returning to work tomorrow.'

Nicole sank further into the mattress as her sister-in-law prattled on about physiotherapy and painkillers and possibly flying over to see them in a few weeks. Tamsin clearly hadn't been the person helping Ethan. Nicole still had no idea who had been, who it was that had fallen foul of Zeglov and his crew. Maybe she would never know. But at least Ethan hadn't turned to his sister, one small mercy.

She forced herself to make polite conversation, then ended the call, promising to phone her sister-in-law back soon.

Now she had the day to herself to prepare. She lay back on the bed, willing Ethan to message. Because time was running out.

–

The message came through at 8.59 a.m.

> Hi, darling. Meet me in Applewood Lane, near Bricket Wood. It's a long winding country road with a dip in the middle. There's a row of lime trees at the bottom of the dip. I'll meet you there at 12 p.m.

The full address and postcode appeared on the screen.

Nicole's hands trembled as she typed the details into Google Maps. It was a remote location. Forty minutes' drive from Highgate. And... she froze. The postal address was St Albans. Not Ashford. Nowhere near the park where they met last week, and less than twenty minutes' drive from where Ania had her accident, and where Ethan had last met with Zeglov.

She texted back, four simple words.

> Okay. See you there.

Then sat back in her chair and tried to quell the nerves fluttering in her chest. Three more hours...

The buzz of her iPhone made her jump. Ania.

Ania didn't bother with preamble. 'How are you?' Her voice was low, barely a whisper, as if she was concerned about being overheard. 'I haven't slept a wink.'

'I'm okay.'

'Have you heard?'

'I have. Just now.'

The ensuing silence was loaded.

'Oh God, Nicole, I don't like this. If it wasn't for my leg…' Her voice cracked. 'Be careful, won't you? And call me when you are done?'

'I will. Don't worry.'

Only now did Nicole know exactly what she should do. She rang off, scrolled down and selected another number. The phone rang out one, two, three times before a female voice answered.

'DC Sharon Crossland?'

'Hi, Sharon. It's Nicole Jameson here.' She drew a breath. 'Do you have a moment? There's something I need to talk to you about.'

Chapter 65

Later that day, the road ahead darkened, chilling the car. Nicole entered a tunnel of trees, switched her wipers down a notch, relishing the respite from the torrent of rain lashing her windscreen, and hiked up the heater. The clock on the dashboard read 11.52 p.m. Eight more minutes.

A shiver slid down her back. Eight more minutes before her life changed forever.

Oh, God, she hoped Ethan was there. That he hadn't had a change of heart. That something else hadn't prevented him from making their rendezvous point. Because she couldn't bear to think of the consequences.

Rain seeped through intermittent gaps in the leaves, puddling on the tarmac. She flicked on her headlights, slowed to a crawl. It was a gloomy summer's afternoon, the gunmetal-grey sky loaded with heavy clouds.

A fleeting glance in her rear-view mirror at the unmarked car behind her. She longed for a cigarette. To drag the nicotine deep into her lungs. Watch the smoke seep out and slowly disperse into the air. But she didn't smoke anymore, she gave up when she was expecting Katie. Threw away her emergency stash when Ethan discovered them, tucked beneath the *Homes & Gardens* magazine in her bedside drawer. Not that she could have one now anyway.

Nicole steered around a bend and the road opened, the trees fading into rolling countryside reaching to the horizon. A crisscross of hedges carved up the landscape of rich arable fields.

There wasn't another vehicle on the road, not apart from her and her secret convoy.

She passed a lay-by, a haggard old oak. Almost there.

A sharp turn off the main road, down a narrow lane. She swerved to avoid the potholes. The car rocked and rolled over the uneven ground. She rounded a corner. The car behind was hanging back now. Another corner, down into a dip, and then she saw him.

He was standing beneath a row of lime trees, the thick canopy providing welcome cover from the unrelenting rain. Just as they'd arranged. He was wearing a long rain mac, a flat cap pulled low over his brow. He looked up as she approached.

Nicole depressed the brake and the car crawled towards him. Trepidation kneading her as she teetered between her lives, old and new. She could taste freedom in the air. Freedom mingled with fear.

He started towards her. She was not only complicit in fraud, she was now going to be complicit in murder. The crimes totting up. The nerves resurfaced, buzzing around her chest.

When she'd phoned the detective earlier, Sharon had sounded weary. There'd been no new sightings of Ethan and they'd found no CCTV footage of him either. The sighting sounded more and more like a hoax. Good. As far as everyone was concerned, Ethan was already dead.

Her chest hardened. Why should she, Nicole, be implicated in Ethan's criminal dealings? Why should she face charges of fraud, watch her children, her parents suffer for him? No. She wasn't about to subject her family to more heartache. This wasn't only justice for her, or for Zeglov. This was for her children, and for Ania's family too. Ethan had drawn them all into his little plan and deceived the lot of them.

The BMW rounded the corner. Ethan didn't see it at first. He was bending down, about to look through her passenger window when he spotted it.

His jaw dropped, he cast a stricken look at Nicole, and then he ran.

Brakes screeched. Zeglov's men jumped out of the car and made chase. They were faster than him. Closing in as they chased him across the field.

Nicole reeled in a jagged breath, turned over the engine and pulled away. Her work here was done.

–

Back in north London, the rain had abated and the sun was breaking through the clouds, mopping the pavements with its powerful beam. Nicole navigated the streets until she spotted a deli on the corner, a bin outside. She pulled over, tugged the burner phone out of her pocket and climbed out of the car, leaving the engine running. She'd already removed the SIM card. When she got home later, she would flush the card down the loo. Then delete @Appletree-208 from her Instagram account. Disposing of every ounce of Ethan's contact.

She chucked the phone in the bin and climbed back into the car. She needed to cancel that holiday too. Finally, she was taking control. Seeking justice for herself and her family. Her way. And it felt good.

Epilogue

Nicole sat in the car, droplets of rain streaking the glass, and looked out at the black front door, the tulips engraved into the panels of glass. Almost two weeks had passed since she had led Zeglov's men to Ethan and the Russian had been true to his word: she hadn't heard a peep from him. And, what's more, there had been no cars outside their homes, no strange men calling, no one watching them. She barely felt the need to check over her shoulder these days. Life was starting to settle. Gloriously uncomplicated days tumbling into each other. She was even thinking of going back to work in September, after the school holidays.

She pulled the memory stick out of her pocket and flipped it over in her hand. The inquiry into the plane crash was ongoing. There'd been no news from Sharon since her phone call to check on Ethan's sighting, and nothing from Ethan either. Not that she expected to hear from Ethan. She wasn't proud of herself for giving her husband up to Zeglov, but he'd brought it on himself, allowing himself to be drawn into their criminal underworld, then exploiting his position, fuelled by his own greed. Murdering Conrad in cold blood, then attacking Ania, pushing her car off the road. No thought of the consequences of his actions, or the damage it might inflict on the families, the children. No consideration for his loved ones.

'Are you sure about this?' Ania said, looking down at the memory stick. She looked better, brighter. Nicole had called or visited most days since she'd been discharged from hospital.

Ania was on crutches, her leg still in plaster, but her bruises had disappeared, and she seemed to gain strength as each day passed.

Nicole nodded.

'How's he going to access it? I thought you said it was password-protected.'

Nicole had been thinking about this since she'd raised the issue. Sitting around Ania's kitchen table, swirling the mug of tea in her hand. 'He'll have connections. He'll find someone to break into it, I'm sure. Anyway' – she looked up at the house again – 'it's dirty money. We don't want this anywhere near us.'

'Maybe we should give it to the Harrisons.'

'We've been through this,' Nicole said. 'If we give it to the Harrisons, we'd have to admit our part in Ethan's demise. No.' She shook her head. 'We keep this secret to ourselves.'

Nicole was slowly distancing herself from David and Olivia. They weren't friends, she realised that now. They were business acquaintances who manipulated associations, forcing themselves into family life, cementing their positions to get what they wanted. She recalled David's barefaced lies, denying all knowledge of Mags when she'd visited his office.

'Are you sure the Harrisons weren't involved in Ethan's agreement with Zeglov?' Ania pressed. 'I mean, if they attended his gatherings...'

'Zeglov says not,' she said in a low voice.

'Do you think we should warn them about him?'

As much as Ania loathed the Harrisons, the fact that she didn't want to condemn them to Zeglov's seedy world was heartening. Nicole thought of them, at the party where their husbands were openly having sex, performing in front of an audience. No. They kept their fair share of secrets. She couldn't help but wonder if that was why David had offered to go through Ethan's paperwork, why he'd been so keen to look through his study. To ensure she wouldn't find any connection between Zeglov and them. 'I think they're quite capable of taking care of themselves,' she said.

Nicole pulled an envelope out of her bag, wrote *Mr Zeglov – In Confidence* on the front, then tucked the memory stick inside, stuck it down and climbed out of the car. The rain was coming down hard, little needles pummelling the pavement. She yanked up her hood, rounded her car and approached the house. Looking up at the security camera, she pulled her hood back, stared for several seconds to ensure her face was recorded, then posted the envelope in the letterbox and moved back to her car. The accounts on there might go some way towards paying off what Ethan owed, which, in Nicole's mind, meant she and Zeglov were even.

—

Back in Leytonstone, the wind had picked up, wiping the clouds from the sky and making for a dry July afternoon.

Patryk and Robert were on the doorstep by the time Nicole cut the engine. Blanka ambled down the pathway. Ania's family, poised to welcome her home. Such a happy, joyous sight.

Nicole waved at the boys as she climbed out of the car, retrieved the crutches from the back and helped Ania out. They rushed to greet their mum, almost knocking her over, then talked at her, a million words a minute, while Blanka led her down the path. Nicole smiled. Her own children came out to meet her and she hugged them tightly. They had their difficult days, but, generally, the kids seemed to be adjusting well to Ethan's passing. She'd finally shared the baby news with them yesterday and they were both thrilled, looking forward to welcoming another sibling into their little family.

'Everything okay?' Blanka asked as she entered the hallway.

Nicole waited for the kids to trot into the front room, out of earshot. 'All done.'

Poor Blanka. They'd told her they were visiting Conrad's grave, paying their respects together. Intent on keeping the secrets behind the plane crash firmly between the two of them.

Now they'd completed the final stage of their plan, they needed to put it all behind them and move forward.

Blanka helped Ania off with her jacket and, suddenly, Nicole felt surplus to requirements. Ania looked beat. The morning's trip across London had taken everything out of her. It was time to give them space. And… there was something else. She and Ania had been drawn together by shared adversity. Forced to make a murderous decision. A decision that most people never faced in a lifetime. A decision that would stay with them for the rest of their lives. But, without talk of the crash, of conspiracies, of retribution, what did they have left? 'Right, I'd better round up the kids and get going,' she said.

Blanka looked up. 'Why don't you stay and have some coffee with us?'

Nicole wrinkled her nose. 'I don't know.'

Ania turned, surprising her by breaking out into a smile. 'Please, do stay. I'd like you to.'

And Nicole's heart filled with joy. It was still early days, but it felt like a seminal moment, an early shoot in the growth of friendship. 'Okay, just for a few minutes.'

Blanka moved into the kitchen to make drinks just as the sun came out. Ania hobbled out to the yard with Nicole. It was lovely to enjoy the simplicity of a fresh breeze. The clouds above drifting to expose an aqua sky. For so long, Nicole had been hunched up, knotted within. Finally, as each day passed, she could feel herself unfurling and it felt good.

The kids wandered out to join them and talk turned to butterflies. Finlay was telling them about Cape Town. 'They have butterflies bigger than your hand there,' he said. 'My auntie sent me a photo of one.'

Patryk looked awestruck. 'Really?'

'Yup. And you can go on safari and see lions and elephants and zebra.'

'We should all go together when Mummy's leg is better,' Nicole found herself saying. Maybe they could surprise Tamsin, save her ailing back and take a trip over there instead. 'My treat. Blanka too.'

Blanka carried out the drinks, passed them over and smiled. 'That would be so cool!'

The kids clapped their hands. Katie squealed.

'We could take Grandma and Grandad,' Nicole said to her. 'I'm sure they'd fancy a short break.'

'The more, the merrier,' Blanka chipped in. 'Your mum has got a book on Polish butterflies,' she said to the boys. 'Come and see.' She herded the children back into the house.

'Thanks,' Ania said when they'd gone. 'It's a lovely thought. But you must know we can't possibly join you. I can't afford it.'

Nicole took a sip of coffee and met her gaze. 'Of course you can. Aside from the life insurance, Ethan had a bonus due before he died. David's honoured it.'

'It's not my money.'

'It's not mine either,' Nicole said, glancing back into the kitchen. Blanka had a book open on the table and was poring over it with the children. 'We'll call it a holiday on Harrison Dunbar. I think they owe us that much, don't you?'

Acknowledgements

As always, so many people have helped behind the scenes to bring this story to fruition.

First, I hope the people of St Albans will forgive me for using artistic licence with their beautiful city – South Wood Services is a figment of my imagination and doesn't exist.

Huge thanks go to Charlie Kimbell, who advised on piloting single-engine aircrafts and provided general background on aeroplane safety and aviation.

To Annie Welsford, who passed on her knowledge about issues relating to pregnancy. Your midwifery insight was much appreciated.

My dear friend Ian Robinson, who guided me on locations for St Albans, Luton and London, and supported me so much with this novel. Also, my friend Martin Sargeant, who was able to assist with finding Bricket Wood.

Agata Dunliniec for her valuable advice on Polish culture. The next coffee is on me!

To my agent, Caroline Montgomery at Rupert Crew – totally lovely and always at the end of the phone, a fact I'm endlessly grateful for.

Gratitude to Louise Cullen for her keen editing eye; the book wouldn't be what it is today without your input. Also, to Francesca, Sian and all the team at Canelo for believing in this, my second standalone domestic thriller, and championing it.

Once again, the wonderful book community which I'm honoured to be a part of. My author friends, especially those in CS, all the fabulous book bloggers and reviewers, and the amazingly supportive book clubs, both online and in person. I know I say this every time, but I couldn't be more grateful for your ongoing support.

So many friends have listened to my musings and generally offered a shoulder to lean on. Most notably, Colin Williams, Rebecca Bradley, Nicky Peacock, and Philip and Abi Bouch.

Finally, to my beautiful family – David and Ella. You're always mentioned at the end, and you really should be at the beginning. Thank you, for absolutely everything!

Jane loves to hear from readers. Visit her website at www.janeisaac.co.uk where you can join her Readers' Club to receive updates on new releases, and message her through the contact page.